NICK PEARSON

MISSING LINK

First published by Napper Publishing 2025

First edition

ISBN (paperback): 978-1-9191915-1-5
ISBN (hardcover): 978-1-9191915-2-2

This book was professionally typeset on Reedsy.
Find out more at reedsy.com

For my darling wife, Kim
Thanks for your love and support

Sometimes the past is best left alone

Acknowledgments

I am not sure if writing gets easier with subsequent books but I must acknowledge the support of two people who have played a big part in helping to get my first novel published.

Janet Humphrey, published author of the Dust book series, has been amazingly helpful in guiding me through how to self-publish a book.

My wife Kim has been there throughout the process and encouraged me when the going got tough and when work got in the way of writing. Thanks, babe!

And hopefully a pre-acknowledgement to anyone who buys and reads my book. I hope you enjoy it and please do let me know your feedback.

Finally to the publishing house that agree to publish my second novel after the roaring success of Missing Link. Well this is fiction so this kind of statement is allowed!

Nick Pearson, September 2025

1

PROLOGUE

July 1976

The summer of '76; endless sweltering hot days, overcrowded beaches, a drought and a crazy hit record by Ray Stevens telling the story of Ethel the streaker! In so many ways it was a summer to remember.

Simon Letwin and his family spent the whole six weeks of the school holidays by the sea in their caravan near Scarborough. Simon's grandparents, William and Margaret Steele, managed to spend a few days with them but since William ran the family brewing business and with the summer months being busy ones for the industry, he found it difficult to get away for more than the odd weekend. Simon, unlike his younger siblings Mark and Annabel, was not a lover of the sea, preferring to sit on the beach reading a good book. His brother and sister, meanwhile, splashed and screamed in the water for most of the six weeks with the hundreds of others who just wanted to enjoy the unprecedented good weather while it lasted.

Not that Simon was a loner, he just preferred his own company. He did spend some time in the sea when his mother Carmen's cousin and her children travelled to Yorkshire from their home in Essex to stay with William and Margaret and, as part of the trip, visited the Letwins' at their coastal retreat.

Sonia Croft was a few years older than Carmen Steele, but the cousins had hit it off from the first time they had met as young girls and both had always looked forward to their annual reunion during the summer holidays. One year Sonia and her parents Eric and Elisabeth would travel and stay with the Steele's and the following year the journey would be reversed for a fun holiday together in Essex.

By the 1970s, with Carmen and Sonia both married and with young families of their own, the tradition continued. Ronald Letwin and Gerry Binns, the two spouses, did not have a lot in common, Ronald being a GP who enjoyed photography and reading whilst Gerry owned a cycle shop and was athletic and ran every morning. However, the two men took the view that if their children and wives were happy then this was something that they would both embrace and enjoy.

The Binns' children Graham and his younger sister Ashleigh loved visiting the Steele's because it was the only time of the year that they got to spend time at the coast. Living close to Ilford as they did it was over 60 miles to the nearest sandy beach at Clacton-on-Sea, so trips there were rare. Graham was twelve years old, two years Simon's senior and Simon looked up to the elder boy as children often do. The boys got on very well together and Ronald was happy to practice his hobby, capturing for posterity the highlights of the summer holidays in monochrome. Pictures in the sea, pictures building sandcastles and pictures playing beach cricket with the occasional accident as one of the children tumbled over some poor unsuspecting individual who got in the way of an attempt to take a spectacular catch.

Photographs that would sit for years in an album, largely forgotten, the annual trips to Yorkshire and Essex dwindling as the two families got older and the grandparents passed on. Forgotten until one photograph, innocent enough in itself, triggered a chain of events that would wreak havoc within these same families decades later.

As he sat on the beach soaking up the sun along with thousands of other happy souls, carefree in his youthful innocence, Simon Letwin was totally unaware of just how dangerous life would get when he reconnected with the Binns' family many years after the picture of him with Mark and Graham sitting on the seashore had perfectly captured in freeze frame the fun and excitement of that glorious summer of '76.

2

CHAPTER 1

14 August 2016

"So, it is pretty obvious to anyone with half a brain that we have made the right decision in voting for Brexit and we now need to get on with it and get rid of these bloody Eurocrats once and for all!"

Hannah Letwin threw her arms in the air as if to demonstrate that her point was made and was irrefutable unless you were a moron. Which, in her opinion, her younger brother Greg was. That no doubt explained why he responded in the way he did.

"Han, anyone that voted for Brexit is selfish and short sighted and did not think for one minute about what is right for the future. I bet you would vote for a return to colonialism if there was a bloody referendum on that. You know most young people like us realise that Britain belongs in Europe and that being in the EU brings so many benefits and opportunities. It was mostly the older generation who supported Brexit and many of them are not even going to be around to see the results of their decision. I can only think it is those loonies that lecture you that have warped your mind."

Hannah was a final year Politics student at Hull University and was hoping to work in Westminster or to join the Civil Service when she graduated. She saw herself as principled and committed and had little time for people who were wishy washy or who subscribed to what she saw as trendy Eurofads. She was of the opinion that Greg, at 17, currently fitted both of those descriptions and she hoped that he would shake off these undesirable qualities when he went to university himself. However, given his intention to study Sociology, which she viewed as one of those degrees that were a complete waste of time and money, she seriously doubted that he would.

"Let's see. If it means I can have my fish and chips wrapped in newspaper again and that we do not have to pay farmers not to produce stuff – which bright spark dreamed that one up? – it will be happy days and even you might agree with me."

Simon Letwin smiled to himself as he listened to his children take such resolute positions on the topic of the day. Brexit had really sparked polarised debates about whether Britain was better off inside or out of Europe ever since the Prime Minister, David Cameron, had agreed to let the people decide the answer to this question. Now, after all the indicators suggested that the vote would be to remain inside the EU the result itself, to leave, had surprised almost everyone.

Simon was the Chief Executive of the family brewery, Steele's Ales, a role he had occupied since 2007 when his uncle, Keith Steele, retired and became Chairman of the company. Simon was a Steele through the maternal side of his family, his mother Carmen having been Keith's elder sister. Sadly Carmen had contracted cancer and died at the age of 57 in 2001. As a business which operated purely in the UK except for a few sales of their flagship Steele's IPA to the expat markets in Europe and the USA, the company was not as potentially exposed to the ramifications of Brexit as many other UK companies were. This was, in Simon's opinion, just as well since he had enough on his plate with a potential takeover of the firm and the internal wrangling this was causing without having to cope with the threats posed by disrupted supply chains, duty changes and the general instability which loomed ominously over those whose businesses were highly dependent on the European markets for their sales.

"And another thing," continued Hannah, her voice rising as it tended to do when she was talking about something that really mattered to her. "It will also give us the chance to reclaim our fishing rights from the French who seem to think it is their God-given right to plunder 80% of the total stocks in our bloody waters! Who else but Britain would have put up with that bullshit?"

Greg sighed as if this was some dreary task he had to attend to every day and regretted the time wasted in attending to it

"That is typical of you, Han. We the Brits do not consume anything like enough fish to even use up the 20% you claim is left, let alone the 80% you allege we give away. That is a typical Hannah Letwin argument, heavy on volume and almost devoid of substance.

"Oh, Mr Know It All has woken up..."

Simon did not hear the conclusion of the discussion that his offspring were engaged in as he had decided that it was time to handle a few work emails in preparation for the week ahead. He and Dani could then relax for a couple of hours in front of the TV which was the typical way their Sundays ended. Dani was Simon's wife of 23 years and he still loved and fancied her as much as he had when they first met. He was not a bad looking guy he had to admit, but it still amazed him that of all the eligible men at Durham University it was him that Danielle Glover, widely regarded as one of the hottest students on campus, had chosen to be with. Despite the fact that she had given birth to two children and was in her late forties, Dani still had the looks to make eyes turn and Simon would secretly smile inside when this happened.

Simon closed the door of his study to extinguish the sound of his combative children and sat down at his desk. As he did so he noticed the photograph album he had been looking at with his brother Mark and his nephew Jack a few days earlier which was still sitting on the bookshelf next to his desk. Jack was 12 and had recently developed an interest in ancestry since watching a television series where famous people discovered their relatives from generations past. Mark had told Jack that Simon had inherited most of their father's photographs when Ronald Letwin had died in 2009 and suggested to his son that he should ask Uncle Simon if he could see some of the old pictures next time they were at his house. This had led to more than two hours of poring through album after album of mostly black and white pictures of the family back as far as Jack's great-great grandfather Horace Steele who had been born in 1887. To Jack this seemed a positively prehistoric era! There were also photos of William Steele, Simon and Mark's grandfather, who founded the family brewing company in 1947 and a variety of Letwins, some of whom neither Simon nor Mark could put a name to. Jack had been fascinated by all of this history and Simon had been happy to see the passion his young nephew was showing for something that clearly interested him.

Simon picked up the album from the bookshelf at first trying to remember why he had not put it away with the rest of the photos after Mark and Jack had left. As he flicked through the pages and came to one particular photograph, he remembered why he had left this album out. The picture was of three young boys sitting at the water's edge on Scarborough beach in the sweltering summer of 1976. Simon and Mark Letwin and their cousin Graham Binns. It seemed to be the only photograph of Graham amongst his father's collection and there were no pictures of any of the other members of the Binns family. That was probably not surprising given that the family holidays had been started and continued by their grandparents so that once they had passed on it was probably inevitable that the frequency of these trips would diminish until they finally ceased altogether.

Eric Croft, Graham's maternal grandfather, had died in 1972 but it was really after the deaths of William and Margaret Steele, three years apart in the eighties, that the family holidays stopped for good. The final member of the quartet of grandparents, William's younger sister Elisabeth, had died in 1990.

Graham's mother Sonia had been Eric and Elisabeth's only child. When William Steele founded the brewery after the war he had asked his sister if she and Eric wanted to invest in the new family venture and even take up and active role in the management of the business. The Crofts had considered the offer but decided not to take up William's invitation. They were settled in Essex and Eric enjoyed life as a chef to one of the titled families in the county. Besides, the wages of a chef and a housekeeper, Elisabeth also being in service at that time, were scarcely enough to live on let alone consider an investment of the sort William was suggesting. Looking back at the success that Steele's had enjoyed and its market value today it could be concluded that Eric and Elisabeth had missed a great opportunity to secure their family's financial future, but then hindsight is a wonderful thing!

Simon stared again at the photograph of the three boys and wondered where Graham was now and what he was doing. How long was it since they had last had any form of contact? He was not even sure that he himself had met Graham and his family again after 1976 although he assumed there must have been more holiday visits whilst his grandparents were still alive. Even if there were it must have been at least 35 years since Graham had been in Ingleby where William and Margaret had lived. Simon certainly had no idea of what had happened in the intervening years. Was Graham even alive?

As he contemplated this he suddenly remembered that Graham's father had died at quite a young age apparently as a result of injuries sustained in a vicious attack. Was that right? Was his name Gerry? It had only been mentioned briefly by Simon's parents if he could remember correctly which was totally understandable if the circumstances suggested foul play. And what of Sonia, his mother's cousin and close friend? As these thoughts and memories continued flooding into his mind he was suddenly struck with the realisation that his own children did not know that the Binns family even existed and that once he, Simon, died the two families might never be in touch again assuming that neither Mark nor their younger sister Annabel would make a proactive move in that direction.

Did it matter? He had had no contact with Graham Binns or his family for decades so what did he think was going to come out of re-establishing lines of communication now? Would Graham even remember who he was? Had Graham ever thought about Simon and the Letwins since they were last in contact and wondered what had happened to them over the years?

Simon rubbed his eyes and decided that he needed to try to contact Graham just to say hello and see how he was. It might just be a brief exchange of words followed by a resumption of the years of silence but Simon was now possessed with a desire, almost a need to know what had happened to his second cousin.

The next question was how to try to re-establish contact. It was alright concluding that he wanted to speak with Graham but he had no phone number, no email address, not even a physical address (although whether he would have written and posted a letter if he had was a matter of conjecture). Simon did not use mainstream social media so that was not an option either. As he thought this through his laptop pinged and a notification came through that someone had viewed his profile on Link Up. Link Up! Yes, that might work. Link Up was a social media business network that had seemingly become the default tool for recruitment and for getting in touch with professional people from all over the world.

Simon was not an avid regular user but he had built up a network of over 300 connections without really trying. Certainly he had accepted contact requests from people he did not know, mostly people looking either to supply the brewery with products or services or looking for employment. Recently a lot of people had viewed his profile given the rumours surrounding the potential sale or takeover of Steele's that had been swirling around for months like a pint of insipid ale.

Simon clicked on the Link Up icon and then opened his home page. In the search box he typed Graham Binns and found that there were at least 20 people with that name, mostly in the UK but a few in Canada, the USA and even one in Colombia. He went back to the search box and added Essex but this did not yield any more targeted results. So he scrolled down the list of all Graham Binns and checked those with display pictures. There was a software engineer and a publishing manager but neither looked anything like the young Graham in the photograph. Not that he might be easily recognisable 40 years after the beach photograph was taken.

Simon scrolled further down and saw a picture of a Graham Binns which looked a much better resemblance of what he imagined the 12-year old in the picture might look like now. He clicked on the profile name and scrolled down to the details on the work and education section. This Graham Binns ran his own accounting firm based in London and had graduated from Birmingham University in 1985. Simon had graduated in 1987 so since his Graham was two years older than him this would have been exactly the time to have expected him to graduate assuming of course that he had gone to university. This seemed promising. Simon screwed his eyes up and enlarged the display picture. There was a definite resemblance to young Graham. The profile contained no further clues as to whether this was the Graham Binns he was seeking or not. What should he do?

He could have sent a message and explained who he was but he was only a third level contact to this person so his only option was to send a contact request and wait to see whether he got a response. What would happen when his request landed in Graham's notifications assuming he had the right person? Would he see the name Simon Letwin and realise who it was? If he did, would he bother to accept the request given the years and years of silence between them? The only way to know that, Simon concluded, was to send it anyway and wait. He clicked on the contact icon and watched as his request disappeared into cyberspace.

Returning to thoughts of his original reason for coming into his study, Simon opened his work email inbox and scanned down the collection of new items that had arrived since he had last checked on Friday evening. Updated sales figures, brewery production numbers, supplier confirmations of orders, all the usual topics that the CEO of a business like Steele's Ales would receive every day. There was an email from Mark asking him for his comments on a presentation he had prepared for the upcoming Board meeting. Mark was the Chief Financial Officer at Steele's, the money and numbers guy who Simon had to say was an invaluable support to him as the CEO of the business. They tried to keep their private and business relationships separate in order to ensure that one did not interfere with the other. This was helped by the fact that they had very different personalities despite being close. Mark was quite introverted and someone who liked things to be in good order and as predictable as possible in an industry which was notoriously unpredictable. Simon, in contrast, was gregarious and outgoing and not averse to creating mini crises from time to time to spark some of his more laid back colleagues into action.

Simon opened the presentation and started to read through the slides which Mark had put together. Overall, he had little to add in terms of content since Mark had, as usual, prepared and researched his topic thoroughly. There were a couple of areas where Simon dropped a comment but it did not take him long to finish and return the presentation to his younger brother. He glanced at the rest of the new messages and decided that everything else could wait until tomorrow morning.

Simon looked again at the photo album sitting on his desk open at the page containing the picture on Scarborough beach. He was now almost desperate to find out what had happened to the Binns family over the past 40 years and wondered if this was a totally irrational piece of behaviour on his part. He had sent the contact request on Link Up but was this even the right Graham Binns? If it wasn't how on earth would he find the right one? If it was the right person, would he ignore the request or not even remember who Simon was? He sighed and was about to close the laptop down when it pinged again and a message flashed up on the screen.

Graham Binns had accepted his contact request.

3

CHAPTER 2

November 1937

"I really hate having to snatch time together like this and I keep wondering if we will ever truly be able to be together without having to hide it all."

The man had a pained expression on his face as they hugged each other. As their eyes met, he saw the same depth of sadness as he himself felt.
"You are still sure she does not suspect? I know we do not see each other very often but it is really difficult keeping something like this from the person you live with. And work too. Suspicions can mount there as well."
"Work is not a problem, I have flexibility there, so I am not worried on that score. I just have to be very careful on the home front. I am pretty sure she does not suspect there is anything going on. Anyway, as you said we hardly see each other so it is not as if I get away very often."

He sighed and they kissed briefly, brushing their lips together as they tightened their grip on each other.
"I was just thinking last week seeing Princess Elisabeth looking so happy when she married her prince that it is so unfair that we are not able to be like that. I so wish things were different and that we were free to follow our instincts."

His partner looked deep into his eyes and a weak smile formed. They both realised the sheer impossibility of that ever happening.

Even if he were to divorce his wife.

In 1937 it was illegal for two men to do what they were doing.

4

CHAPTER 3

9 August 2016

The previous week at Steele's Ales there was a knock on Simon's door but before he could open his mouth to say anything the imposing figure of his uncle was already heading towards his desk.
"I can't support this plan and nor will the other members of the Board. We have discussed this over and over recently and nothing changes anything. I didn't build this business up to where I did it to see it snaffled from under our very noses by people who would not know decent beer if someone tipped a keg of the bloody stuff over their heads!"
Keith Steele was neither a man for small talk nor one who waited to be invited into someone else's space. Simon would probably have been more offended by and animated at the rudeness of the chairman had he not long-ago developed the ability to resist such behaviour. It was as if there was a vaccine for Keithitus of which Simon had received his protective jab many moons ago.

Steele's Ales was still a wholly family-owned business, and Keith and Simon were the family representatives on the board of directors. The Board was made up of five people, the three additional directors having been appointed by the family to provide external corporate expertise. Simon would also have added privately that they played a mediation role whenever his uncle got on his high horse about anything, which was a regular occurrence, and which was seemingly becoming ever more prevalent as the Chairman aged, not altogether gracefully.

"I'm not so sure that the Board will be as much against it as you think, Keith. It is not every day that an offer which values your business at a 35% premium to the owners' current valuation comes along. It is all about how to create shareholder value. Yes, it is the family business, but at some stage all kids leave home, and a different phase of your life begins."

Keith glared at Simon, his trademark withering look evident all over his round red face.

"Old William would be turning in his grave, lad. How can you sit there blathering about shareholder value as if this was some tinpot operation rather than the family heritage? Well, my family heritage at least. It is quite clear that the name Steele means a lot less to you than it does to me. Mind you, maybe that's because you are not actually a Steele, are you, Mr Letwin?"

Below the belt even by Keith's low punching standards.

Simon could easily have lost his temper but chose to remain calm. Keith was so predictable. Simon was sorely tempted to point out that the Keith Steele years in the CEO role had been a period of stagnation and profit destruction for Steele's Ales rather than the era of wine and roses that Keith always tried to portray it as. The business had completely lost its way by 2007 leading to Keith being asked by the Board to step back and take on the role of chairman. Keith told anyone who would listen at the time that he was retiring to start work on a venture that would benefit the family business but, like most of Keith's claims, it was more bluster than substance. It had taken Simon three years as the incoming CEO to repair the effects of Keith's stewardship of the company and it was only in the last five years that positive growth had resumed. That was why companies such as Vinbrew, their current suitor, were so interested in adding Steele's to their growing portfolio of global beverage businesses.

As he fought to avoid entering into a slanging match with his uncle, Simon suddenly wondered as he had on several occasions recently if there was another reason why Keith was so adamant that the company would not be sold. What reason could that be? Would he be more receptive to selling to another family brewery rather than an international powerhouse such as Vinbrew who many traditionalists felt produced "plastic" beers unlike the "real" ales that a company like Steele's brewed? Or was there a different reason for his opposition, something not readily apparent, something floating below the surface hidden from view? It was not that Simon did not admire people who resolutely refuse to sell out something they love and believe in; it was just that in the case of Steele's Ales the offer on the table from Vinbrew was one that might not be repeated any time soon given that the beer industry was fickle and unpredictable to say the least.

"Ultimately, Keith, the decision is neither solely yours nor solely mine, so I suggest we do not waste any more time or breath until it is considered at next week's Board meeting."

"Waste our breath? Waste our sodding breath?" For a moment Simon was genuinely afraid that his uncle was on the verge of having a heart attack as his face grew redder than normal and spittle started to pour liberally from his quivering mouth. "I'll waste every last gasp of my breath, lad, if it keeps my company in the hands of those that built it. You will carry me out in a box before I allow Vimpoo or whatever they're bloody called to get their grubby paws on this business. In fact,..."

Keith's rising tirade was cut short by the appearance of Mark Letwin whose brow was furrowed as he entered his brother's office.

"What on earth is going on in here? I thought the roof was about to cave in. I couldn't hear myself think next door."

"Nothing really," said Keith, rocking his head from side to side, "only that the CEO is trying to engineer giving the family jewels away, so I just stopped by to make sure they are safely under lock and key and that the bloody key is firmly in my pocket."

"Keith, let's wait for the Board meeting before we get excited and take our eyes off the most important thing which is managing the day to day business to make sure it continues to grow. After all, that is why big companies like Vinbrew are interested in us in the first place. Which is also why I came to see Simon as the July accounts are ready for his review before next week's Board meeting."

"Mark, you are like a miniature Simon, do you know that? It is as clear as day that you two are trying to get this thing through the back door thinking that nobody is looking. Well, I am standing in front of the back bloody door and I am not moving an inch until this flavour of the month fad disappears once and for all and you two regain your sanity." With that, and leaving no room for any response, Keith spun on his heels and marched theatrically out of the office, almost colliding with a bronze African statue Simon had bought recently and muttering under his breath as he left.

"He has certainly got his pecker up today," said Mark, enjoying the post-Keith calm that had descended on Simon's office.

"He is a stubborn old bastard," replied Simon, "but I cannot get rid of this niggling feeling that there might be more to this than just Vinbrew. I have no basis for that thought and certainly no idea what it might be but one thing I am is perceptive. Something is definitely up."

Mark hummed and rubbed his chin. "It could just be another confirmation that he is getting older and more obnoxious as time goes by. It seems more and more the case that if everyone turns right uncle Keith will definitely turn left just to be bloody minded. It is in his DNA."

As he said this Mark was also thinking about what his brother had just said. Keith's argument certainly seemed to be based more on feelings of the heart than logic of the head.

Everything suggested that they should at least give very serious consideration to the Vinbrew takeover offer rather than dismiss it unconditionally as Keith was doing.

Why was their uncle so against selling the business? Was he afraid of something coming to light if the business was sold? Did Steele's, despite its stellar performance over recent times, have something dark and troubling lurking in one of its closets?

5

CHAPTER 4

14 August 2016

Simon stared at the screen where the confirmation that he had a new connection on Link Up sat in the bottom right-hand corner.

"Bingo!" he said to himself as a broad smile appeared on his face. He clicked on the box and was immediately taken to the Link Up site where he was encouraged to send a message to his new contact, something he fully intended to do without delay. He began typing.

"Hi Graham, this is Simon Letwin. Before I go any further can I just check that you are the Graham Binns that used to come to Ingleby with your parents to visit my grandparents William and Margaret?"

The response was immediate.

"Hi Simon. Yep, it is me! I was surprised to receive your contact request given that we have never really been in touch. What prompted this if I might ask?"

"To be honest, Graham, it was a spur of the moment thing. I was looking at some old photographs from my dad's collection and saw one of you, me and my brother Mark on the beach at Scarborough. It got me wondering what happened to you and your sister - I cannot even remember her name, I am afraid. Maybe it is the onset of old age, but I then decided I really ought to get in touch and at least re-establish a connection. I hope you do not mind."

"It is absolutely fine, Simon. I must admit I have not really thought about those summer trips for years, but it is really nice to hear from you. What have you been up to these last forty years?! The executive summary, of course!"

Simon launched into a brief history of his university days, joining the family brewing business in 1988 and rising to become CEO twenty years later. His marriage to Dani in 1993 and becoming a father a few years later.
"What about you, Graham?"
"After graduating I joined one of the big four accounting firms and worked for them for years until I decided I had had enough of the corporate world so set up my own company about 12 years ago. We specialise in accounting services for medical professionals, and it has proved a really good niche to be in. I am married to Sarah, and we have one daughter, Bridget, who is 22 now and just starting out as an accountant too. I did not push her in that direction before you ask!"
Simon smiled to himself. As if half a dozen sentences could do justice to four decades of someone's life!

"Sadly, my parents are both dead," Simon continued, deciding to offer this up front before Graham asked. He did not want his second cousin having to apologise for something he could not possibly know. "Mum got cancer in the late nineties and then Dad died in 2009. How is your family?"
"I am sorry to hear about your parents," Graham replied. Simon thought what a strange phrase this was, used by everyone when informed of a death. What had the other person to be sorry about?
"Yes, my mum Sonia is still alive although she lives in a care home now and has worsening dementia. She is 77. She has her good days and then for no reason cannot remember who Ashleigh and I are. You asked about my sister, by the way, her name is Ashleigh. And Dad, you might know that he died in 1991 when he was 50."

Simon was obviously aware that Graham's father had died young and waited for Graham to give a bit more information about his father's death but it never came. He assumed that the circumstances of his passing must have been very difficult for Graham and the family and was probably not something they talked about at least not with relative strangers like Simon.

"Simon, I need to go as I promised that I would help Bridget with an assignment she is working on, and she is shouting at me to ask if I am ready! It has been great having this little catch up."

Simon thought the same. At least he now knew that Graham was alive and well.

"I am not sure if you are up for this, but it would be great to meet up in person one of these days." People often said this when they reconnected with someone, but Simon genuinely meant it on this occasion. Their families were related and at least the previous generations had been very close, sharing family holidays and enjoying each other's company over many summers.

"Sure, why not? Do you ever get down to London?"

"Not very often," Simon admitted, "but I might need to be down there in the near future." Simon was thinking about the possible takeover of Steele's which might require him to be in the capital soon to either move this forward or to build a defence if the Board decided to rebuff the approach. Their retained lawyers had offices in the capital and a meeting there soon was a distinct possibility.

"If you are coming down just let me know. It would be good to catch up, I agree. Must go now. Cheers!"

Simon closed the Link Up page and then closed the laptop. He was feeling pleased with himself for having found Graham which had at least allowed him to satisfy his curiosity regarding the fate of the Binns family since they last met. As he stood up and headed back towards the lounge where the family was watching TV he did not yet know that very soon he would meet up with Graham Binns, a meeting that would draw him into something he could not imagine where lives would be put at risk and where events that had happened decades earlier would be dug up and pulled violently from their hiding places where they had been buried for years, deep in the past.

Buried deep where at least one person wanted them to remain, someone who would not shy away from doing everything they could to keep these particular secrets hidden from view.

Forever.

6

CHAPTER 5

14 August 2016

At the same time as Simon Letwin was exchanging his first words with Graham Binns in forty years, another British man was enjoying a cold San Miguel beer in a bar on the Costa del Sol. In fact, he was the owner of the bar and sometimes he still could not believe how lucky he had been to have the opportunity to set up a business like this in the sun-drenched Mediterranean.

It would soon be twenty-five years since he first set foot in Marbella, newly arrived from England with the keys to a business that would secure his future. Who would have guessed? Certainly not those who labelled him a lazy bugger, a dropout, a stain on the family, a good-for-nothing wastrel, the black sheep of the litter. Fuck them, he thought, smiling at the irony and the fact that most of these poor, sad people slaved fifty weeks of the year to be able to afford a fortnight in the place he now called home.

He took a long, satisfying mouthful of cold beer and remembered the day that all of this had been made possible. They say that the key to success is being in the right place at the right time and he for one would not argue with that. The memory of that Saturday afternoon came flooding back to him. He had been listening to the radio following his football team Leeds United as they played a top of the table league match against Manchester City in a season where they finished in third place. Whenever Leeds played there was very little that could distract him, yet the sound of raised voices and a great deal of banging piqued his curiosity such that he abandoned the radio and went to investigate what was happening. As he approached the kitchen, he saw that the door was closed which was unusual as nobody ever shut the doors in their house. The loud voices were coming from inside the kitchen which probably explained why somebody had decided to close the door on this occasion.

"You have known this all along, but you kept it quiet to suit your own selfish bloody purposes."

Silence.

He did not recognise the voice of the man who had spoken and wondered if it was a business contact of his father's that had been wronged. No, a business contact would not be in their house, surely any meeting to discuss work would have taken place outside. So, who was this person and why was he hurling accusations around like this?

"Well, we want our share of it now and we are going to get it. In fact, I won't rest until this wrong has been made right and I will do whatever is necessary to make it happen. You might want to keep this grubby little secret hidden from view, but I am sorry, the genie has been released from the lamp and there is no way to put it back."

The other man in the room remained silent. If what the first man was saying was true, there was probably not a lot he could have said. The young man continued to listen from outside the kitchen and it was the next sentence spoken by the unknown voice that really made his ears prick up and stand to attention. As the full implication of what was being discussed was made clear to him, he started to understand what the grubby little secret was. Except in his view, if what the visitor was saying was even half true, it was far more than a grubby little secret, it was a stick of dynamite waiting to be lit. It was at this moment that the man who had remained silent started to speak.

"If you dare utter one word about this it will be the last word you ever speak. I will not let you or anyone else ruin things. We can talk and see what we might be able to do, but what you are suggesting is never going to happen. I will personally make sure of that."

"There is no way I am going away quietly now I know what happened and you had better realise that. I will not rest till we have back what is rightly ours."

He took another swig of his beer and the satisfied smirk returned to his face as the memories flooded back. He had retreated from outside the kitchen back to his room, worried that the two men might open the door and find him listening outside. He was delighted to discover that Lee Chapman had scored to put Leeds in front in a game they would eventually win 3-2 .

Several days after the heated exchange in the kitchen he heard another conversation, this time over the phone, which again caused him to stop and listen. Ordinarily he paid no attention to such things, but it was what was being said that stopped him in his tracks.

'Dead. Suspicious circumstances. I could not believe it. Apparently, he was in perfect health so I really do not know what must have happened. But the police are involved."

He had listened to the rest of the conversation and as he did so a dawning realisation had crept into his mind that maybe the events being discussed on the phone call were linked to what had happened in the kitchen a few days earlier. Was the dead man the unknown stranger who had been making the accusations of a cover up? It would not be long before he found out.

Yes, in this life you make your own luck because nobody is going to make it for you.

"Maria, dame una cerveza, por favor." He was not fluent in Spanish, despite all the years living there, but he did know how to order another beer. As he slurped the cold liquid, he congratulated himself on having been perceptive enough to take advantage of the circumstances that had presented themselves to him.

Right place, right time.

He would bloody well drink to that!

7

CHAPTER 6

17 August 2016

The Steele's board meeting turned out to be exactly the kind of lively affair that could have been predicted given the dramatically differing views of the two camps that had formed regarding the potential takeover of the business. Keith Steele did his best to convince the Board that the family jewels should never be available for sale but in the end the Board voted in favour of doing some more detailed work on the Vinbrew offer and also looking proactively to see if any counter offers might be forthcoming as a way of ensuring that if the final decision made was to sell Steele's that the best price was being obtained for the company.

In terms of concrete actions, it was agreed that Simon and Mark would have a meeting with the firm of mergers and acquisitions lawyers the Board had identified who would advise on the best way of assessing whether what Vinbrew was offering was the best deal they could get. That would then allow the Board to decide if they could ask more for the business or not which in turn would be considered as part of the final decision as to whether they agreed to sell Steele's Ales or not.

Keith was predictably hostile after the Board meeting finished and left nobody in any doubt that he viewed the decision to move to the next stage rather than kill the takeover offer outright as being somewhere between an act of sabotage and a complete failure to recognise what the phrase "family business" meant.

Simon deliberately avoided speaking directly with his uncle after the meeting as he had other things to focus on to do with the business. He found that even a short time in Keith Steele's company was extremely energy sapping and he could not afford to be anything other than ruthless with his time management if he was to get home at a reasonable time this evening. Before he dived into the issues he needed to work on he called Judith, his PA, to come to his office.

"Jude, Mark and I need to go to London next week to meet with the guys at Westmann Buck. You know, the lawyers we have identified to help us with the Vinbrew offer? Can you contact Peter Westmann and see when he is available for a meeting. Check my diary and Mark's and see if we can schedule something for early next week that works for all of us."

Judith smiled in her usual efficient manner and left the office.

Simon spent the next three hours working on the important tasks in hand and finally closed his laptop and packed his bag just after six thirty. It had been a long and somewhat bruising day with the events at the Board meeting, but things had at least gone the way he had hoped and they now had the green light to do a proper evaluation of the Vinbrew offer. He had not yet finally made his own mind up whether a sale was in their best interests, but at least they would be able to objectively look at both sides of the coin before reaching a definitive decision.

The forty-minute drive home was largely uneventful and Simon allowed his mind to wander as he drove more or less on automatic pilot. Before he reached home, he had thought about the Vinbrew deal, the winter skiing holiday he and Dani planned to go on and the reconnection with Graham Binns which might hopefully advance a little further now that he was heading down to London sometime next week. He would wait for Judith to confirm the date and then send Graham a message to see if he was free to meet up.

"Hi babes," Simon called as he opened the front door and stepped into the entrance hall. The smell of something delicious wafted from the kitchen.
"In here, hun," came the reply and Simon found his wife sitting in the lounge reading something on her tablet.
"Something smells good. What's on the menu?"
Dani smiled at Simon. "Salmon en croute. I know how much you love it, and I reckoned you would have had a stressful day with the board meeting so this is like a massage for the palate!"
Simon grabbed Dani's arms, hoisted her out of the chair and wrapped his arms around her tightly.
"You always know how to push the right buttons, babes, that is why I still love you as much as I ever did." He kissed her and took in the familiar smell of her perfume, intoxicating and intriguing.
"So how was the Board meeting? More importantly how badly behaved was Keith?"
Dani was not involved in the business (her choice – she had always told Simon working and living together was a recipe for disaster) but she was usually fully up to speed with happenings at Steele's and had seen enough of Simon's uncle in the twenty seven years she had known her husband to be in no doubt as to what kind of man he was. Their paths rarely crossed these days, and she was certainly not complaining about that. She had been heard to say on numerous occasions that if she had one more direct encounter with Keith Steele it would be one too many.

Simon launched into a resume of the day's happenings. The rancorous exchanges at the Board meeting and the silent pleasure he had got following the majority decision to consider the Vinbrew offer. He had particularly enjoyed watching the wind rapidly deflate Keith's sails as if somebody had stuck a pin into his preciously guarded party balloon.

"So, Mark and I will go to London next week to meet the lawyers and start looking at the next steps in assessing the offer on the table. I am not sure yet which way this will go, and I am certainly not going to play any part in giving away the family jewels as Keith is accusing me of doing. However, if the offer is right for the business and, more importantly, for the shareholders, I would give strong consideration to supporting it. Especially given that we are a key shareholder!"

The shareholding of Steele's was split equally between the families of the two children of William Steele who founded the brewery in 1947. Keith Steele owned 50% of the shares with the other 50% now divided equally between the three children of the late Carmen Letwin (nee Steele), Keith's younger sister and mother of Simon, Mark and Annabel. Whilst Simon and Mark had worked in the family company since graduating from university, their sister had chosen to pursue her love of art and now ran a very successful gallery in Cambridge with her husband Paul.

Dani went to check how dinner was progressing and ten minutes later she and Simon were sitting at the dining table ready to tuck into the salmon.
"I have chilled one of those bottles of Marlborough Sauvignon Blanc," she said. I was pretty sure you might need some fortification after the day you seem to have had."
Simon raised his glass. "Cheers to us babes, and here's to the future, whatever direction it may take us in". They clinked glasses and started their dinner.
"By the way, the trip to London will hopefully allow me to meet up with Graham Binns as I mentioned last Sunday. Judith is sorting the meeting timings and then I will send him a message to try to fix something up."
"This thing seems to have got right into your system, love," replied Dani. "Is there something about this that you are not telling me? Forty years of silence and then out of the blue you are planning to meet for dinner."

Simon had to admit that his wife's observation was valid. She had never heard of Graham Binns a week ago and now here he was infiltrating her husband's thoughts and making him hopeful that he could get down to London to meet up with his second cousin. From what Simon had told her, apart from the annual family holiday, which grew out of the strong fraternal bond between William Steele and his sister Elisabeth, and had ended when William and Margaret had passed, the families had not spoken in decades. Dani was, therefore, more than justified in her scepticism.

"I can only put it down to the onset of old age," said Simon chuckling. "I just got it into my head that it would be awful if we died without ever speaking again and that Graham and I are basically the last links between the two families. If we both popped our clogs that would be that, finito."

"Are you sure Graham is as keen on this as you seem to be? I mean, God forbid that he might think you are some kind of weirdo popping up out of the blue one day wanting to pry into the last forty years of his family goings on having shown zero interest in any of them since you were a child."

A fair question, thought Simon but he did not say this out loud. The salmon was delicious and the white wine a perfect accompaniment to dinner. By the time he had finished eating Simon felt that most of the day's stress had dissipated and he looked forward to an hour watching the news before heading up to bed. With thoughts of Keith, the Board meeting and takeover bids firmly parked at the back of his mind, Simon stood up, kissed Dani and retreated to the lounge.

8

CHAPTER 7

July 1938

As a young girl Elisabeth Steele had loved the life in Ingleby with her brother William and their parents and it would certainly be true to say that the Steele family was a very close-knit one.

Going into service at the local manor house in 1933 at the age of 14, Elisabeth's life was dramatically changed a year later when she met Eric Croft. He had moved to Ingleby with his family from Essex since his father had been transferred to the local RAF base.

Eric was a trainee cook and was also hired by the Earl of Ingleby's household to work in the kitchens alongside Elisabeth. From almost the very first day in his new job, Eric began to flirt with Elisabeth, commenting on how beautiful she was and telling her that she was far too smart to be working as a mere kitchen hand.

Nobody had ever spoken to her in such a way and in truth she saw herself as very ordinary compared with some of the other girls who worked at Ingleby Hall. Perhaps this was why she fell hook, line and sinker for Eric, who was more softly spoken and gentle compared to the boys Elisabeth had mixed with before.

Most of them were cocksure and full of themselves, believing that they could snap their fingers and have any girl they chose come running. Eric was different and Elisabeth loved the way he treated her as an equal and with respect. He was two years older than her but at eighteen was still just a boy.

Over the next two years their relationship moved forward at breakneck speed. Within six months Eric had asked Elisabeth to marry him, having first approached her father Horace to gain his approval.

Horace Steele was a traditionalist and believed that marrying one's daughter off at a young age and in full bloom was preferable to waiting and risking her becoming less attractive to the male species, ending up with an undesirable husband, so he gave Eric his blessing without much ado.

At the same time, Eric's father was posted back to Essex and Eric told Elisabeth that he would like to follow them as he missed his home county. At first Elisabeth was not keen to leave Yorkshire and her family particularly as both she and Eric had jobs working together with the Earl.

Not to be deterred, Eric contacted his former employer, the family that owned Humberton House, just outside his home town of Ilford, and managed to secure not only a cook's role for himself but also a job for his wife to be.

In love and keen to support her future husband, Elisabeth agreed that a move to Essex would be fine with her. The couple were married at St Jude's Church in Ilford in October 1936 and started to build their new married life together in Essex.

However, within a few months of moving to Ilford Elisabeth started to notice some fairly dramatic changes in Eric. Whereas earlier he was attentive and would do anything for her, he now seemed to be growing distant and to be preoccupied with things other than his wife.

At first the changes were subtle, such as neglecting to kiss Elisabeth goodbye before he left the house, but gradually things became much more obvious, and Elisabeth was at a loss to understand what had changed.

She tried to ignore the situation, even wondering if the apparent changes in Eric had come about as a result of something she had done, but she could not identify the root cause of the issue.

Then one afternoon, whilst Eric was working and she was on a break, she folded some washing and went to put it in Eric's wardrobe, noticing as she did the corner of a white greetings card poking out from amongst her husband's shirts.

Initially telling herself she should not pry, she was nevertheless curious as to whether this was a card that she herself had sent to Eric. Puzzled and keen to allay any fears, she reached out and picked it up.

As she looked at the greeting on the front and then opened it to read the message inside her face froze and she was momentarily paralysed with shock. She had feared that she may not like what she read, but the message that the card contained, and its implications, were far worse than she could ever have imagined.

* * *

"I just don't know what to do, Margaret, I really don't. Since I found the card a couple of weeks ago, I have been wandering around like a mad woman. I knew I was coming here to visit and that I could confide in you. Honestly, I do not know anyone else I could discuss this with."

The hopelessness painted across Elisabeth's face was stark and Margaret Jones, whilst believing herself to be a good listener, wondered as she heard the other woman's story what she could say that might make the situation even marginally better for her friend.

Margaret was engaged to be married to William Steele, Elisabeth's elder brother, and was two years older than her. Because of the distance between Ingleby and Ilford the two women did not see each other very often since Elisabeth had moved south, but they wrote to each other on a very regular basis.

Margaret had received Elisabeth's latest letter only a week earlier and had been counting down the days to her visit given the worrying hints that the letter contained, suggesting that all was not well with her and Eric.

Now that Elisabeth was explaining the source of her helplessness Margaret understood exactly why the younger woman felt the way she did.

"Have you given any hint to Eric that you found the card?" Margaret was fairly sure she knew the answer to that question, but she did not know how else to move the conversation forward.

"My goodness, no," replied Elisabeth, "I have not said anything of that nature."

"And I do not think you should", said Margaret, "unless and until you are prepared to walk away from your marriage."

Elisabeth looked at the other woman, a mixture of pleading and despair etched all over her face.

"But how can things ever work after this? I told you Eric has changed since we got married and I am pretty sure that this is why. So, if this is going to continue, and I see no reason to doubt that it will, the Eric I fell in love with will never come back. What is the point of being married to him?"

Margaret, who was excited at the thought of her own future betrothal to William, thought that Elisabeth might be overreacting. Firstly, a card in itself, no matter how suggestive the words it contained, was not necessarily proof of a full-blown affair.

In her view it was in the nature of men to flirt with other women and this card might simply be from someone with whom Eric had done just that, giving the other person the idea that there might be more to his words than there actually was.

For example, Eric may not have revealed to the card sender that he was married, which could have completely altered the other person's view had they only been aware.

"I know it is worrying for you, Elisabeth," said Margaret, "but I would suggest that you don't rush into anything which you may well later regret.

At least give yourself some time to see how things develop. You never know, this other woman may just be a temporary distraction for Eric until he gets whatever it is out of his system. You know men, they are stupid and don't use their brains half the time!"

Elisabeth looked at Margaret and slowly shook her head. Without saying anything, she reached into her bag, retrieved the card and handed it to her friend. The greeting on the front of the card proclaimed "Special Greetings for the Love of my Life" but it was the words written inside that caused Margaret to utter a high-pitched "Bloody Hell!".

"To my darling Eric.

You cannot imagine how much I love and want you however impossible that might be. I hope we can continue to snatch moments like last week when you can get away.

Robert x

9

CHAPTER 8

23 August 2016

"This is your table, sir. I'll leave you the menu and wine list to browse through whilst you wait for your colleague." The waiter smiled efficiently, turned and retreated to deal with another table.

It was Tuesday evening and Simon had just arrived at Mendoza, one of London's up and coming Argentinian steak houses. Simon was a self-confessed carnivore and never missed an opportunity to enjoy a thick rib-eye steak when the occasion presented itself. This had in recent times caused some fairly heated debates with his youngest son, Greg, who, the previous year, had announced that he was becoming a vegan. He claimed when asked by Simon that this was a decision made on health grounds, but Hannah lost no time in correcting her brother's version of events announcing at the dinner table that it was actually because the girl he fancied at school was a vegan and he reckoned that this might put him ahead of other suitors in the chase for her affections. Greg's hostile, ultra-defensive reaction to his sister's revelation was, to Simon's mind, clear evidence that the girlfriend theory trumped the health theory by a considerable distance, and he had smiled inwardly at his son's evident discomfort at having been found out. To date, there had been no outward sign of Greg's progress in the vegan girlfriend stakes but who knew what was happening behind the scenes? Teenage kicks, teenage angst, thought Simon and he rather hoped that Greg was making more progress than he seemed to be.

As he looked around the restaurant for any sign of Graham Binns (they had agreed to meet at 7.30 and it was still only 7.25) Simon's thoughts shifted to the meeting he and Mark had had earlier that day with Peter Westmann. They had sent the lawyer a large amount of information as pre-reading for the meeting so thankfully they had been able to move fairly quickly to the heart of the discussion once the personal introductions and the mandatory bout of small talk had been dealt with. Westmann was, Simon was pleased to note, fairly un-lawyerly in his demeanour and approach so the discussion, far from being heavy in technical detail and legal speak, was refreshingly straightforward and to the point.

"My initial reaction is that the offer on the table is quite fair and realistic from what I understand so far about Steele's business, so I think you have a basis from which to move forward if you choose to do so. Very often the initial offer is derisory but in this case I think that as an opening salvo it is a reflection that these guys are quite serious about wishing to acquire your company. Clearly there is a whole raft of work to be done and you will find that this will be a huge drain on the ability of those involved to focus on their day-to-day responsibilities, but it is critical that you do your due diligence every bit as thoroughly as Vinbrew will be doing theirs. I think we could also up the ante a bit with Vinbrew by trying to attract some alternative interest in Steele's, real or not. We have plenty of experience in that area and I would happily help you to put that in motion."
Peter Westmann smiled, satisfied that he had said more or less what he was sure Simon and Mark were hoping to hear. Since the fee he would earn from a successful conclusion to the matter was not inconsiderable, it would have been surprising if that was not the case.

Whilst Simon was meeting Graham, Mark was taking advantage of being in London to catch up with an old university friend of his who had been a fellow member of the Bristol University Cycling club and who now lived and worked in Hampstead. As Simon's thoughts returned from the offices of Westmann Buck to the present he became aware of a presence next to the table.

"Sir, I believe your colleague has arrived."
Simon looked around in time to see the waiter showing Graham Binns to the table and pulling back the chair with the invitation to sit down and make himself comfortable.
"Hello, Simon, it is really good to see you again."
Graham offered his hand and Simon smiled and reciprocated.
"Graham, it's great to see you in the flesh after all this time! We used to have a school song that started with the line "Forty years on when afar and asunder" and that could have been written for this occasion!"
The two men laughed and there was a small period of silence as if they were two actors on stage not quite remembering which of them was supposed to speak next. Simon broke the deadlock.
"The good thing is we both went through the elevator summary of our last forty years when we chatted on Link Up so we probably do not need to do that again. I am just pleased that we are getting to meet up and re-establish contact. I was saying to Dani the other day that I almost feel we owe it to our parents and grandparents to do that given how close they were during the 60s and 70s."
"Yes, I agree," replied Graham, "I was telling Sarah about you and your family after I accepted your connect request and she was amazed that I had never once spoken of you during all the time I have known her. She asked me why that was and to be honest I could not find a really convincing answer to that question."

It was a fair question to ask. Indeed, it was a question that had been occupying Simon's mind quite frequently since he reached out to Graham a few weeks earlier. Why did people lose touch? What was it that suddenly turned a close family connection into a void of nothingness? It was not just families like the Steele's/Letwins and the Binns, it was everywhere. Simon had several of his old university friends, people he saw pretty much every day for three years and grew very close to, that he had intended to stay friends with for life but who, soon after graduation, had disappeared from his radar (as he had surely done from theirs). How many were dead? Married? Divorced? Successful? Dropouts? He thought about Mike and Rob, the two guys he shared a dilapidated student house with in his second year who were such diametrically opposed characters that Simon had had to hone his mediation skills to a razor-sharp level by the end of the academic year. Mike was a committed socialist, introverted, glass half-empty sort of person to whom life seemed to deliver blow after blow (some of which Simon was sure were overblown or non-existent) whilst Rob came from a landed farming family, was an extreme extrovert, cheerful and bouncy and spent most of the year goading Mike and playing on the latter's natural lack of self-confidence. This frequently provoked screaming outbursts as Mike's low coping threshold burst through the dam and filled the house with streams of abuse and, at times, floods of tears.

"Are you okay, Simon?" Graham's question brought Simon back from the streets of Durham into the slightly more salubrious surroundings of the steak restaurant.

"Yes, Graham, I'm fine. I have been asking myself the same question as Sarah asked for a while now. Does something suddenly happen that makes people grow apart or is it just a natural consequence of moving on to the next phase of your life? A bit heavy and existential, I know. Should we order drinks and look at the menu?"

They agreed on a mid-priced bottle of Malbec which turned out to be very good. Simon had already decided to have a rib eye and Graham chose a fillet steak. With the ordering done Simon brought the discussion back to the family memories which had led to this meeting

"It feels strange that we are related but not really knowing very much at all about your family," he started. "I vaguely remember meeting you all at my grandparents' house and of course I have the famous picture of you with Mark and me on Scarborough beach but that aside it is almost as if we were

total strangers."
"Yes, "replied Graham, "it is a bit weird. You know in those days people did not go on foreign holidays, so Ingleby was about as exotic as it got for people living in Ilford!" He laughed at this, and Simon nodded.

"So, you said your mum is still alive, Graham, although suffering from dementia?"
"Yes, she is. She started to develop the symptoms about seven years ago and we eventually had to move her into a care home. She has her good days when she is fairly lucid but increasingly she forgets who Ashleigh and I are. It's really upsetting when that happens to someone you love."
Graham looked wistful and Simon thought he noticed a small tear in his second cousin's eye. He quickly moved the subject on to his own parents.
"As I said, mum died at 57 in 2001 when she developed bone cancer. We thought she had beaten it, but it came back and unfortunately she could not fight it any longer. It is never easy to watch your nearest and dearest slip away like that."
"And what about Ronald?" asked Graham.
"Dad was a paragon of health until the last couple of years. Then he just went downhill and in the end it all happened very quickly. He was a GP but that is no protection when your time is up."

They had spoken about three of the four parents and Simon wondered whether it was now an appropriate time to enquire about Gerry. The initial discussion on Link Up had revealed no details on what actually happened to Graham's father. Simon hesitated because he already knew that the man had met a nasty and untimely death and was sure it must still be a tough thing for the family to talk about. In the end he did not need to say anything as Graham brought the subject up himself.
"I am sure you heard about my dad. He was attacked and killed in the cycle shop in 1991. As you can imagine, it was hell, and the hurt is still there. It hit mum particularly hard as you can imagine."
"I did hear something at the time, Graham, but as I was just a kid I never

really understood exactly what happened and why."

"The why is still something of a mystery. They arrested a local guy called Michael Spedding within days and he is in prison serving a life sentence for murder. He had a history of robbery and had committed a fair few crimes but this was seemingly the first time that any physical violence had been involved. The strange thing is that Dad never kept a lot of money in the shop, and it is quite difficult to steal enough bicycles to have made him a worthwhile target."

"Was there ever a challenge to the verdict? I mean, as you said, it seems an odd choice of target if you are a big-time crook whilst if you are a petty thief who has never used violence before why you would start on this occasion?"

Graham sighed. "No, the verdict was never challenged. The police said the evidence was strong and they found a discarded cigarette butt in the shop which the forensics guys matched with the records they had on file for Spedding. So, I guess that they must have got the right person."

"I am really very sorry, Graham, it must be so hard losing someone in that way."

"Yes, it has been hell." From the look on Graham's face this was still a raw and open wound for him.

"Rib eye medium rare?"

The waiter's arrival was perfectly timed, and Simon was glad that he did not have to deal with the silence which seemed inevitable after the discussion about Gerry.

"And here is your medium fillet, sir. Can I get you anything else?"

"I think we are fine," replied Simon as Graham shook his head.

"Please enjoy."

The steak was every bit as good as Simon had hoped it would be and from the way Graham tucked into his fillet it seemed that they were both of a similar opinion. The Malbec was a perfect match for the food and neither man said anything significant whilst they ate dinner. As the waiter cleared away the two clean plates Simon patted his stomach and smiled.

"Well, I have to say I enjoyed that. My son would no doubt protest vehemently, but I could not become a vegan or a veggie because I would miss this too much."

"I agree," said Graham. "Sarah and I occasionally do a veggie week but if I thought that would be the last steak I ever ate I would be mighty disappointed."

The waiter returned to ask about desserts but neither man took up the invitation although Simon had half hoped that Graham might want one which would have allowed him to justify to himself that he should keep him company and order a New York cheesecake.

"I have really enjoyed catching up," said Simon, "we should not leave it another forty years before we do it again! In fact, if you and Sarah fancy a trip up to Ingleby we would be pleased to host you."

"That is very kind. Yeah, it was really nice to see you too, Simon. I will mention your kind offer to Sarah and let's stay in contact."

Simon drained the last of his wine, they split the bill and then shook hands before heading their separate ways. For Simon, this involved a short tube ride to the hotel which he had booked knowing it would be a late night and one which involved too much wine for him to drive back to Ingleby. He would do that in the morning, refreshed and after a decent night's sleep.

For some reason the sleep he was looking forward to after an early start and a long day did not come and he lay in bed thinking about the discussions with Graham. Gerry's death had clearly been a violent one and according to the police was a closed case. Forensic evidence backed up the circumstantial evidence which showed that the local criminal who was arrested was indeed the person responsible for murdering Gerry. Yet for a reason which he could not put his finger on, Simon felt that there was more to this than initially met the eye. But what did this have to do with him?

It had happened 25 years ago, and life had moved on. The pain would no doubt have eased somewhat for Sonia and the Binns family as the years went by and reopening the wounds which must at least have started to heal would only be justified if there was any doubt that the police had got it wrong. Furthermore, any re-examination of the case would have to be at the request of the Binns family, it had absolutely nothing to do with Simon.

Still, he could not shake the feeling of discomfort and his sixth sense told him there was something that had been missed or had not been said. What he was even more certain of was that Graham had similar doubts. His second cousin had not said anything to suggest this at dinner, but Simon was an intuitive person and he could feel the tension brewing in Graham's mind as he explained the death of his father. It was no doubt far easier for Graham to keep his thoughts bottled up and, anyway, why would he even venture to share any misgivings about the original verdict with Simon who had had no contact with anyone in the Binns family for forty years?

That did not of course mean that the police had got their deductions right or that this Michael Spedding was guilty beyond any reasonable doubt. As he lay in bed willing sleep to come to clear his mind of what could well turn out to be fantasy, Simon was sure of one thing.

The case might not be as closed as everyone assumed.

10

CHAPTER 9

May 1939 – Middle Winton, Somerset

As the English Spring moved hastily towards Summer with the sun beating down on one of the most beautiful villages in one of England's most picturesque counties, the word idyllic, so often overused, was not an exaggeration when describing this particular Sunday afternoon in Middle Winton.

In the garden of Nettle Cottage, a 17th century Grade II listed building, three young women sat drinking lemonade and playing Monopoly. The game had been launched in England three years earlier and was becoming very popular as a form of family entertainment particularly since the Great Depression had affected people's finances and meant that money was short for other forms of entertainment.
"That will be £230 please, "said one of the women with a triumphant look on her face. She was the only child of the family that lived at Nettle Cottage, and she worked as a typist in the offices of a local company in nearby Minehead.
"I will get the hang of this game one of these days!" The second woman laughed and handed over a fistful of notes to her friend whilst the third girl chided her about her continuing bad luck.

The other two young women had been staying in Middle Winton for the past three weeks and it was envisaged that they would be there for a few months more given the condition of one of them. Her fiancé had decided that the best way to treat her health issue was to send her down to Somerset away from her normal existence, somewhere it was felt that she could rest and recuperate in relative privacy. She could also come and go more easily, avoiding the need for difficult explanations to worried or quizzical family members and friends. Outwardly she did not look sick which was hardly surprising since medically there was nothing wrong with her. The reason she was in Somerset, miles from home, was precisely because she needed to avoid being seen out and about in her local neighbourhood. Removing her from home would avoid the need to suffer the gossip which would inevitably result from her being noticed by those that knew the family and from having to explain her condition. Furthermore, for her fiance such a revelation might be much more than embarrassing, it could potentially scupper his plans to set up his own business given the social stigma attached to their predicament.

The girl was not married.

But she was pregnant.

11

CHAPTER 10

24 August 2016

Despite his sleepless night in London, Simon had set off for Yorkshire bright and early the following morning and was sitting at his desk when Mark walked into his office at 10.30.

"Hey, Simon, how was the dinner with Graham?"

"Morning bro," replied Simon, using a Hannah-ism as if he was still in his formative years rather than entering his fifties. "The dinner was excellent; you must try the place sometime. The meeting with Graham was very interesting too and it was really good to catch up with him. At least the two families are back in contact and my somewhat irrational fear of losing that forever has been exorcised."

"Did anything new come out of filling the gaps of the past forty years?"

"I am not sure." Simon had decided to be a bit cagey about the subject of Gerry's death if and when he spoke about it to Mark or anyone else on the Steele or Letwin sides of the family. After all, he might be blowing things out of all proportion, and he had absolutely no evidence to suggest that Michael Spedding, whom he did not know from Adam, was innocent of the crime he had been jailed for committing. Simon had spent the time during the drive north thinking more deeply about the whole matter and decided that he had perhaps been too hasty in adding two and two to get five and that he should rather leave the whole matter where it currently stood, closed and over. In any case, it was, he had reminded himself, none of his business.

"I also had a great catch up with Billy, so it seems we both made the most of our time in the capital. I did get the late train back though and it was a short night by the time I finally reached home. By the way, have you heard from Uncle Keith since we spoke with Peter Westmann?"

It always amused Simon that Mark continued to refer to the Chairman as "uncle". Indeed, when they were children, their uncle was adamant that they simply call him Keith.

"I am too bloody young to be your uncle, makes me sound like an old git."

When Simon had revealed this conversation to his mother Carmen, she had confirmed that her brother was, if not yet an old git, well down the road to becoming one. In truth, it was the understatement of the year to say that Keith and Carmen lacked sibling affection, he believing his sister to be too pushy "for a woman", she of the opinion that her brother had clearly inherited some rogue genes from somewhere. A prime example of their disjointed relationship had occurred on Simon's ninth birthday when Keith bought him a hunting knife in a leather scabbard more to annoy Carmen than because Simon had ever expressed a desire to own one.

"No, the old git has been unusually silent these past twenty-four hours."

Simon had segued seamlessly from his thoughts about the younger Keith to the present day but felt the "old git" mantra was definitely appropriate for the present time.

As if on cue and with the timing of a seasoned actor Keith Steele burst into Simon's office without knocking or in any way pre-warning the CEO of his imminent arrival.

"Oh, do come in, Keith, please don't worry about knocking to make sure I am not in a meeting." Simon refused to be intimidated by his uncle and had some time ago decided that standing up to him was the best way to handle him.

"I didn't realise the Chairman of the Board was required to knock, Simon. Anyway, as seemingly the only defender of this business from external attack I think I am allowed to do whatever is required to stop other people from flogging my company as if we were at a bloody car boot sale."

Simon decided once again not to rise to the bait which was his other strategy for dealing with Keith.

"Yes Keith, we had a fruitful meeting in London yesterday." Simon felt a little sarcasm would not go amiss. "The lawyer feels that the initial offer is a fair one for starters and certainly a basis for the Board to give it serious consideration before we decide how to proceed."

Mark chipped in to back up his elder brother.

"Yeah, I thought it went well too. This is the very first stage in the process but at least we are off to a promising start."

Keith Steele looked from Simon to Mark and back again.

"It is clear that you two have made up your minds about this already, but I repeat that it will be over my dead body that Steele's Ales will be sold to these Vimbro guys. You cannot just muscle in on seventy years of family history brandishing your cheque book like some American sports magnate buying up football clubs."

Simon considered himself a patient man who was happy to let people have their full say but Keith's tedious and repetitive rants coupled with his unsubtle, even nasty suggestions that he, Simon, was not passionately committed to the family business, was pushing him closer and closer to the edge.

"Keith," he began, "I understand that you have been part of this business for a very long time and that you have strong opinions about our future direction but please stop insinuating that I am any less committed to our family's well-being than you are. I have given 28 years of my life to Steele's, and I will continue to give my everything for as long as my everything is required. I suggest we park the discussion about takeovers, defence battles and the like until the Board has something concrete to discuss."

For a split-second Simon thought his words might have broken through Keith's hard shell but he soon realised that his uncle was not about to cease his tirade any time soon
"If you think you can silence me so that you can push your grubby scheme through think again, lad. I will continue to shout and scream until someone listens and turns back from this crazy notion that the family is better off if Steele's is sold rather than rescued from the clutches of those grabbing bastards."

"Oh, by the way Keith, I met someone last night from our dim, distant family past!"
Simon decided that the best way to halt the onslaught would be to completely change the subject and try to deflect Keith's attention from his present obsession.
"And who would that be?" said Keith, more dismissive than interested, but Simon thought a response of any kind was welcome if it tempered the flames of his uncle's wrath.
"Graham Binns. I am sure you remember Sonia and Gerry and their family who used to stay with Grandma and Grandad when we were kids. Your memory of them stretches back further than mine although I assume you probably avoided Mum and Sonia like the plague given the apparent lack of fraternal affection if what Mum used to tell me was true."
"What brought about this little reunion if I might be as bold as to ask? It must be years since any of us saw one of the Binns family and I am pretty sure their visits to Ingleby had more or less stopped by the time you were growing up."
"I know it sounds dramatic, Keith, but I was worried that once the present generation on both sides died out that would be the link severed forever. Call it the early onset of old age or whatever but I just had this notion that it was something I needed to do. We connected on Link Up so there, if required, is absolute proof of the power of social media."
Keith half snorted and half grunted as he listened to Simon's story.
"So, what are you hoping to achieve from rekindling this particular fire, lad? Is this the great reconciliation or is that your curiosity satisfied for another

few decades?"

Simon was taken aback by the hint of vitriol lurking thinly veiled behind Keith's words. It was true that Simon hardly remembered the summer visits, but he was not aware of any hint of discord. His mother had always spoken fondly of her cousin and the family she had subsequently had. It was true that Keith had been something of an urchin as a child in contrast to Carmen who had been an A grade student and a model daughter according to what he had picked up at the time. Nevertheless, he could not imagine what the Binns family had done to occasion such a disinterested and almost acerbic response.

"I am not hoping to achieve anything specific, Keith. I simply had the urge to find out what had happened to Graham after I found an old black and white photograph Dad took of him with Mark and me on Scarborough beach when we were kids."

"Just be careful you do not poke your nose too far into other people's business, Simon," said Keith. "You have no idea what any of them have been doing for the past however many years and with little to be gained from re-establishing contact you might be better directing your energies to stopping that bunch of highway robbers from stealing our family business from under our noses. I'm off to the pub for a pint."

Simon had managed to temporarily shift Keith's train of thought away from the Vinbrew matter but clearly not for long. What had he meant though with his warning to his nephew not to poke his nose into the business of others? In this case, "others" were a branch of their family who at least outwardly were nice, normal people who for many years had been close to and had brought great pleasure to his grandparents and to his mother. Had something happened that he was unaware of to make Keith wary and reticent where the Binns family was concerned? As he watched Keith walk across his office, he felt more than a slight concern at his uncle's reaction to the mention of Graham Binns.

CHAPTER 10

If he had been able to see his uncle's face as Keith opened the office door, he would have been more than concerned, he would probably have felt a chill of fear slither down the length of his spine.

12

CHAPTER 11

7th November 1990

Gerry Binns had been expecting his mother-in-law's death for some time given that she had suffered with ill health for the past few years, but it was still a big shock to him and his wife Sonia when it finally happened. Elisabeth Croft had never been what could be termed a "healthy" woman. She suffered more or less perennially from the kind of minor ailments which most people tolerate and simply get on with their lives but which, in the case of Elisabeth, seemingly caused her to experience more profound effects and to stop her from doing the things she needed to do. Gerry would have used the word "seemingly" because he sometimes felt that Sonia's mother's "glass half empty" approach where her health was concerned was a far greater contributor to her various maladies than any actual sickness she may have been dealing with.

Even as a child, Elisabeth Steele had been the polar opposite of her elder brother William when it came to coping with everyday life. Where he was a gregarious, energetic and ambitious boy, she was frequently absent from school and seemingly unable to demonstrate any real passion for the things she was engaged in. Sonia, as daughters would be expected to do, usually defended her mother against any accusation that she might have been faking illness or might make a normal case of the sniffles seem like full blown flu, but Gerry was less magnanimous in matters of his mother-in-law's catalogue of infirmities.

Perhaps the only surprising thing was that Elisabeth had outlived Gerry's father Eric by almost twenty years. Eric had been a fit man and despite a career in the catering industry as a chef remained trim and in shape until he was unexpectedly diagnosed with hepatitis at the age of 52, an illness which three years later ended his life. The loss of her husband seemingly only added to Elisabeth's propensity to fall ill on a regular basis, and she lived out the rest of her life more or less permanently suffering from one ailment or the other.

On a warm Sunday morning, having buried Elisabeth a week after her death, Eric and Sonia set about the unenviable task of dealing with the various administrative issues, sorting out the contents of her house and deciding what to do with the property given that they already had a family home of their own. As the only child, Sonia inherited everything that her mother left. In reality, the only thing of real value was the house itself, a basic two-up two-down in a less than desirable location. Whilst the cash would be very useful it was hardly a life-changing windfall. Elisabeth had a couple of thousand pounds in the bank and a PEP that she had invested in when they were introduced in 1987 plus, of course, a house full of items of varying value, financial or sentimental, amassed over the seventy-one years of her life. Sonia suggested to Gerry that she would start downstairs, going through the kitchen and lounge/dining room whilst he went upstairs to sort through the items in both bedrooms. Of the two, the largest was clearly where Elisabeth slept and featured an old-fashioned bedroom suite whilst the other room contained a single bed that was partially hidden beneath a huge quantity of boxes and assorted items including, bizarrely, a cast iron mangle. This room was clearly the one where the accumulation of a lifetime's "junk" (the phrase immediately leapt into Gerry's mind when he saw it) was stored, most of it either unused for years or useless but for some reason never thrown away.

Over the next few hours between several cups of coffee and a tin of ravioli which he found at the back of a cupboard in the kitchen ("I used to eat this regularly when I was a kid" he told Sonia) Gerry sifted through a whole gamut of items ranging from old blankets to rolls of wallpaper to ornaments and gadgets of varying quality and appeal plus a number of boxes containing holiday postcards, letters, birthday and anniversary cards and an eclectic selection of books. As to the latter, it was fairly clear which books had belonged to whom with a selection of Mills & Boon novels sitting alongside books on fishing and cricket which Gerry recalled were two of Eric's passions. Gerry had no time for fishing, his judgment on that pastime coloured for a lifetime by an uncle who had once taken him to the local river where they had spent eight hours sitting waiting for a bite (which never came) and where his uncle insisted that it was Gerry's job to thread maggots onto the line which almost caused him to vomit. Lunch, when they had it, tasted of maggots (at least in his brain) and Gerry had never been as relieved as he was when his uncle announced it was time to go home. Cricket, on the other hand, was a sport Gerry had loved since the time he went to watch England play the invincible Australians in 1948 when the deadly trio of Lindwall, Miller and Johnston tore the heart out of the English batting line up to win the Ashes series 4-0. Amongst the collection of books Gerry found the Wisden almanac for the following year and started to flick through the pages, the memories of that epic test match coming flooding back as he was reminded of the scale of the victories the Aussies had achieved.

As he was about to replace the book in the box an envelope that had evidently lodged itself between the last page and the back cover fell on to the floor with the address side facing upwards. The letter was addressed to Mrs Elisabeth Croft but what attracted Gerry's attention was the blue rectangle in the top left corner bearing the name and address of Dr Thomas Hawthorne, Ilford, Essex. The date stamp on the letter was 12 September 1937. Whether he was intrigued, or just plain nosey, Gerry could not recall afterwards but whichever it was he decided to see what the letter inside the envelope said. He unfolded the single sheet and as he read the short message it contained, he froze, unable to process what he was reading. So much so that he re-read the letter half a dozen times to make sure that his brain was not deceiving him after a long day sorting through Elisabeth's possessions. No, it was not, and the information contained in the doctor's words was crystal clear.

Which led Gerry to ask himself a very obvious question.

The answer to which was seemingly an impossibility.

13

CHAPTER 12

28 August 2016

For the next three days Simon did not think about Graham Binns as he was buried in the follow up work from the meeting with Peter Westmann and with some urgent matters that needed his attention concerning day-to-day issues in the UK brewing market. Beer sales were continuing to decline as consumers tried other types of drinks, some of this due to the power of social media, some due to the changing habits of the younger generation and some due to the financial constraints caused by the rising cost of just keeping a roof over your head. Add to that the rise and rise of gastro pubs, where wine was often the drink chosen to accompany food, and the decline of the "session" drinker in more traditional bars, it was plain to see where the CEO of a brewery such as Steele's would need to focus his mind.

Now it was Sunday and Simon had enjoyed a rare lie in until 9.30, a breakfast of bacon and eggs and a couple of hours buried inside the Sunday Times. Dani had been at the gym in the morning and had returned home to do some pottering in their garden before switching on the oven and putting in a lamb joint which would be their Sunday roast a couple of hours later. She was now sitting in the conservatory with Simon who had just folded up his newspaper and sighed contentedly.

"So, tell me some more about what is going on, babe. You have been passing through here like a whirlwind these past few days!"
Simon gave a slightly embarrassed smile at the accuracy of his wife's description of the second half of the previous week.
"It's just been a bit manic, love" was the best he could manage and from the look on Dani's face his best fell a few yards short of what she was expecting to hear. Not that Dani was in any way possessive or demanding, but she did like to be kept in the loop with everything that led to her husband's behaviour in the domestic setting.
"You seem to have been distracted," she said. "It would be good if you could share it."
Simon nodded and hummed. He had intended to have a whole day where he did not think about work but he realized that this was not going to be possible since Dani was clearly intent on hearing what had caused him to be so occupied and so neglectful of her in the process.

"I didn't realise how much the last few weeks has taken out of me, babe," he began. "The takeover stuff has actually been a hell of a distraction if I am honest even though it could be very good for us as shareholders. Keith's ranting has not helped however immune to it I have become, and I have maybe come closer to saying something to him I might regret than I have for a very long time."
Dani gave him a look that suggested this was a good start but nowhere near enough to satisfy her.
"And then there is all the ongoing stuff that just seems relentless in its ferocity," Simon continued. "Our numbers are holding up pretty well and the new lines are performing better than we dared to hope but that could all fall apart tomorrow. This business has changed beyond recognition and you have to keep running at full tilt just to stay up to speed with what is happening. I honestly do not believe that Keith realises just how different things are since he was running the business and he wants to try to keep everything just the way it has always been. That is just not realistic but try telling him that. Keith Steele, the brewing industry's King Canute if I ever I

saw him."

Dani's expression had softened, and a smile emerged from her lips.

"You are not getting any younger, babe, you need to look after yourself and make sure that you don't go the way of the traditional boozer. I am far too young to be a widow and you still have a ton of stuff to do on your bucket list."

Simon felt a bit like a heavyweight boxer who had just let down his defences and been punched full on in the gut. He had been stretching every sinew these past few days and he knew that Dani was more than entitled to express her concerns.

"In fact, Dani continued, "you have been so concerned about Steele's that I have not heard you utter a peep about Graham Binns for the best part of four days! That is some sign of the pressures of work given that you had seemingly become obsessed with the guy."

That is very true, thought Simon, and once again Dani showed herself to be so perceptive and right on point when it came to her husband.

"You are right that I have not given him much thought this week, "he said. "I still believe that there is something not right and I have this itch that needs scratching to find out what it is."

"With all the stress and pressure of work, Simon, are you really sure that you have the time for trivialities like this? You are already working all hours at Steele's and now you want to spend time on something firstly has nothing to do with you and secondly is almost certainly the result of your overactive brain going into overdrive. And while you do this, you'll neglect me and the kids in the process."

Simon was quite shocked. Dani never referred to him by his name, it was always "babe" or "hun", and this sudden shift to relative formality troubled him. Added to that she was clearly not impressed at his sudden interest in a distant relative about whom nothing had been heard for decades.

"I'm sorry, babe, I realise that I have been a bit preoccupied this week. It has been crazier than usual at work although I will say it before you do, when isn't it? Hopefully things will ease up once we have clarity on where this takeover matter is heading."

"I do not mind the long hours, babe,“ said Dani, "I know that comes with the turf and I am not trying to stop you from doing what I know you have to do in the interests of the company. I just hope that you will then devote the rest of your time to the family and not go off at a mad tangent chasing distant cousins and creating intrigue where none exists. Anyway, I had better check on the lamb and put the roast potatoes in." With that, Dani stood up and headed for the kitchen leaving Simon alone with his thoughts.

So that was that. In the 27 years of knowing his wife Simon had never seen Dani utter such an unambiguous indication that she disapproved of what he was doing and that she was actually not prepared to entertain its prolongation. Playing cricket on both Saturday and Sundays when they were first married had been a source of much debate and he had needed to employ all of his charm to get away with that but get away with it he did to a large extent. This was somehow different, and the message was very clear. Simon had not realised that Dani was unhappy with him for pursuing Graham Binns and it was clear that she would not put up with him spending any more time on what she felt was a whim. She had not objected to him meeting Graham for dinner but rather to the subsequent intrigue that the meeting had seemingly given birth to. As he sat alone thinking through what his wife had just said Simon himself began to question whether he was simply imagining intrigue where none existed. One thing he was certain of, he did not want to do anything which might jeopardise his marriage or his family. So, reluctantly, he began to think that he should forget Graham Binns and the events of years gone by to make sure that that did not happen. "Deal," he said out loud, "deal."

Unfortunately, his resolve to forget his second cousin would last less than twenty-four hours. A phone call was it all it would take to undo the deal he had struck with himself and put him firmly back on a collision course with Dani over long forgotten events that would place not only his marriage in jeopardy but potentially his life.

14

CHAPTER 13

17 November 1990

Michael Spedding had lived in Ilford his whole life. Having never travelled much beyond the county boundaries of Essex he was not really in a position to judge whether his home town was a nice place to live or not but to anyone who asked he would have described his Ilford as "a bit of a shithole". Anyone who knew Michael Spedding, however, would probably have described him in similar terms and might have classified his view of Ilford as somewhat clouded by his own inadequacies.

Spedding had been something of a dropout at school, always in trouble with the headmaster and frequently caned or put into detention for a wide variety of offences spanning insubordination, playing truant and fighting with anyone who remotely antagonised him. It came as little surprise to anyone, including Michael himself, when he flunked his GCSEs, and he simply could not wait to get out of an institution where he felt he did not belong.

The absence of a father figure in his life had often been cited as a reason for his behaviour but his mother would not have countenanced such a belief. She worked hard to provide for Michael and his younger sister and presided over what she felt was a loving home. The fact that her eldest child chose not to appreciate her and her efforts could not be blamed on the wastrel who had fathered him and whom she had ditched unceremoniously when his womanising and general lack of husband-like qualities became too much for her. Michael's sister Tabatha, three years his junior, had managed to avoid her elder sibling's failings and eventually left school at 18 with a clutch of GCSEs and three decent "A" levels which allowed her to pursue her dream and to gain a place at journalism college.

The winter looked like being a harsh one and already in most of the UK, including Ilford, the freezing nights and dark, dreary days were becoming the norm. The fabled green shoots of Spring were months away so it was a case of grinning and bearing it for a while. Michael Spedding, unemployed, and in the view of many who knew him unemployable, wandered through the town centre as he did on most days as morning turned to afternoon. Staying in the house where he would doubtless fall foul of his mother for some reason or other (though he never attributed their fallouts to his own behaviour) was not an option he ever considered so every morning he would walk into town and spend a couple of hours in the bookmakers deciding if there was anything worth spending his unemployment benefit on before heading into the high street to see what, if anything, was happening there.

On this particular November day his stop at the bookmakers had yielded nothing that he wanted to stake any money on so he headed into the centre and found himself standing outside Binns Cycle World which is where he often stopped to light a cigarette and observe the activities of the local population. The shop was opposite a trendy café where he occasionally went to take a mug of tea but was also close to the Nags Head where he more regularly called in at lunchtime for a couple of pints of Adnams Southwold bitter. He told his mother that he could not afford to pay her board and lodge as well as feed and water himself during the day and she seemed to believe him. He was never sure if she knew of his almost daily drinking habit but if she did and did not complain then who was he to enlighten her?

Drawing on his cigarette and deciding whether to call into the Nags Head today (he was running short of cash and the next dole cheque was five days away) Spedding noticed a figure in the window of the café who seemed to be staring at him in a peculiar way. Normally when someone seemed to be taking the piss and giving him the eye, he would have confronted them and asked what they were doing but he did not want to create a scene in the café. When the person saw Michael was looking in their direction, they quickly turned their head ninety degrees, picked up a cup and started to drink. Michael drew on his cigarette whilst continuing to ponder whether or not the Nags Head was going to be the recipient today of his dwindling pile of liquidity. Maybe he would compromise and have just one pint instead of his regular two. Yes, that was the answer he was looking for and he smiled, happy that he had reached an agreement with himself. He looked at his watch and saw that it was 12.25. Definitely Adnams time. He pinched the almost smoked butt of his Marlborough, dropped it on the pavement and strode purposefully towards the front door of the Nags Head.

The pub was fairly quiet which was not unusual for a chilly Wednesday lunchtime in November, but he did spot a few regulars who like him seemed to be perpetual visitors to the establishment. Not that he ever engaged with any of them, being more of a loner than a socialite, and more so not trusting himself to avoid getting into some kind of argument which might lead to something he regretted. He had never understood why he seemed incapable of having a conversation or forming normal relationships with people without the ever-present fear that he might just thump them if they said anything he disagreed with. That was probably why he had only ever had one girlfriend and even that particular relationship, if it lasted long enough to be referred to as such, had done little to convince him that relationships were something worth pursuing in the future. He sat cradling his pint sipping it more cautiously than he normally would, presumably because he knew this was the only one he would be having today. Channel 4 racing was on the television, and he watched the 12.40 from Wincanton more for something to do than because he had a particular desire to know who won the race. He was only interested if he had a bet on and so it was of little interest to him when Pot of Gold came storming over the final fence romping to a 5-length victory at 16-1.

Ten minutes later he downed the last few drops of his beer, wiped his mouth on the sleeve of his jacket and stepped back out into the street. The rain was beginning to fall, and he decided it was time to head home even if that probably meant another row with his mother. He glanced at the window of the cycle shop as he zipped up his jacket and was surprised to see the Closed sign showing on the door. As far as he knew from his many hours spent standing outside the shop it did not close for lunch. The days when retail shops took a lunch break were long gone in today's ultra-competitive world and he wondered why Gerry Binns might have decided to close early on this particular day. He put his hands up to the window and glanced into the small shop. He was about to walk away when he noticed two bicycles lying in a heap on the floor at the back of the shop as if someone had thrown them down in a fit of pique. Michael knew how expensive mountain bikes were these days and he wondered why Gerry Binns might have allowed his valuable stock to be left lying on the floor in this way. Ever curious he decided to investigate given that he had nothing to hurry home for. He walked down the passage which ran alongside the shop and led to the back of the premises. The rear of the cycle shop was surrounded by a wooden fence and the gate leading to the door of the premises was open. Michael peered round the gate and, noticing that the rear door was ajar, which was completely at odds with a shop that was apparently closed, he pushed open the gate and headed towards the building. And stopped abruptly in his tracks. Through the partly open door he saw the head of a man, but it was the pool of red liquid slowly gathering around him that told Michael that something was very wrong.

For a few moments he just stood there staring at what he had discovered before he came to his senses and realised that he needed to fetch help. He turned round and bolted out of the gate almost colliding with a woman pushing a shopping trolley. He stopped and blurted out "He's dead" which

was the limit of the words that he could form in his brain. The woman frowned and pushed open the gate following the route Michael had himself just taken. When she saw the blood, she let out a scream followed by several "Oh my Gods" as she clamped her hand across her mouth. She hurried back through the gate to where her shopping trolley stood and stared at Michael. "You're that Spedding boy, aren't you?" she said with a strong degree of distaste, "I know your poor mother who must be an angel given the reputation you have. Did you kill him then?"
Michael stared at the woman and shook his head, unable to form any more words.
"I'm calling the police."

With that she took off down the passage heading into the high street. As luck would have it one of the local constables was on duty in the vicinity and within a few minutes the woman and PC George Lovelace were standing at the gate to Binns' Cycle World. Michael Spedding, however, was nowhere to be seen. When the woman had run off to find the police, he realised that this did not look good and having a lifelong hatred of authority, and in particular of those in blue uniforms, he decided it was better if he made a hasty exit. Whilst he would not personally have described himself as a criminal his reputation did tend to go before him as the woman herself had suggested, so he had decided that flight was preferable to waiting around given the grimness of the crime scene that would greet the soon-to-arrive long arm of the law.

Less than thirty minutes later after a knock on the door of the Spedding household and a few cautionary words, Michael was sitting in an interview room in Ilford police station where he was subjected to four hours of questioning before being held overnight in a police cell. By the next evening a Marlborough cigarette butt had been found next to the body of Gerry Binns and when a DNA test was performed and shown to be a perfect match with Michael Spedding's DNA the police had their man. Three months later the case was closed when a life sentence was handed out to him for the murder of Gerry Binns.

What Ilford police did not realise was that Michael Spedding had committed no crime more serious than dropping a cigarette butt on the floor in front of Gerry Binns' cycle shop. Unfortunately, that small act was all that the person sitting in the café opposite had needed and they quickly moved to do what they came to do and disappear, framing the unfortunate Spedding for it and ensuring that no trail leading to them would ever exist.

15

CHAPTER 14

29 August 2016

Like most people Simon had always hated Monday mornings but when he realised that a hatred of Mondays also then infected the second half of Sunday as the weekend drew inexorably to its end, he decided that it was time he started to embrace Mondays and make sure his weekends were not tainted. His strategy for this revolved around setting tasks he really enjoyed for Monday morning as a way of easing himself into the new week. After several bouts of trying things and deciding what he found the most motivational he decided that anything that involved speaking with customers or discussing the sales performance of the company with his field managers was positive whilst poring over financial data or dealing with the Chairman were comparatively negative.

Thus, he avoided Keith and Mark like the plague on Monday mornings and set up a series of calls with the Area Managers to get to the nub of what had been going on over the previous week. He also asked the telesales team to give him the contact numbers of 6 pubs that purchased from Steele's so that he could call them and ask for some honest feedback on his company's performance in their eyes. He really enjoyed the fact that the customers he rang were largely amazed that the CEO of Steele's was calling them directly and he was sure this helped to secure their loyalty. Finally, he set up the weekly tasting panel where a cross-functional team of executives would taste the range of Steele's ales and score them based on a set number of criteria. This meant that by 1.00 when he opened his lunch box, he was feeling energised and positive and ready to face most things that the rest of the week could throw at him.

Most things except Keith, he had discovered. His uncle's ability to introduce rain clouds over whatever rays of sunshine his Monday morning routine had delivered convinced Simon that he simply had to grin and bear the wrath and rants of the Chairman. The good thing was that Keith was definitely not a Monday morning person so Simon's start to each week was largely chairman-free, a small mercy for which he was extremely grateful.

Simon had looked forward to this particular Monday morning more than usual as he needed to get some space away from the house after his heavy discussion with Dani the previous day. As he drove into the office he was still surprised and shocked at the strength of his wife's feelings on the subject of his re-acquaintance with Graham Binns. He had to admit to himself that the pressure of work over the past few months had been increasing and with it the lateness of his arrival home on many occasions. Dani had never once criticised him for this as she understood that there were periods when Steele's Ales demanded more of her husband's time. Clearly, she did not extend the same level of understanding to what she presumably viewed as his perceived dalliance with his second cousin. Reluctantly he resigned himself to doing what he should probably have done after the dinner with Graham, namely being satisfied that he had re-established lines of communication whilst putting all thoughts of intrigue in the matter of Gerry Binns' demise firmly out of his mind.

The morning progressed well, and he went into the tasting panel at 11.30 feeling highly motivated following his calls with the Area Managers. It seemed that the company's new promotion scheme was driving significant extra sales in all regions, a supposition seemingly confirmed by the customers he subsequently spoke with. He had tasted the first two products in the panel and was about to move to the third when his phone buzzed. He stared at the screen as the name Graham Binns flashed across it. He was about to step outside and answer the call when he remembered his promise to himself earlier that morning. He pushed the red decline button and put his phone away out of view. Nevertheless, he could not take his mind away from why Graham might be calling him, especially during a working day. The rest of the tasting panel passed by in a bit of a haze as Simon kept wondering why his second cousin might be trying to get hold of him.

As he headed back to his office after the tasting panel Simon took his phone from his pocket and saw that he had another missed call and a message. When he saw that both were from Graham Binns he frowned and opened his message inbox. "Hi Simon, I called twice but guess you must be busy. Sorry to bother you, just wanted to tell you something and ask your advice. Graham." Simon stared at the message as conflicting thoughts went through his mind. On the one hand he was reminded of his promise to Dani and to himself that he would ignore the potential intrigue surrounding Graham's family in favour of focusing on the myriad issues and challenges in his own life at the moment. However, he was certain that Graham had not told him everything at their dinner (and why should he have done that anyway?) and now that he had proactively contacted Simon did that mean that there really was something important to share? Simon shook his head and silently cursed himself for his stupidity. Dani had made it clear that it was both foolish and unfair to his own family for him to devote time to some fantastical whim about some long-forgotten relation's family and he promised himself that he would drop the matter and move on. Determined to do just that, he nodded to himself and walked over to his PA's desk.

"Jude, can you get in touch with Peter Westmann and see if he has finished the documents he was preparing on the next steps regarding Vinbrew? He said they would be with us by the end of last week."

"Sure, Simon, let me call him once I have finished with the invites for Keith's dinner. I want to get them out because he has already been on the phone this morning asking if I have finished." Simon shook his head and sighed. His uncle organised periodic dinners for a bunch of his cronies supposedly to the benefit of Steele's Ales and naturally using the brewery's funds to pay for it. He claimed that his guests were movers and shakers in the industry. Simon preferred the term "piss heads" having once stumbled on one of these evenings where the only moving and shaking he witnessed was a bunch of inebriated old fools staggering around and spouting unintelligibly, clearly the worse for wear. He smiled to himself as he remembered an old joke; what is the definition of testiculating? Answer, waving your arms around and talking bollocks! Keith and Co were certainly professional testiculators!
"OK, well you had better do the old man's bidding but try to get me an update from Peter in the next hour or so. We need to move this Vinbrew matter forward one way or another".

Back in his office Simon opened his inbox and checked the emails he had received during the course of the morning. He usually got upwards of 50 emails each working day and was constantly battling to encourage his colleagues not to copy him on communication unless it was really necessary. Despite telling people that they could take a decision within agreed guidelines without involving him he continued to be included in discussions on the most mundane of matters. Although technology had advanced in leaps and bounds it seemed as if good old fashioned arse covering was still very much alive and kicking in its traditional format! The thought brought a big smile to Simon's face as he selected the messages that seemed to really require his input and left the rest to remain unopened on the basis that if any of the latter really required his contribution someone would come chasing him at a later date. In his experience that rarely happened.

Having dealt with his inbox and heard from Jude that Peter Westmann had apologised for the delay and would be sending the documents over by the following evening, Simon realised that it was almost 3.30 and that he needed to check that he had everything he needed for the weekly management meeting that started at 4pm. As he read through his notes his thoughts turned back to Graham Binns and the two missed calls and the message he had sent earlier in the day. Try as he might he could not put this out of his mind and was desperate to learn what his recently rediscovered second cousin meant by wanting his advice. Maybe it was nothing to do with Gerry's death but rather a piece of business or personal advice that Graham was seeking. Somehow Simon doubted that and was sure it was linked to the violent demise of the older man. Simon felt like someone who has an itchy rash and knows they should not scratch it for fear of making it bleed and of causing permanent scarring. For Simon, this situation was definitely an itch which was becoming unbearable to leave untouched.

Convincing himself that he had everything he needed for the management meeting and realising he had 17 minutes before it started Simon decided to address the itch and to hell with the consequences. He was going to reply to Graham's message to ask if he was free for a call but decided on a more direct approach and pushed the dial button on his phone. Three rings later Graham's voice echoed down the line.

"Simon, good afternoon. Thanks for ringing me back."

"Sorry it wasn't earlier," replied Simon, "I was in back-to-back meetings until just now." He did not say what he knew he should say – "sorry Graham, I really do not have the time to get involved in any intrigue as I have far more important priorities closer to home" – but instead asked Graham up front what had precipitated these calls totally out of the blue.

"To be honest, Simon," Graham continued, "I have been debating whether to call you since we met for dinner – I need to share something with somebody I trust but that someone must be objective and be prepared to listen. Based on our dinner conversations and having spent a couple of hours in your company I think you meet my criteria!"

Simon winced at the compliment. He knew that if Dani could hear this conversation, she would have been very direct in her approach – "Simon, if you even think about responding positively to this, I am divorcing you without further delay" – but he found himself encouraging his second cousin almost involuntarily.

"Wow, Graham, I am flattered to hear that. I am all ears. Actually, I have about a quarter of an hour before my management meeting, and I do need to be on time for that"

Graham let out an audibly deep sigh at the other end of the line.

"Right, where to begin? Okay, I do not know whether you picked anything up from our dinner conversation but when I said that the evidence against Michael Spedding seemed incontrovertible and that the police were right, I was not quite sharing my actual viewpoint. I have my very strong doubts that Spedding was responsible for dad's death. I certainly do not have any real evidence to prove that yet, but something is definitely not right."

Hearing Graham's words down the line Simon found himself smiling in spite of the fact that talk of death, especially death by violent means, is not usually something to incite happiness. He was smiling because he had sensed that there was something wrong from the very beginning of his re-acquaintance with Graham Binns and maybe, just maybe, he was right.

"So, what exactly led you to that conclusion, Graham?" he found himself responding. As he said this, he was aware of an illusory presence whispering in his ear that he had promised both to Dani and to himself not to get involved but by now he was powerless to stop himself.

"When dad died it was exactly the time that Sarah and I were getting married and setting up our own home so once the funeral was over and we had started to come to terms with what this meant, I did not really discuss it much more with mum. She was obviously heartbroken, and grief stricken, and I felt it was best to not bring the whole thing up in conversation and make matters worse. We lived a fair distance apart and so we did not see each other that regularly. Not that you forget the person, or it matters less, it is just that I was settling into married life, building a career and so on. And based on what the police said it was an open and closed case so nothing to do on that score."

Graham sighed loudly again and was silent for a few seconds. "Over the years we actually spoke very little about Dad in terms of what happened that day, although of course we remembered the happy family times like Christmas and birthdays and what a great and loving father he had been to us. Anyway, as I told you before, mum was diagnosed with dementia seven years ago and I started to see her more often as you tend to when these things happen in your family. She went downhill pretty quickly, like in less than two years she went from being mildly forgetful to having days when she didn't even recognise me. We had to move her into a home because she started to need the kind of constant attention that neither Ashleigh nor I could provide given our own family situations. Like many sufferers, her dementia was the kind where she cannot recall something that happened the day before but remains extremely lucid when it comes to things from the distant past."

Simon was eager for Graham to get to the point of the call, checking his watch to make sure he was not going to be late for the management meeting.

"So did she say something about your dad that suggested an alternative to the police theory about Michael Spedding?"

"No, not that, I am not sure whether she ever had her suspicions about the officially recorded cause of death, but she has never suggested anything like that to me if she had."

"So, what has made you suspicious or seeking to question the official police verdict?"

Graham was quiet for a few seconds and Simon anxiously checked his watch. 3.55pm. He had five minutes before the management meeting started. Of course, he could always be late, it was his meeting, but that would make him feel bad as he had always insisted on colleagues turning up for meetings on time and berated those who failed to do so as lacking respect for the rest of the attendees. Finally, Graham answered his question.

"When we moved mum into the care home I volunteered to act as removal man and chauffeur. We decided not to sell her house, at least not immediately, and so we set about getting her essential possessions together in order to get her established in her new home. In her wardrobe I found a small suitcase, which apparently belonged to my dad. It was basically his stash of important documents and memorabilia including his cycling awards and medals. I am not even sure mum knew it was there. At the bottom of the case I found a small folder which contained a letter from a doctor addressed to my grandma and a copy of mum's birth certificate together with a sheet of paper with some notes made by my dad. Out of curiosity, I read the letter and the notes and I realised that if what was being said was true, the implications were potentially shocking. I do not think that dad managed to follow through with his investigations into what he found, but I do believe that this episode could throw a whole new light on why he was killed."

It was 3.59 and Simon really needed to step next door into the management meeting. He cursed under his breath.
"Graham," I have my management meeting starting right now and I can't be late. We will not finish until after 6 so can I call you in the morning to hear what you found? I am really itching to know; it feels a bit like one of those cliff hanger moments you get at the end of an episode of a TV drama!"
"Yes, sure, Simon, you can even call after your meeting if you like. I really need to get an objective view as to how I should handle this. If not, I am free until 10 tomorrow if that works for you."
Simon was tempted to call later in the evening but knew that he had better get back home to Dani rather than spending time on the phone with someone he had promised both himself and his wife that he would forget..
"9.00 tomorrow is good, Graham. Listen I must dash."

Simon cut the call, grabbed his laptop and headed for the board room. What had Graham found? Was his father's murder not as straightforward as the police had concluded? Simon was desperate to hear the answer to those questions and worried that he would not be able to concentrate on the management meeting. He must though, given all that was happening in the business at the moment. Especially, he had to admit sheepishly, given the promise he had made to himself and to Dani. Nevertheless, he could not wait to speak to Graham the following morning.

He walked into the Board room and was slightly embarrassed and uncomfortable to see that the rest of his management team were sitting waiting for him like enthusiastic schoolboys on the first day of a new term. He decided to put the conversation he had just had with Graham to the back of his mind and focus on matters closer to home. For the next two hours he largely managed to do that. However, had he known what this discussion with Graham Binns had started, what dangers it would end up exposing him and others to, he would certainly have stuck to his promise to Dani and turned his back on the whole saga.

Once and for all.

16

CHAPTER 15

7th November 1990

Gerry was still staring at the letter when Sonia walked into the bedroom startling him as he had not heard her coming.

"I thought you might like another coffee, love" she said as Gerry, like a guilty schoolboy who has been found doing something he should not fumbled with the letter and thrust it back into the box of papers.

"Oh, g-g-great love," he stuttered as if his embarrassment had incapacitated his tongue.

"What was that you were looking at?"

"Ah, nothing really, it was some old letter from years ago which I find fascinating reading. There are loads of them in here, look." Gerry fished out the first document that he could put his hand on and passed it to Sonia. His wife studied the paper and looked at him half-suspiciously.

"This is just an old TV rental bill from Rediffusion. I am sure whatever you were reading was far more interesting given the look on your face when you realised I was here. What was it?"

Gerry blushed and tried to keep a control on his body language.

"As I said just an old letter. Thanks for the coffee, love, have you found anything interesting downstairs?"

"Not really," replied Sonia. Gerry was mentally crossing his fingers that

Sonia was not going to insist on seeing the letter which he simply had to avoid at all costs. Ultimately there would have to be a discussion about its contents at some stage, but Gerry judged quite categorically that that time was not now. What he needed was to get Sonia downstairs so that he could search through the rest of the documents and to see whether he could shed any more light on what he had read in the doctor's letter.

"What are we doing for food tonight?" asked Gerry, desperately trying to change the subject. "We could either go to the Brewers Arms or grab some takeaway fish and chips or a Chinese if you fancy that. We do not want to start cooking after we finish here."

"A takeaway sounds fine," replied Sonia. "Let me go and see if I can finish in the kitchen and let's pack up by 7 even if there is still stuff to be sorted."

With that she headed out of the bedroom and down the stairs much to the eternal relief of Gerry. He let out a big sigh and grabbed the letter again from the box. It just did not make sense. Try as he might Gerry could not fully get his mind around the implications of the words he read again for the umpteenth time. Before he even thought of asking Sonia if she could make sense of the letter, he needed to do some digging and some further investigation to see if he could shed any more light on what Dr Hawthorne meant by what he had written to Sonia's mother. The message was clear but the explanation as to why he was saying what he said was shrouded in mystery.

"What are you telling us, doctor" he muttered to himself "what on earth are you suggesting?"

Gerry placed the letter back in its envelope and laid it on the bed. He then started to riffle through the rest of the contents of the box where the letter had been found. He knew exactly what he was looking for and was working on the assumption that if this was where Elisabeth kept her most important correspondence this was probably the place he needed to focus on. The box was crammed with papers and letters, and it took him some considerable time to sift through them until he finally found what he wanted inside an envelope stamped 'Registry of Births, Marriages and Deaths'. The document was a birth certificate for a baby girl and clearly stated her name, the name of the mother and father and the date of the registration of the birth. Everything looked perfectly normal and said exactly what anyone who know the family would have said that it should say. Perfectly normal unless you had also read the letter from Dr Hawthorne. Anyone who had seen both documents, as Gerry now had, would probably be thinking the same thing that Gerry was.

Something was wrong.

Something was very, very wrong.

17

CHAPTER 16

30 August 2016

Simon had enjoyed a very pleasant evening at home following the Monday management meeting. Despite wanting to wish away the hours before he could call Graham back, he had decided to leave both work and intrigue firmly locked away and to focus his attention this evening on Dani. Whether that was the result of feeling guilty at his decision to do the polar opposite of what he had agreed with her or guilty because he realised how distant he had been recently, he was determined to give his wife his full attention. They ate dinner, watched a movie of her choosing and then went to bed early. They had not made love recently and Simon was determined to ensure a passionate end to the evening. He was hoping that Dani felt the same and was happy when he realised that she did.

Refreshed and feeling better about his deception after an enjoyable evening, Simon drove into work early on Tuesday morning and dove straight into his inbox over a cup of strong black coffee. By the time 09.00 came around he had broken the back of his emails and was ready to speak with Graham. Before doing so he opened his office door and asked Jude to make sure he was not disturbed until he finished an important external call.

"Simon, good morning." His second cousin picked up on the first ring suggesting he had been waiting for the call. "I hope everything is good at the brewery."
Simon smiled ruefully to himself as he thought about the truthful response to that question. If he even started to explain to Graham the shenanigans going on around the Vinbrew takeover situation he would have no time to talk about the real reason for this call. So he decided to be totally non-committal.
"All good, Graham," he replied, "the usual challenges but nothing to get excited about. So, I have been really keen to hear the conclusion of what we were discussing last night."
"I have been keen to tell you, Simon."
Simon glanced towards the door as if he expected someone to be there spying on him as he spoke with Graham. Talk about a guilt complex!

"I really do not know where to start, Simon. The doctor's letter revealed something to my grandma that if it was true would mean that what had supposedly happened could not have actually happened. Based on dad's notes regarding the birth certificate, the whole family situation was being called into question."
Simon was listening intently and trying to anticipate what this story regarding Graham's grandma was leading to. He had to admit to himself that despite his promise not to get involved he was fascinated by mystery and the whole sleuthing thing such that he knew it was pointless trying to resist.
"So what did the doctor say?" Simon asked what he thought was the obvious question.
"Well, this is where it gets very interesting," replied Graham.

The door to Simon's office opened and he was about to shout at Jude to say that he had requested not to be disturbed when he saw the look on his brother Mark's face.
"Graham, just hold on a second." Simon put the call on hold and looked up at Mark.
"Mark, what's up?"

"I just had a call from Peter Westmann who had tried calling you but was told you were busy."

Simon winced slightly, embarrassed at missing a call from their M&A advisor when he was on a personal call with Graham Binns.

"Apparently Vinbrew have now formalised things and have submitted an Indication of Interest to Westmann Buck. In return they are asking for a period of exclusivity to allow them to start formal due diligence," continued Mark.

"We have not agreed to sell yet," replied Simon, "so there are a few steps to take before any due diligence process starts."

"Graham who by the way? Are you going to keep him on hold?"

Simon got Graham back online and asked him if he could call back, apologising profusely that there was an emergency at the company he had to deal with.

"Graham Binns," he replied, ending the call and turning his attention back to his brother.

"What is going on with him?" asked Mark. "And why would you ask Jude to hold all of your calls while you spoke with him? Seems a bit extreme unless I am missing something."

Simon wondered whether to tell Mark any of what had been happening with their second cousin these past couple of days. He decided that there was no harm in sharing the developments such as he knew them. After all, thought Simon, family is family.

"When I met him for dinner in London and the conversation touched on his father's murder, I sensed that he was not telling me everything. Then yesterday morning he called me twice out of the blue and when he could not get me, he left a message. I had told Dani about my suspicions following the dinner and she went apeshit at me, telling me I was already neglecting her and the kids with everything going on here and that if I wanted to go chasing red herrings and involving myself in the lives of people I had not seen for forty years, I would basically be spending the rest of my days alone."

"Ouch," said Mark, "where on earth did that come from?"

"She is right, Mark. This business consumes you and eats into your personal space without you realising. We are so wrapped up in Steele's that you forget that there are people outside these four walls who need you and rely on you. Maybe you manage your work life balance better than me. Anyway, I ignored the commitment I made to Dani and to myself and called Graham back.

He started to tell me about what he had found out, but we ran out of time since the management meeting was starting. I agreed to call him back this morning and told Jude not to disturb me. I know it sounds overly dramatic, but I really wanted to know more and I especially did not want Keith barging in and upsetting the flow. I see the old bastard is in this morning, or rather I hear that he is in. Even the deaf could not mistake his dulcet tones echoing around the building, door locked or not. Then you came in and broke the thread of the conversation!"

"Sorry," said Mark, "I just thought that the future of the business might merit me overriding your instructions to Jude."

"Of course, Mark, I was kidding. So, what is Peter suggesting?"

"Well, he wants to speak with you of course, but essentially, he told me that it would be good if we could possibly get back down to London to see him and discuss where we are face to face. He says that there is also genuine interest from a second company that he is following up on and would hopefully have more information over the coming days."

Simon smiled. "Hmmmm," he mused.

"What?" asked Mark

"Well, if we need to go down to London again I could meet up with Graham in person and find out exactly what he discovered about Gerry's death. It seems that all attempts to do that over the phone at the moment are doomed to failure. Let me call Peter Westmann back and see what he suggests. Then I can update you on what I have learned so far from Graham."

Fifteen minutes later Simon had spoken to their M&A advisor and texted Graham to say that he would be in London on Friday morning and wondered if

Graham was free for lunch. Mark returned to Simon's office more to pander to what he saw as his elder brother's wild imagination than to any real interest in the Binns family whom he could only ever recall having met once.

Simon continued with the story.

"So, it seems that the police might have made a mistake arresting and charging this guy Michael Spedding and that there could be a more sinister explanation for Gerry Binns' death which has something to do with a doctor's letter and some issues with his mother's birth certificate. I think Graham was about to reveal more to me when you came into the office".

Mark listened patiently, feigning more interest than he actually felt, and then gave Simon his honest opinion.

"I am sorry if this is not what you want to hear, Simon, but I think Dani is absolutely entitled to be angry at what I think, based on the little you have told me so far, appears to be something that does not merit your time given all the other things going on at the moment. I know we are related to the Binns' but we have not been in contact since we were kids and whilst I know you love a good murder mystery, this is likely to be a flight of fancy that leads nowhere. Stick to reading Robert Goddard and Lisa Jewell, and leave Graham Binns where he has been for the last forty years."

Simon was taken aback by the directness of his brother's words. Mark was someone who did not normally say much and preferred to stay below the parapet rather than stick his neck out and risk taking a sniper's bullet. Simon was wounded but not defeated and he needed at least to respond to Mark's advice.

"I know this sounds like some schoolboy fantasy, but I genuinely believe that something in all of this is not right. Graham certainly thinks so. Look, I take your point about priorities closer to home and I would be devastated if anything happened to Dani and me. Let me see Graham on Friday and listen to what he has found out and I promise you that I will share it with you, and if you still believe I am wrong to get involved I will call a halt and forget all about it. Is that reasonable?"

Mark sighed and shook his head.

"I think you should stop now but you are clearly not going to do that. You are a stubborn bastard sometimes. Alright, meet Graham on Friday but promise me, no rather promise Dani and yourself, that once Agatha Binns has shared the rest of this fantastical plot with you that you will file it under "closed" and get back to the real world. Deal?"

Simon blushed at what he knew to be the truth but just could not admit to himself.
"Deal. You are probably right that I am adding 2+2 and getting 5 but let me just hear him out and then move on."
Speaking these words Simon knew that he did not really mean them but at least it would get Mark off his back until he had had a chance to find out what Graham was so urgently seeking to share with him. And Dani would suspect nothing since his trip to London was for Steele's business and not for anything likely to incite her anger further.
He felt pleased with himself for navigating the choppy waters caused by his wife's and his brother's verbal tirades.

He was looking forward to Friday and to finally understanding what Graham had discovered.

He did not realise just how choppy the waters surrounding him were about to get, nor that they were building up into a tsunami that would very soon be heading ominously in his direction.

18

CHAPTER 17

06 December 1939

Herbert Wilson sat behind his desk in the local registry office in Minehead and peered over the top of his horn-rimmed spectacles at the young man sitting opposite him. Herbert looked exactly like the archetypal image of a man whose job it was to deal with the very serious and sombre business of births, marriages and deaths. His thick tweed suit gave him an air of quiet efficiency whilst his almost bald pate perhaps suggested that the gravity and rote nature of his job had caused his hair to prematurely fall out through a combination of a lack of excitement and variety. He squinted in an almost pained manner as he spoke deliberately and as if he had to examine, consider and approve each word he uttered before it was allowed to escape his lips.
"This is a most peculiar request, sir, and certainly not something that is within my remit to execute. In fact, it is so peculiar and so unusual shall we say (the word 'unusual' was almost chewed before it emerged suggesting that the registrar had chosen it particularly carefully before letting it out) that I think it would be best if Sir were to leave my office now and we will say no more about this." As if to emphasise that the discussion was over, Herbert Wilson made a great show of very deliberately closing his registry book and

patting it twice as if to suggest that it would certainly not be reopened in the presence of his current visitor.

The visitor had expected exactly this reaction and made no attempt to vacate the chair he was sitting in. Instead, he smiled benevolently at the registrar and chuckled as if to suggest that he had a solution to whatever was making Herbert so cautious and reticent to accede to his request.
"Mr Wilson," he started in a manner that one might use when confronted by a whiny child that refused to eat their vegetables. Which was ironic in some ways since Herbert Wilson was several decades older than the visitor. "I totally agree that this is not the kind of request you are likely to get every day, but one has to look at it on its merits. There are very good reasons why I am asking for your assistance with this as I have already explained, and it is clear that making these small changes on a piece of paper will not result in anyone dying nor will it endanger the well-being of our country. Unlike the actions of Mr Neville Chamberlain and his antics in Munich."

The visitor clasped his hands together on the desk and looked expectantly at the other man. Herbert Wilson's face resembled someone who had just taken a mouthful of fruit squash from a glass and realised as they swallowed it that they had forgotten to dilute it with water.
"My dear boy, "the registrar said, "I will repeat once more that this is a most noxious and unfortunate request and one that I certainly wish you had not made. I have served my country and this town for more than 30 years and I have a reputation which I have built and which I have no intention of letting anyone jeopardise for their own selfish reasons. I am sorry to be so direct, Sir, but I really must end this meeting right now."

"Okay, Mr Wilson, you make yourself very clear. I will leave your office as you request and will not bother you again. It is a shame that you did not allow me to conclude what I had come to say, namely that as a devout Christian I wished to discuss making a donation to the St Mary's organ restoration appeal. I understand that you are indeed the organist at this very church and a capable and talented musician at that. It must be a matter of considerable personal disappointment to you that you are currently unable to play this fine instrument and honour the Lord as I know you would wish to. A man who serves his local community both within and outside the church is indeed someone I am sure the good people of Minehead appreciate enormously. The Great Depression and its knock-on effects have a lot to answer for including making church services here just that little bit lacking in musical accompaniment due to a severe dearth of funding for the essential repair work." The visitor smiled and looked at Herbert as might a poker player who has just put a royal flush on the table after one of his opponents had expectantly revealed that he had four of a kind. The registrar pursed his lips and looked down at the contents of his desk as he seemingly considered all of the possible replies to this new strand of information. Eventually he raised his head again as if his desk had yielded up the selected response which he could now share with his interlocutor.

"Might I enquire what kind of support Sir had in mind?"

The young man smiled benevolently at Herbert Wilson on hearing his response. There was no build up to the question he asked as one might expect when the matter concerned the delicate subject of money, just a direct to the point enquiry about how big the man's wallet might be.

"Well, Mr Wilson, that very much depends on the level of satisfaction I imagine I might get from hearing that beautiful organ ringing out in St Mary's again. I am the kind of man who has no problem with generosity if my benefaction is suitably rewarded."

"I-I-I, well yes, erm I am sure that erm you you you would be very satisfied with with the I mean the sound of the organ and we would indeed be most grateful."

Ten minutes later the visitor walked out of the registry office clutching an envelope which contained the piece of paper he had come for. He was smiling, content in the knowledge that he had nullified the very serious threat to his financial well-being that the original certificate had posed. It was surprising how changing two small pieces of information on an official document could make such a difference. Yes, there might be some form of impact on one certain person in the future but that could not be helped and hopefully it would never come to light anyway.

"Needs must," he said out loud to nobody in particular and congratulated himself once more on the potential calamity he had just avoided.

19

CHAPTER 18

31 August 2016

Simon was sitting at his desk reading through the latest documents that Westmann Buck had sent through. He had suggested to his advisors that they send the information for Friday's meeting in advance so that he could pre-read the papers and make the actual meeting in London as efficient and quick as possible. He had not, of course, told Peter Westmann that he had an ulterior motive for keeping the visit a short one, namely his lunch appointment with Graham Binns.

He was particularly interested to read what the advisors had prepared on the second and newly revealed potential purchaser, a UK based private equity company called Eldrich Global. He had vaguely heard of them before their formal declaration of interest in Steele's since they had been buying up small but growing wine and spirit brands in Europe, Australia and the USA as part of their strategy to build an alcoholic beverage portfolio. They had not yet ventured into beer, but it appeared that the news that Steele's was the subject of interest from Vinbrew had piqued their curiosity and they had now signalled their intent to seek an initial meeting to find out more and present their credentials. Of course, Vinbrew was still very much the front runner in the takeover stakes assuming that the Steele's board continued to allow such interest to be rewarded with the potential of a sale, but Simon rather liked what he read about their new suitor. Steele's was a business which competed against the big boys on a quality and a "real ale" ticket and it seemed that the companies Eldrich Global had been acquiring were similarly the creation of passionate family entrepreneurs like his grandfather William had been.

When Peter Westmann had first sent the information outlining the private equity interest on Wednesday morning Simon had wanted to share the news with Keith more out of devilment than anything else but had been told by Jude that his uncle would not be in the office for the rest of the week as he had been invited to a reunion in Leicester with a few old friends from his younger days. Keith never told his nephew when and if he would be in the office or not and so it was always through his PA that Simon found out about the chairman's latest escapades . Simon was actually quite glad that he did not have to incur the predictable wrath of his uncle who would no doubt see only negativity in a competitive bid for the company rather than an opportunity to drive the further shareholder value that a potential bidding war might bring.

The rest of the morning passed fairly slowly for Simon as his thoughts were entirely on the meeting with Graham the following day and, to a lesser extent, on the discussions with Westmann Buck. By one o'clock he was feeling peckish having only had a small bowl of muesli for breakfast so decided to eat the sandwich he had made before leaving home. As he sat down again, he reached for the remote and turned on the television that was fixed to the wall next to his desk. He had installed this largely so that he could keep up with the test match series when England were playing, but occasionally he would put Sky News on for half an hour at lunchtime to watch the latest developments in British political life. The Brexit debates had occupied much of the news agenda over recent months and Simon was fascinated by the ebb and flow of the relative arguments and the 'will they? won't they?' nature of the referendum. He was halfway through his ham and pickle sandwich when his ears pricked up at the breaking news story that the anchor had started to

talk about.
"Police in London have revealed that they were called to an office in Camden early this morning after a 52-year old man was found apparently stabbed to death. Early indications are that the man was self-employed. Relatives have been informed but the man's identity is not being released at this time. A police spokesman says that they are treating the case as murder."

Simon stopped eating his lunch in mid-bite and stared at the television. The next story concerning waiting lists in the NHS was already being discussed by a medical expert, but his thoughts were still firmly focused on the previous news item. Graham's office was in Camden. Graham was 52. Graham was self-employed. Before he panicked Simon told himself that there were probably several 52-year old self-employed businessmen in Camden but that barely reassured him. What could he do? How could he find out if it was indeed Graham? A wave of blind panic came over Simon and he stood up and headed out of his office to find Mark. His brother was not in his office and Jude confirmed that he was in a Finance review meeting with his team.
"Are you OK, Simon? You look like you have seen a ghost."
Jude looked genuinely concerned. Simon wondered if he should tell her what was bothering him but decided to keep it to himself. He did not really believe in coincidences and the rational side of his brain told him that the victim was probably far more likely to be some other London based businessman than it was Graham Binns.
"I am OK, Jude, just a bit overwhelmed with all the stuff going on at the moment."
"I can understand that" said his PA, "it is a bit manic at the moment even by Steele's standards! By the way, Martin Donaghue rang you earlier and asked if you could call back when you have five minutes." Donaghue was one of the Steele's non-family Board members, a successful business owner in his own right and an expert in strategy and investment which had been immensely useful to the brewery over recent years as it grew and expanded its reach and its portfolio.
"Thanks, Jude, I will call him now."

Simon headed back to his office, thoughts of the breaking news from Camden swirling around in his head. How long would it take the police to confirm the identity of the dead man? If they had already informed the next of kin what would the delay be? He would leave Sky News on this afternoon hoping that sooner rather than later the story would unfold further. Reaching for his mobile phone Simon sought out Martin Donaghue's contact details and pressed the call button.

"Simon, hi, how are you?"

"Hi Martin, pretty good considering everything that is going on at the moment. How are things at Donaghue Capital?"

"We keep adding new clients, Simon, and thankfully all the uncertainty surrounding Brexit, which is making people reticent, seems to be missing us. Long may it last! Anyway, I called you to discuss Steele's business not mine. I wanted to know where we are from your point of view with the takeover interest. Keith rang me yesterday to underline his total opposition to it and to say he expects the Board to back the view of the Chairman."

Simon gave a small half-laugh at the news that Keith continued to lobby for the status quo. It summed the man up in his opinion, stuck in a bygone era which he believed to have been the best of times.

"It is all progressing despite the best efforts of my uncle to dismiss it out of hand. You heard about Eldrich Global I assume? Look, I do not know whether either of these potential buyers is right for us and whether we will ultimately sell the business, but we owe it to ourselves to at least let the process evolve. Keith is not prepared to countenance this, and I personally think that is wrong. In fact, I have a second meeting with the M&A advisor in London on Friday."

"You know I am with you, Simon. It makes absolute sense to allow this process to continue provided you remain in control of what happens. There is no commitment to sell however aggressive the would-be buyers become so let them move forward. I wanted to let you know that I have a bit of an inside track on Eldrich Global as they purchased a couple of whisky brands last year from a large client of ours. The guy that heads up their business is a bit of a maverick and has a reputation of being an arrogant sod but he seems to run a good operation and they are certainly making waves in the industry. Steele's would be a much bigger purchase for them than their deals to date, but I guess you should be prepared to listen to them. Not sure how this guy and Keith would get on, I assume there would probably be fireworks!"

"Thanks Martin. I will go into the next stage with an open mind and see where it takes us."

1

After a few closing pleasantries and enquiries about the health of each other's family Simon ended the call and looked at the television to see if there was any update on the Camden murder story. There wasn't according to the news stream at the bottom of the screen which still just referred to a 52-year old self-employed businessman.

There was a knock on the door and Mark walked into the office.

"You were looking for me, I think?"

"Yes, I was but I am not sure having thought about it that I still am."

Simon blushed slightly as he spoke.

"Oh, ok. What is going on, you look like a schoolboy who has just been caught smoking behind the bike sheds?"

Simon was wavering as to whether or not to tell his brother about the Camden murder. Given Mark's reaction when Simon first mentioned that Graham had discovered something interesting about his father's demise suggested that silence might be the best approach. On the other hand, Mark knew that he was planning to meet Graham on Friday and, whilst he had not exactly bestowed his full blessing on the reunion, he had at least claimed to understand why Simon felt a need to meet their second cousin for one final time. He was itching to confide in somebody about the story currently trending on Sky News. On the other hand, was he being ridiculous? Who would murder Graham? Yes, he claimed to have evidence that his father's death had not been caused by Michael Spedding, but he had told Simon quite clearly that he had chosen him to confide in suggesting that he had not told anyone else. How then could anyone who might be threatened by this information becoming widely known have learned of Graham's new conclusions? It did not make any sense.

"Are you sure you are ok, Simon? What has got into you?" Mark shrugged his shoulders as he sought to understand the worried look on his brother's face. "Ok, Mark, I do want to share something with you concerning Graham Binns. Well, when I say concerning Graham Binns, I mean potentially concerning Graham Binns. Well, it concerns him whether it is ultimately him or not I guess."

Mark looked at his brother, frowned and shook his head.

"You are usually such a direct person, Si, I am the one who thinks and cogitates before speaking. What has changed?"

"There is a story trending on Sky News that a man who matches Graham's profile has been murdered in his office in Camden. Before you say it, I know what you are going to tell me and I am even telling myself the same thing. There are likely plenty of 52-year-old self-employed businessmen working in Camden. It just seems such a coincidence and quite frankly I am concerned."

"I really do not want to repeat the comments I made on Tuesday, Simon, but you need to get a grip on yourself where it concerns this whole charade. It is starting to become more important to you than other parts of your life. You seem to forget we have a takeover battle in full flow and that you have a wife threatening to cut you adrift if you do not stop trying to emulate Sherlock Holmes, yet you continue to see intrigue where none lies in this one-man soap opera where you have awarded yourself the lead part. Sorry if this sounds unfair but someone needs to hold a mirror in front of your face."

Simon was shocked at the severity of his brother's words and for a few moments he was unable to find any words with which to respond. Eventually he found his voice and was about to mount some kind of defence when he noticed that Mark was staring at something behind him with his mouth hanging open. Simon turned around and realised that his brother was looking at the television mounted on the wall. As he did so Simon caught the words scrolling along the bottom of the screen in the news bar.

"Police have just confirmed that the 52-year-old man found stabbed to death in his office in Camden early this morning is Graham Binns, a self-employed financial advisor from Ilford in Essex."

20

CHAPTER 19

11 November 1990

Gerry Binns did not like lying to Sonia but on this particular occasion he could see no way to avoid it without having to explain something he preferred at this stage to keep a secret. At some point he would have to ask his wife about the documents he had discovered at his mother-in-law's house but that time, he deemed, was not now. He had invented a story about a conference for cycle shop retailers in Bristol and was crossing his fingers that Sonia would not want or be able to check whether there actually was such an event happening. He really had driven along the same route he would have taken had he genuinely been going to Bristol, along the M4 then down the M5. It somehow made him feel that his lie was less serious than if he had travelled in a totally different direction.

However, when he reached the Bristol exit, he did not leave the motorway but rather continued south until he came to the turn-off for Taunton. From there he drove straight until he reached the A39 and followed this all the way to his destination. He had never been to Somerset and so had not even realised that the town of Minehead was on the coast! As he drove towards the town centre Gerry told himself that he and Sonia should seriously consider

Somerset as a potential short holiday destination next time they wanted a break from suburban Ilford. However, holidays were far from his mind on this particular November day. He had a very specific objective to try to accomplish whilst he was in the town.

The registry office was situated in Bancks Street and, much to his surprise and relief, Gerry managed to find a parking space close by. He walked the short distance to the building and then entered through the heavy wooden doors. Whenever Gerry went into this type of council office he had the impression that he was stepping back forty years with the smell of wax polish on the mahogany furniture and the fact that the people who worked here tended to dress very conservatively in a jacket and tie or a floral dress. It gave an aura of formality to the place and the impression that it was trapped in an earlier period, unlikely ever to escape from there. As he walked over to the reception area, Gerry wondered whether he would be able to find the information he had come for and indeed whether he would even get past the first hurdle. In this instance the first hurdle was a rather dull looking woman whose lapel badge identified her as Marjory Jillings and whose role in the office was apparently the Front Desk Administrator. In Gerry's experience of dealing with local councils on a myriad of issues related to his cycle shop anyone who administered things tended to believe that such administrative duties included examining things from every feasible angle and asking countless questions of dubious value as if they felt a need to spin even the simplest of tasks out in order to ensure that their job was justified. Preparing himself for the worst, Gerry approached the front desk with a sense of trepidation, but he need not have worried. Belying her somewhat fusty appearance, when she spoke Marjory Jillings was the very epitome of positivity, her face beaming as she addressed her visitor.

"Good morning, sir, how can I be of assistance on this wonderful day?"

Gerry's initial reaction was that the Front Desk Administrator was taking the mickey and poking fun at his expense, but he soon realised that her enthusiasm was genuine and heartfelt. Which led him to ask himself what on earth she was doing working in such an austere place when she clearly had the skills required to be a cheerleader running activities at a summer holiday camp. Reminding himself of his single purpose in coming to Minehead that morning, Gerry brought his mind back to the matter in hand and laid out to Marjory Jillings what help he was seeking.

"I am trying to understand an apparent anomaly on my wife's birth certificate and wondered if you might be able to help throw some light on the matter."

"I can try, Mr....erm..."

"Binns, Gerry Binns."

"Mr Binns. Is your wife with you today? We do have a rule that documents can only be accessed by the person whose name appears on them. Unless, of course, the person in question is dead."

Marjory Jillings pronounced "dead" as if it was a word that belonged in another ether, not present in the English language dictionary with every other word but rather an invader, a word that had attached itself like a scheming parasite to the end of her sentence.

"She is not exactly dead," said Gerry, who, having anticipated this objection, had prepared a response that he hoped would be plausible enough to convince the relevant people to divulge information without Sonia being present. "My wife has been suffering from a serious stress trauma brought on when it was suggested in a long-forgotten letter that there were serious anomalies in the recording of her birth. The circumstantial evidence concerning these anomalies seems to be very strong, but her birth certificate appears to be as we always believed with no suggestion of any impropriety. We need to understand why this is. She is not well enough to travel such a long distance which is why I have made the journey all the way from Essex to hopefully get clarity on her behalf."

Gerry looked expectantly in the direction of Marjorie Jillings, silently praying that what he hoped had been a convincing performance was indeed viewed that way by her.

The Front Desk Administrator looked at Gerry over her large round spectacles and gave a small cough.

"Mr Binns, first of all I am sorry to hear about your wife's condition and I do hope that it will just be a temporary state of affairs until she gets clarity on the situation that led to her stress. Unfortunately, as I said earlier, without the presence of Mrs Binns to sign and authorise this I am not in a position to divulge any information to anyone else. I know that is not what you had wanted to hear but the privacy and protection of personal information laws have become so much tighter as I am sure you are aware."

"I see." Gerry wondered if his initial impression of Marjory Jillings as a bureaucratic battle-axe might indeed have been right, and that her bright and breezy welcome had been but a façade.

"Mrs Jillings," he continued, "Marjory if I might be so bold. This is a really sensitive matter and one that needs some clarity as soon as possible so as to avoid any nasty consequences, particularly in respect of my wife's health. I have spent four hours driving here because of this and I run a business in Essex which means is it really is difficult to get time off. I am begging you to help."

Marjorie Jillings' expression was difficult to decipher, and Gerry looked imploringly at her as she seemed to be weighing up an appropriate response. Finally, she sighed and moved closer to the counter and closer to Gerry.

"Mr Binns, here is what I can do. I will go and speak now with our registrar Mr Lockwood and, assuming he has no objection, I will look into the archives and see what I can find. I will not be allowed to give you any sensitive information, but I will try to find out if there is any substance to what you say seems to have happened. Is that fair?"

Gerry smiled and told Marjorie that this was very kind of her, and he would be very grateful if she could help to throw some more light on what seemed to be contradictory records. Depending on what she did come back with he could obviously try to push more, but at least he had made progress compared to her first response.

"This might take a bit of time, Mr Binns, so you might want to go for a walk and come back in an hour or so. There are some very interesting shops in

the high street, and I am sure a nice cup of tea or coffee would be welcome. I would not recommend the vending machine in this building by the way." Marjorie Jillings laughed out loud as if she had just told a potential winning one-liner at the Edinburgh fringe.
"Thanks for the tourist advice, Marjorie!" Gerry smiled and confirmed that he would be back within the hour.

In the event Gerry did not visit a café as he instead stumbled upon a cycle shop and decided to invest the time he had in conversation with Ian Mellor, the owner, to compare notes and try to get some ideas for his own business. After his hour-long busman's holiday, Gerry returned to the registry office to see what Marjorie Jillings had been able to discover.

"Mr Binns," she chimed as Gerry came through the entrance, "I have managed to look into the matter and I hope you will deem your journey to have been worthwhile."
Gerry did not want to raise his hopes too much despite Marjory's chirpy, upbeat welcome. He had been here before and that almost ended in disappointment.
"Thank you," he replied in the hope that what she had for him would indeed take his investigation further forward.
"So, I went into the records for 1939 and found your wife's birth certificate. I believe that she was born on the eighth of September. The certificate records her parents as Eric and Elisabeth Croft (nee Steele). I am assuming that these are your wife's parents?"
Gerry nodded.
"However, there is a note in the margin of the register stating that this was a replacement certificate since the original, dated 19th of September, contained an error which needed to be corrected."
A thin smile appeared on Gerry's lips. A cautious but obvious smile. Was it indeed possible that his suspicions may indeed be validated by the new information that the registry office was able to provide.
"Apparently," continued Marjory, "the error was indeed a pretty serious one

which seems most unusual. Often in these kinds of situations it is a matter of correcting a spelling mistake or changing the date of birth by one day, particularly when a baby is born close to or at midnight. In the particular case of your wife the change requested and carried out was about as major as it was possible to get.

Mr Binns, your wife's original birth certificate contained different names for both her mother and her father."

CHAPTER 20

31st August 2016

Simon sat looking at the Sky news feed with his whole body feeling as if it had just suffered paralysis. He was literally rooted to the chair as if he had been struck dumb. Mark looked similarly stunned as he sat motionless staring at the television. He was the first to find his voice;

"Oh my God!" It seemed as if no more words were necessary as an initial reaction.

Eventually Simon found his tongue.

"I knew something was not right. I just knew it." He shook his head and covered his eyes with his hands. Then he frowned as if something new had just come to him.

"But hang on...are these two things connected? I mean the thing with Gerry and..and..and this?"

Mark looked across at his brother.

"I don't know, Simon, but this is shocking. I have no idea whether everything you have been saying recently is true or not, but this is someone we know, someone we are related to. Seemingly murdered in cold blood. It is horrific."

Simon continued to stare at the television even though the news feed had

moved on to other stories and there was no mention of the murder from the news anchor. It was as if he had been turned to stone. Eventually he spoke very quietly.
"I just can't believe it. I mean, can it be a coincidence that he wanted to tell me something about his dad's death and then within 48 hours he is dead himself. Not just dead but murdered!"

Simon looked at his brother as if seeking an acknowledgement that his assertion was correct. Mark sighed.
"Simon, I do not know what to think. Up until a few minutes ago I believed you were becoming obsessed with some triviality at a time when there are much bigger fish, both personal and professional, to fry. I still think that that is maybe still the case, but the news of his death is nevertheless quite a shock."
"There has to be a connection, Mark. Sure, you sometimes see such coincidences but that cannot be the explanation for what has just happened. Graham knew that his father was not murdered by Michael Spedding. I am not sure if he knew or suspected who did do it, but he knew that the police had got the wrong man. Of that I am utterly convinced."
"I am assuming from your last comment that you intend to continue what you have started? Though how you would be able to do that without Graham around I am not sure as he was the only link you have into the theory that someone else killed his father."

Simon looked pensive as he listened to what his brother was saying. Mark was absolutely right but it would be unforgivable to Simon's mind if he simply abandoned Graham now and let sleeping dogs lie.
"I do, Mark, and right now I cannot think straight about how to do it. I need to get my head around what has happened first."
"You need to get your head around the potential sale of Steele's, Simon." Mark, ever the practical one, realised that things were moving apace with the potential acquisition by Vinbrew together with the arrival of a new suitor which added complexity to the situation. "We have a meeting in London to

prepare for and I want to make sure that this has not disappeared from your radar whilst you are busy playing Poirot."

"I know, Mark, I know."

"I suggest that you finish that sandwich while I grab my lunch and that we meet in the boardroom at 2 to review how we want to play the meeting with Peter Westmann on Friday. I have pulled together some more information on Eldrich Global to add to what you already have so we can make sure that by the close of business we are ready."

With that Mark stood up and headed for the door. As he was leaving Simon's office he turned round and looked earnestly at his brother.

"Si, I know this is shocking news and I also know that you will not let this thing drop but please remember that you are the CEO of this business and also a husband and father whose family needs him to continue to be just that wherever this other situation might lead. Make sure you think long and hard about what I am saying."

Simon sighed, pursed his lips and looked blankly ahead at nothing in particular. His head was swirling with a myriad of thoughts and emotions. The potential acquisition of the Steele's business. His personal situation and the whole work-life balance issue which was clearly and understandably high on Dani's agenda. And the Binns murder case – now a double murder case – which had been thrust into his line of sight after 40 years without him ever having thought of his relatives in Essex. He knew that Mark was right and that the first two of these matters were the ones he should focus on. Was it the right time to consider selling Steele's? Could they get the right deal that made it a good decision for the family? How could he convince Dani that he was still a devoted husband and father given all the competing demands on his time? Yes, he knew Mark was right, but he was now totally captivated by the third matter and knew that he had fallen for it hook, line and sinker. It was absolutely beyond the pale in terms of letting go and forgetting about Graham Binns and his family. Quite how he was going to pursue this further with his second cousin dead, as Mark had pointed out, he had no idea, but pursue it he knew he would, whatever the consequences for his other priorities.

What began as simply an impulsive desire to reconnect with Graham Binns through Link Up had now seemingly morphed into a tale of murder and intrigue every bit as compelling as a novel by his favourite author Robert Goddard. Try as he might he knew it was far too late to disentangle himself.

Even if such entanglement put him squarely in the path of danger.

22

CHAPTER 21

April 1939

It was Easter Sunday and with the first flowers of Spring starting to appear Ingleby was the very picture of Yorkshire beauty. Ordinarily William Steele would have been looking forward to the long weekend and an extended break from his job as a Production Supervisor at the local brewery, but on this occasion the news he had received the previous week had shocked him and had been playing heavily on his mind ever since. William was generally an optimist and someone who believed that any problem could be solved if one was either patient, creative or willing to compromise. However, since he had been confronted with this current situation, he had been genuinely unable to see a way out of the mess. He could not deny that he was partly responsible for the matter in hand which made it even more difficult to find a solution. That was not true, he thought, as he contemplated the issue for the umpteenth time. There were two obvious solutions, the problem was that neither of these would be an acceptable outcome in this instance. As he thought once again about the likely reactions of others impacted by what had happened were they ever to find out about it, William covered his eyes with his hands and let out a resigned sigh. No matter which way he looked at it, a solution that would avoid the likely disaster seemed unattainable.

His thoughts were interrupted by the arrival of his fiancée Margaret with whom he would be going to church later. Margaret lived with her parents on the other side of Ingleby and worked as a clerk in one of the government offices in the nearby town of Richmond. The couple were to marry the following year and plans for this special occasion were well developed. As thoughts of the wedding resurfaced upon seeing Margaret again, William was once more led to wonder what on earth could be done to tackle the problem that had arisen. It was not beyond the bounds of possibility that a failure to tackle this issue might even jeopardise their wedding the following June if his father reacted to events as William thought he would. What on earth was he going to do?

"Happy Easter, my sweet," said Margaret, although she did not look happy in William's view. She was probably thinking about the same thing that he was given that the problem could have a dramatic impact on both of them.
"Yes, Happy Easter, pumpkin" he replied in a tone that in truth was more melancholic than happy. "Are you okay? You look a little bit down in the dumps if I might say so."
Margaret looked at William and the pain etched on her face seemed to intensify. She shook her head.
"Not really," she admitted, "I am worried about Elisabeth."
William frowned. This was not the explanation for her demeanour that he had expected Margaret to share given the enormity of their own issue that had been troubling him for days. A surge of anger hit him, and he allowed it to creep into his next comment.
"What the hell is the matter with Elisabeth that preoccupies you? I think we have other problems to tackle much closer to home." He instantly regretted raising his voice, which was so unlike him.

Margaret bridled at her fiancé's harsh tone which in truth she had never witnessed before. She was also worried that William might be angry when he

discovered that she had not said anything about what Elisabeth had shared with her the previous year. Margaret had intended to keep her future sister-in-law's secret to herself, but the letter she had received the day before had made her want to confide in William, who after all, in addition to being Elisabeth's elder sibling, would be Margaret's husband in the near future.
"It's Eric, he's not normal," she blurted out as if her words were propelled by jet force.
"What do you mean he's not normal? Is he ill? What is the problem?" asked William.
Elisabeth opened her mouth to respond but for a few seconds nothing came out. Eventually her verbal paralysis subsided, although her embarrassment continued.
"He...he's...he has a boyfriend. There I have said it." She let out a heavy sigh of relief and looked expectantly at William, whose expression was akin to that of someone who had just been told that the earth was flat.

"You...you mean he is a.....homosexual? An actual homosexual? And..and..and is he doing things with another man? I mean, despite being married?"
Margaret nodded. She stared at William whose mind seemed to be weighing up what possible additional comment would be appropriate in the circumstances. After a few moments of silence, and to Margaret's utter surprise, a broad smile broke out on her fiancé's lips. This was the last response that Margaret had expected, and she found herself feeling a mix of relief that William's earlier anger had completely dissipated and utter bewilderment that he found the news of his brother-in-law's homosexuality so funny.

"Interesting, very interesting." William's face now sported a smug look as he muttered these words, leaving Margaret completely and utterly bemused.

23

CHAPTER 22

02 September 2016

The shock that Simon felt at the violent death of Graham Binns had hardly dissipated when he and Mark travelled to London on Friday morning for the second meeting with Westmann Buck. As the train sped south Simon thought ironically that it should also have been his second meeting with Graham had circumstances not so rudely intervened. When he reached home on Wednesday evening, he had decided to say nothing to Dani about the events of the afternoon given the promises he had made to forget the whole Binns saga and concentrate on his family and the business. He deliberately avoided putting Sky News on, telling Dani that he would much rather talk and then watch the next episode in the Netflix series that had caught both of their imaginations. However, whilst he was at work on Thursday Dani had discovered the story for herself in the morning newspaper and was more than keen to discuss the matter once Simon arrived home.

"I have to admit that it is quite spooky, him being murdered like this after you had laid out your concerns about his father's death. Still, that will be a job for Scotland Yard to investigate, not you." As she uttered the last sentence

Dani gave a small laugh which could have been interpreted in different ways. Simon thought he knew what she was hinting at and got the message loud and clear. He had been thinking about this very topic all afternoon, trying to work out how he could stay close to events as they unfurled over the coming days and weeks without incurring the wrath of his wife. The answer, he concluded, was the very same Scotland Yard that Dani had just mentioned.

"Yes," replied Simon, "I am sure that Scotland Yard are already all over the crime scene and interviewing witnesses and close family members as they try to make sense of the whole tragedy. In fact, I am sure that they may want to speak with me given that I met him for dinner very recently." Simon neglected to add that he had also received a call from Graham earlier that week with concerns about his father's death and that they had intended to meet again in London on Friday. Simon judged that keeping that information to himself was probably critical if marital harmony were to be maintained. "I doubt that they would even know that you had dinner with him, and, anyway, having dinner together hardly makes you a prime suspect for the crime. Would they also want to speak with the petrol station attendant that filled his car up during this week?" Dani, as usual, was sharp and direct, and on this occasion added a dash of sarcasm for good measure.

Simon winced internally. Scotland Yard did want to speak with him after he had called them on Wednesday to outline to them the conversation he had had with Graham Binns following their earlier dinner appointment at Mendoza. The police were particularly interested to hear that the two men were supposed to meet again on Friday for Graham to outline his findings and concerns to Simon who seemed to have become something of a confidant. Simon had told the Senior Investigating Officer, Allan Broughton, that he was coming to London for business on Friday and had agreed to meet with the detective at 2.30. Simon had already started to think about how he needed to play this meeting which he had organised to find out what the police knew about Graham's murder rather than out of any real sense of public duty or as a witness with background information that might be useful to the investigation. The good thing was that using the cover of the meeting with Peter Westmann as the reason for his London trip, Simon did not need to breathe a word to Dani about his upcoming interaction with Scotland Yard.

Having changed trains at Darlington, Simon and Mark were on a direct train to King's Cross which was scheduled to arrive at 09.37 meaning that they would have more than enough time to reach the Westmann Buck office for their 11.00 meeting provided the train was running on time. This was by no means a given based on recent performance where the reasons for delays included leaves on the track, the weather being too cold, the weather being too hot and rolling stock in the wrong place as well as the more usual reasons such as congestion and strikes. Fortunately for the brothers, the train today was on time, so they entered the tube station at 10.00 arriving at the meeting destination 40 minutes later.

In truth, and he would certainly not admit this to Mark, Simon was distracted, and his mind was not fully on the meeting with their advisor. His perfectionist streak chided him for this, and he was not happy to admit to himself that he was much more focused on the second meeting of the day with Allan Broughton than on the one about to start. He knew that the Steele's agenda was far more important in the great scheme of things than what Dani described as his dalliances with a second cousin he had not even thought of during the past 40 years, but that was not how things felt this morning.

The meeting was certainly very informative and added to Simon and Mark's grasp of the various elements in play. This was needed for the Steele's Board to be updated on the options with a view to concluding on the relative merits of a sale compared to keeping hold of the crown jewels, as Keith referred to the company. Despite his mind not being fully on the subject, Simon listened to Peter Westmann as he provided more details on Eldrich Global about whom they knew much less than they did about Vinbrew.

"Eldrich is certainly making waves in the industry with its prolific acquisition strategy, " said Peter, "they seem to have a very clear and well-defined approach. What is interesting is that Steele's would be their first beer acquisition and would represent a significant statement of intent. The companies they have invested in seem happy with the experience, and they are particularly keen that the management team of the businesses they buy stay on and work with them to grow the top and bottom lines and create conditions for their exit. That is unlikely to be the case if Vinbrew were to purchase Steele's. In their other acquisitions, and most of those have been beer companies, they put in their own leadership team from day one and whilst they may retain the outgoing CEO and one or two other key people as transition consultants, it is very much a case of "use them and then spit them out" in our experience. Of course, after the acquisition you may not wish to stay even if you had the choice."

Simon was not familiar with the modus operandi of private equity firms although he had heard that many were very hard-nosed and demanding as partners or acquirers. He was interested to learn that they usually kept on the leaders of their acquired companies and more or less ran things as "business as usual" with the objective of improving the whole operation. This might be a serious consideration when selecting an acquiring company if a decision was taken to proceed to full due diligence with either or both of their suitors.
"Vinbrew is asking for an exclusivity period to do its due diligence if you recall from our last conversation. If you were to grant them this, it would prevent you from holding discussions with Eldrich during that time. What is the Board's view on whether you would be happy to proceed to due diligence with one or both of these companies?"
"That will be a decision for the Board based on the information Mark and I take back to the next meeting from what we have learned today." Simon nodded and looked at his brother.
"Anything to add, Mark?"
"Do we have a hint as to how Eldrich might look to structure their deal? We already have a clear view of what Vinbrew is thinking."
"That is what we are waiting to hear once we go back to them with a positive response to take things forward, Mark," said Peter. "Vinbrew came straight

in with an indication of what a potential offer might look like to tempt you guys to respond favourably. Private equity companies such as Eldrich tend to be more circumspect and look for a positive sign from their potential target before committing themselves."

After the usual wrap up and confirmation of next steps the meeting ended, and Simon and Mark left the office.

"That was interesting," said Simon, "what was your take?"

Mark did not reply immediately, being Mark he always liked to consider his response before making it.

"I do not see any issue in allowing discussions with both of these guys to go ahead given that we are not committing to anything at this stage. But before that, I think we need a Board decision on whether or not we are prepared to consider selling the company assuming that one of these two acquirers satisfies us. There is no point spending time letting them do their diligence only to tell them after they finish that Steele's is not for sale. And doing due diligence with a potential buyer is not only a lot of work for them but also a heavy lift for the company looking to be acquired. If we get into DD, we will be burning candles at both ends if we want to keep the business going whilst they assess us."

"We need to bring this to the Board on the 14th and align on our strategy. I must admit the thought of going into battle with Keith again is not one I relish but it is what we need to do. My objective at the next Board is for us to decide if we are genuinely open to selling or not. We cannot keep kicking the can down the road." Simon looked rueful as he stated what was clear based on the last time this topic was debated by the Board.

"So, I suppose that you are heading off now to tackle your next agenda item, Sherlock?"

Simon looked a bit sheepish, and he smiled at his brother's sarcasm.

"Yes, it is only 12.30 so I have time if you fancy a bite of lunch."

"I am going to head back to Ingleby, "said Mark, "I promised Annabel I would be home reasonably early this evening as she fancied having dinner at the pub in the village that has just reopened. My only comment to you is for God's sake do not get yourself embroiled in anything with the police. To be honest, Simon, I still do not know why you volunteered the information that you did, but I am obviously not going to dissuade you from doing what you feel you need to. You could have kept this can of worms firmly closed but you have chosen to open it. I hope that you do not regret having done that."

***

The headquarters of the Metropolitan Police, New Scotland Yard, is located on the River Thames at Victoria Embankment just north of Westminster Bridge. Simon strode towards the building well in advance of his agreed meeting time after having eaten a particularly tasty plate of fish and chips in a pub not far from the police headquarters. He had wondered if interviews with the Met actually took place inside their famous building or if it was just an office with desks. He was pleasantly surprised to learn that they did. Somehow that added to the air of intrigue which surrounded the whole case involving Graham Binns.

He entered the building and reported to the reception desk where he was asked to take a seat until he was called through. As he sat waiting, Simon reflected on the last forty-eight hours since the shocking revelation by Sky News that his second cousin had been murdered. Had he reacted too quickly in contacting the police to flag his involvement with Graham? Should he have simply remained quiet and waited to see what happened? His main motivation in calling the Met had been to try to see whether what had happened to Graham was indeed connected with the death of Gerry some twenty-five years earlier. In his haste he had not considered that he might be viewed as a suspect in this matter but now, as he sat in the auspicious surroundings of New Scotland Yard, it dawned on Simon that at the very least the police would view him as a key witness. In which case, what were the chances of him keeping this to himself and from Dani? Had he just committed a serious faux pas? So preoccupied was he by this train of thought that the lady now in front of him had to raise her voice to get her presence noted.

"Simon Letwin? Sir, Detective Inspector Broughton is ready to see you."
Emerging from his deep reverie, Simon apologised and followed the lady through to the interview suites. He had just sat down and taken his notebook from his bag when a tall, curly-haired man with the beginnings of middle-age spread visible on his waistline entered and offered his hand to Simon.
"Allan Broughton," he said in a precise, no-nonsense manner that was totally in keeping with the surroundings of this sparsely furnished room. "Thanks for coming in, Mr Letwin. I appreciate you giving up your time. I am the Senior Investigating Officer in the matter of the unexplained death of Graham Binns."
Simon smiled and indicated that he was here because he wanted to offer his help in the enquiry which elicited an expression of thanks from the detective inspector.

After a few formalities which established Simon's personal details and profession and his relationship to the deceased, Allan Broughton started asking questions in earnest.
"So, can you please explain your recent interactions with the late Mr Binns and why you decided to contact us on Wednesday?"
Simon spent the next fifteen minutes explaining everything from the discovery of the photograph on Scarborough beach and the Link Up request seeking to re-establish contact that this discovery prompted, the dinner at Mendoza, the subsequent calls and message from Graham and its portents leading to their planned meeting in London today. The DI listened to Simon's story and leaned back in his chair and steepled his hands in front of his face.
"Interesting."
Simon was not sure how to interpret this single word from the policeman. It was one of those words that carried a myriad of potential meanings each of them different depending on the context.

"So, let me just get this right," continued Broughton. "You had not spoken with the deceased for 40 years and decided that you wanted to find out what had happened in his life during that period. You met for dinner following which Mr Binns confided in you suspicions he held about his father's death, and you subsequently agreed to meet again today when he planned to give you a more comprehensive insight into his theory of what actually happened to his father Gerry Binns in 1991. Is that correct?"

As an avid reader of detective fiction Simon was used to reading story lines which were very similar to the real-life situation he now found himself in. In novels, the crime squad inspectors had ways of making witnesses feel uncomfortable so that they might let slip something relevant to the case. Simon suddenly felt an aura of guilt descending on him from the way Allan Broughton summarised what he had just been told, in spite of the fact that Simon's interactions with his second cousin had been totally innocent.

"Yes, that about sums it up, Detective Inspector." Simon looked at Allan Broughton for any signs as to what the policemen might be thinking. The latter's next words provided the answer.

"What I am trying to understand, Mr Letwin, is why you suddenly had an urge to contact a distant relative that you have not seen since you were both children who, within a few weeks of re-establishing contact with you, is violently killed two days before he plans to reveal to you something apparently equally shocking about the death of his father. Do you see what I am getting at?"

There it was. Simon's realisation as he had sat in the reception area waiting for his meeting that his decision to contact the police might have been hasty was now being played out in front of his eyes in bold technicolour. He had made the contact with the police in the belief that it might provide him with the information that he was now not going to get from Graham so as not to lose the thread about Gerry's demise. Instead of which he had seemingly opened the very can of worms that Mark had warned him about. He desperately needed to get this discussion back on track before things got even worse and he became a suspect in this case."

"I can see why you might be asking yourself that, yes, Detective Inspector. However, I can assure you that my role in all of this was a totally innocent one. Why would I take the decision to contact you proactively if I was in any way involved in what has happened?"

Allan Broughton looked at Simon in the way a teacher might look at a pupil who had claimed to be behind the bike sheds to study the wildlife there.

"Because, Mr Letwin, maybe you think that by getting your oar in first it will somehow deflect attention from the wider picture."

Simon was speechless. "Seriously, you cannot think that I was responsible for what has happened to my cousin?"

"Second cousin." Broughton smiled as if he had just delivered an upper cut in a boxing match.

Simon was now beginning to feel very uncomfortable and sweat broke out on his brow.

"Look, there was something not at all right about the murder of Gerry Binns. Graham knew that and wanted to unburden himself after the years of silence, and he chose me to do that with. Someone must have cottoned on to what was happening and decided that Graham needed to be silenced. And if you believe that I had a hand in Graham's murder, you can check with any number of people who will no doubt confirm that I have been in North Yorkshire all week. London is at least a 4-hour drive from Ingleby so I can hardly have managed to pop out at lunchtime, commit the deed and get back to my desk before anyone had noticed."

Simon blew out a stream of air, realising that his explanation could easily have been interpreted as that of a man with something to hide. The look on Allan Broughton's face suggested that the same thought might have crossed the detective's mind, too."

"Okay, Mr Letwin, I think we are done. Thank you for coming in voluntarily today and for sharing this with me. We are pulling together all the facts that we can in order to try to solve this matter as quickly as possible."

"Do you have any idea who might have done this," asked Simon. "Assuming I can convince you that it was not me."

The detective inspector looked at Simon and nodded. "It is early yet, and we are still establishing time frames and collating CCTV evidence and the like. You have just supplied us with a potential motive of which we were unaware so that will need to be taken into consideration. We will certainly need to speak with you again, Mr Letwin, so please expect our call. Thanks again for your time today."

With that, Broughton got up and left the room leaving Simon and his thoughts behind. The female police officer who had brought Simon in popped her head round the door and enquired if he was ready to leave. In truth, he could not wait to get out of this building which was beginning to feel oppressive. As he walked towards the tube station to start his journey back to Yorkshire, his mind was spinning as he thought about the conversation he had just had with Allan Broughton.

He hoped that he had not just made the biggest mistake of his life.

24

CHAPTER 23

12 November 1990

Binn's Cycle World was the only independent cycle store in Ilford and had built up a loyal following in the locality since it was opened by Gerry Binns in 1963. Gerry was a keen amateur cyclist who had competed at county level whilst at school and who, after spending seven years working in an insurance office after his 'A' levels, realised his dream of opening a cycle shop three years after he married Sonia Croft. Customers liked the fact that the shop was owned and run by a fellow bike aficionado and often called in just to chat with Gerry about anything from what new bicycles he had in stock to maintenance advice for their machines. Gerry also ran a weekly cycle club for children which was his way of connecting with the local community whilst looking to build awareness and loyalty in the young to hopefully make them lifetime customers. It certainly seemed to be working.

Having returned from Minehead the previous evening, Gerry's thoughts had been almost exclusively focused on trying to make sense of what he had learned and how this tied in with the discoveries he had made at his mother-in-law's house following her recent death. His body was in the cycle shop on this Tuesday morning, but his mind was altogether elsewhere. For the umpteenth time today, he chewed over the key parts of the matter in his mind. Stripping it all down to its lowest common denominator, the problem he was having in even beginning to understand the facts as they seemed to present themselves was that the two most important pieces of information seemed to be totally incompatible with each other. This would seem to suggest that one of the so-called facts was indeed a falsehood, but he had seen the evidence linked to both that confirmed them as being 100% true. Gerry's thoughts were interrupted by the sound of the shop doorbell signalling the arrival of a customer.

"Morning, Gerry, how are you?" Ken Dawson was one of the shop's longest standing clients who had purchased a bike shortly after the shop opened and had since bought two more for himself and one for each of his two children. He regularly called into the shop and had become a good friend of Gerry's over time. "You look to be in a world of your own, Gerry. Dreaming of an exotic trip somewhere over the Summer break?" Ken laughed out loud as if what he had said was much funnier than it actually was.

"To be honest, Ken, I am trying to work out the answer to a dilemma that doesn't want to seem to be understood."

"Well, Gerry, you have the right man in your shop for a task such as that. I can finish the Times crossword in under half an hour and Sue calls me the King of Sodoku!"

Gerry smiled and raised his eyebrows as he looked at the other man. He was unsure whether to say anything to someone who was not really a close friend. He would certainly not personalise it if he decided to share it. As he thought this through, he was struck by the need to share the challenge with somebody and he decided that Ken was as good a person as any.

"So here is the challenge, Ken." Gerry made out that this was a type of logic problem that you might find in a puzzle magazine rather than something that had really happened to his family. He explained the content of the doctor's letter that had been sent to the lady in question and then how her child's birth certificate had been changed some time after they were born. The question is how both "facts" can be true." Gerry wondered if he was making any sense or whether he had lost Ken in the course of telling the story. As the other man seemed to be considering the puzzle, Gerry added his current supposition. "The only solution I can think of that makes any sense is that the child was adopted. However, that does not explain why the birth certificate was changed in the way it was."

Ken Dawson frowned and scratched his nose as if this would somehow help him to decipher the problem. Gerry could almost hear the cogs turning in his brain.
"There is another possible explanation, Gerry." Dawson smiled and stayed silent, as if playing with Gerry and encouraging him to ask the next logical question. Gerry looked at his friend but said nothing. Eventually Ken Dawson continued. As he slowly outlined his thought process and what the alternative explanation might be, a look of horror crossed Gerry Binns' face. Fantastical as it seemed, there was definitely some logic in Ken's solution where it was lacking in his own theory. If this was the correct explanation, it was shocking and its implications would shake the very foundations of his family.
"What do you think, then?" asked Ken Dawson, fishing for a compliment from Gerry.

"If you are right, Ken, I think the people implicated in the puzzle have some serious explaining to do."

25

CHAPTER 24

02 September 2016

It was almost 10pm when Simon arrived back at home after his long day travelling to and from the capital for his two meetings. He was both mentally and physically exhausted, the latter from the roughly nine hours of train journeys and the former from his interactions with the Met Police. In truth, his mental tiredness had been exacerbated by his almost forensic analysis of the pros and cons of his decision to approach Scotland Yard about Graham, conducted in silence on the train back to Darlington. In truth, his feeling as he left the police station that he might have made a wrong move had barely diminished in the hours since, and he stepped through the front door of his house wondering what the next few days would bring.

Dani was in the lounge watching something on the television as Simon took off his jacket and bent down to give her a kiss.
"Hi, hun," he began, "wow what a long and tiring day that was." He had already decided not to tell his wife anything about the meeting with the police not least because it would show that he had earlier lied about what the trip to London was for. He fell back on the lie that he had created a few days earlier.

"So, the meeting with the advisors is at 11.00 and should take a couple of hours, then I have a lunch appointment with a Marketing agency that we are considering as a potential replacement for our current one. You remember I told you about the fiasco with the roadshow programme? Well, these new guys are not one of the big players like the one we are currently working with, but they have had rave reviews in the past couple of years. We need to liven up our Marketing act given that we are being outshouted by some of our competitors." Simon had been surprised by his own ability to lie so brazenly. He needed to remember exactly what the lie had consisted of now that he was back from this supposed meeting. He had also tried to make sure he covered his tracks by outlining his cover story to Mark and requesting his brother's collusion in not mentioning the police to Dani or indeed to anyone else.

"So, was it a fruitful day?" asked Dani, not sounding overly interested and seemingly asking the question because she felt it was what a spouse should do. This was not lost on Simon and made him feel even more guilty if that was possible.
"It went very well, actually. Mark and I will be recommending to the Board that we do progress discussions regarding a potential sale because why wouldn't we? It does not commit us to anything at this stage and it would be stupid not to at least look at what these two companies are offering."
"Keith will not be pleased, to say the least," said Dani, "assuming that he is still opposed to a sale at any price." Dani had flicked the pause button on the TV remote which encouraged Simon.
"Understatement of the year, hun, "he replied, "but it is not his company, there are other shareholders."

"And what about your Marketing meeting? Does that look positive?"
Simon could feel his face redden and hoped it was not too obvious. In reality, the meeting was tentatively pencilled in for later in the month, so he needed to be very careful how he handled this topic both now and later.
"Very encouraging, love. They are a young company but have some great ideas. We will definitely be taking this to the next stage."

"Good, so a worthwhile day, I am glad to hear. Focused on the business and not on that pointless wild goose chase that you wanted to embark on."
Simon felt a surge of fear course through his body. Was that an indication that Dani had sussed him out or was it just a coincidence which his feelings of guilt had manufactured into something more than it was?

"There is so much happening at Steele's at the moment that I cannot take my eyes off the ball. And if I do, it needs to be you I focus on rather than anything else." Simon listened to his words as he uttered them and they sounded false and hollow to him. Hopefully they sounded more genuine than that to Dani. He was grateful to hear her change the subject.
"Have you eaten anything? There is some chilli con carne in the pan."
"I am fine, love" said Simon, "I grabbed a pasty at the station before I left as I knew it would be too late to eat when I got back."
Dani flicked the remote button and the programme she was watching started again. Simon decided that a cold beer was in order and spent the next hour ostensibly watching TV with Dani but, in reality, chewing over the events of the day and where all of this might eventually lead.

* * *

The following Tuesday morning, Simon had an early meeting at the office with the Production team to review current performance and any issues that needed to be discussed. Geoff Willerby, the Operations Director, ran a very efficient ship in the brewery and Steele's production performance was up with the best in the industry. Thankfully there were very few matters of concern beyond a few niggles with raw material availability and the threat of industrial action at their main bottle label supplier.
"Let's make sure we can secure additional supplies from Granby's if Malcolm and his merry men cannot meet our needs. In fact, Geoff, I would place an extra order anyway as a precaution because this strike at Flexible Packaging

seems certain to go ahead based on the call I had with Malcolm a couple of weeks ago."

With the Production meeting over, Simon returned to his office to prepare for his weekly review of the key financial numbers with Mark and his team later that afternoon. Since returning from his London trip last Friday, much of his time had been spent thinking about Graham and the events of the past week despite his assurances to Dani that he was focused on the business and on her. Given the fact that the Met Police were now aware of him and of his recent engagements with the deceased, he had been trying to work out how he could advance his investigations into what Graham had wanted to share with him regarding the death of his father. He had to play it very carefully and not make the police any more suspicious of him than they likely were after the meeting last week, but he would undoubtedly be forced to raise his head above the parapet to learn anything new of value.

With Graham gone, it struck him that the three people he might look to speak with were Sonia and Ashleigh plus Graham's wife Sarah. He was not sure if any of them shared Graham's suspicions regarding Gerry's death and there was only one way to find out. The problem was that it was less than a week since the murder had taken place and Simon was not so insensitive to think that Graham's close family would be anywhere near coming to terms with their loss. Furthermore, he was sure that if he contacted any one of them and they did object, the police would take an extremely dim view of his behaviour and may even assume that these were the actions of a guilty man trying to cover his tracks. He was already inadvertently on their radar after his meeting with Allan Broughton and the last thing he needed to do was to add fuel to a smouldering fire. Not to mention what Dani might say or do. No, he would need to bide his time and see how things developed.

Simon went back to preparing for the Finance meeting and surprisingly managed to keep his mind on this for the next few hours. The main topic for the review was the way costs were creeping up at a pace that was not being matched by either sales growth or the ability to take price increases. Margins were therefore being squeezed and pressure on cash flow was the result. This was one of the major challenges faced by family brewers such as Steele's in the modern age. In Simon's view (and that of many others including the contentious Campaign for Real Ale) the beer that Steele's produced was superior in every way to that of the large breweries but the latter benefited from huge Marketing budgets that allowed them to create totally fictitious brands pretending that they were age-old favourites of drinkers in Spain and Italy then using the power of TV to convince drinkers to seek out the 'authentic taste of paradise'! Fortunately, not everyone fell for this, but it was becoming ever more challenging for the traditional brewers to remain competitive. This was why Simon believed that at least listening to companies like Vinbrew and Eldrich Global was worthwhile. Sometimes an injection of much-needed capital into a business with great fundamentals but with cash challenges could be the catalyst for driving exponential growth and building shareholder value without destroying the heritage present in the business.

The discussion at the meeting was focused on creating a plan to interrogate the main cost areas in the business with a view to saving money without reducing quality or impacting growth.
"We need to challenge every cost centre," said Simon, "there are no sacred cows in this business!"
As they were beginning to wrap up the meeting and summarise the next steps Jude knocked and opened the meeting room door apologising profusely.
"I am sorry to disturb you," she told Simon, "but there is a lady on the line who says she needs to speak with you. Her name is Ashleigh Percival."
"Can you take a message please, Jude? I do not know anyone of that name."
"I suggested that, but she said it is quite important. She also said you may not recognise her because this is her married name.

Her maiden name was Binns."

26

CHAPTER 25

April 1939

The two men sat down next to each other on a bench on the station platform at Nottingham Victoria railway station after agreeing to meet somewhere convenient to them both. The platform was almost deserted, which certainly suited the man at whose insistence this meeting was taking place. The other man had been very reluctant to agree to travel at first, citing the cost, and the fact that it was very difficult for him to get time off work or leave his wife on her own at the weekend. That changed as soon as the first man started to lay out the agenda for the meeting. They knew each other very well and had certainly got on whenever they met, which made the letter that the second man had received from the first all the more unexpected and worrying. The contents of the letter were clear; they must meet within the next seven days, so the sender expected a reply to this request by return post. The rest of the letter explained why the meeting was so important, and hinted rather than outlined in detail at the reason why the second man should agree to come. Better not to commit too much detail to a letter which might find its way into the wrong hands, the first man had thought!

After a few minutes of small talk enquiring about family and commenting on the unseasonably cold weather, the first man began to speak.

"I asked for this meeting because we have a little issue that concerns both of us and I thought it was easier if we discussed it face to face rather than through an exchange of letters that, firstly, take time to arrive and, secondly, are probably the wrong medium for something as delicate as this."

The second man looked at the other man but did not say anything. The first man continued.

"You see, to put it bluntly, my problem is one of timing. What has happened to me was not planned, and, quite frankly, it risks causing me some big problems if it cannot be sorted out. The problem is that the only certain remedy available is not a palatable one for the other party involved, which means it is also unpalatable to me. I hope that I am not talking in too many riddles and that you are following me?"

The other man nodded but still did not say anything.

"Your problem," the first man continued, "is that you are ostensibly a happily married, law-abiding man, but if I strip away the surface sheen, my goodness what do we see underneath? Certainly not something that your wife or your parents would want to see. And I am not sure that the police would be any more impressed to learn about what you get up to when nobody is looking."

A sheen of smug satisfaction adorned the first man's face as he laid out the reason that had brought the two men together.

The second man looked as if he had been struck by lightning. He uttered his first words since he had arrived at the station. He decided to take a combative tone.

"I do not know what you are talking about or where you heard these fantastical rumours. As you say, I am a happily married man and would not dream of doing anything like the things you are suggesting. Unfortunately, I cannot help you to solve your problem, whatever it might be." He looked at the other man and waited to see whether his chosen approach had worked. The look on the first man's face told him that it had not.

"Not the right answer, I am afraid. You and I need each other to get through these little issues, and you will help me because the consequences of your grubby little secret being made public would be worse than death for you. So, let me explain my proposal – I call it a proposal because I am not a presumptuous man, but you will agree to it, of that I am very sure." He then spent the next ten minutes explaining what would happen next. When he had finished, he simply looked at the second man as if there was no response that was possible except blanket agreement. The second man looked as if he was seeking an appropriate reply but, in the end, he managed just one sentence.

"So, how do we do this?"

With a big smile adorning his lips, the first man summarised the way the plan would work. He suggested that what they had agreed to do could even be of benefit to the second man's family given certain things of which they were both aware. At this moment in time, the second man was not in the mood to consider any potential benefits from this transaction, and merely wanted to get away from this horrid situation and spend time with his own thoughts.

And with the huge, life-changing commitment he had just agreed to make.

27

CHAPTER 26

06 September 2016

Ashleigh Binns! That was Graham's sister. Calling him?
"Shall I ask her to call back? I can see you are not finished here yet."
Simon wanted to leap out of his chair and rush back to his office to immediately take the call but decided that he needed to finish this meeting before even thinking of doing that. A glance in Mark's direction told him that his conclusion was right. His brother had a wary, almost accusatory look on his face, or was Simon just being paranoid?
"Can you take her number, Jude, and tell her I will call her back as soon as this meeting is over?"
Jude left the room and Simon apologised for the interruption. "Where were we?"

For the next 15 minutes the team went through the main points from the meeting and agreed the action plan with timings and who would be responsible for each element of the plan. Simon had expected some pointed comment on the interruption from his brother, but Mark said nothing and followed the rest of the Finance team out of the meeting room without a glance in Simon's direction.

Five minutes later Simon was back at his desk and dialling the number that Jude had given him.

"Hello, this is Ashleigh."

"Good afternoon, Ashleigh, this is Simon Letwin. I am sorry I could not take your call earlier."

"Oh, don't worry, I know you must be a busy man!"

Simon uttered a half laugh and considered his next words.

"I...I am really sorry about your brother," he said, "this is just such a terrible situation." As he spoke the words, he wondered if they sounded genuine or hollow, particularly as he did not know the woman on the other end of the line despite her being his second cousin. And he had no idea what had prompted her to phone him. How did she manage to get his contact details? It was if his question had been anticipated.

"You are probably wondering why I am calling, Simon. I hope you do not mind me calling you Simon?"

"Of course not, Ashleigh. Please carry on."

"I managed to track you down through Link Up," said Ashleigh, "which is a bit ironic as I understand that it was the same way that you got back in touch with Graham. Once I saw where you worked the rest was quite straightforward. Do you have time now for me?"

"Yes, of course, I was surprised that you called me like this out of the blue." What he did not add was that he felt guilty about what had happened and certainly nervous at what might follow.

"Well, I thought long and hard before doing it as emotions are obviously still very raw and we are all totally shocked at what has happened. I wasn't that close to my brother and his wife, Sarah, the usual sibling rivalry I guess, but he was my brother and I loved him as such. The police have been with one or more of us for the best part of the last week trying to understand what exactly might have happened and who could have committed this awful crime. They have been asking us whether we knew you and what relationship we had with you, and they eventually told us about your plans to meet with Graham last Friday. They wanted to know if we knew what the meeting was for. We understand that he apparently wanted to share some revelations with you according to the police, which seemed strange to us given that we do not really know each other, and you have seemingly had no contact with either of us since we were kids. Sarah in particular is wondering how you got involved and whether there is a sinister angle to the whole thing. I told her that it was very unlikely, but that I would attempt to contact you just to try and get some reassurance. Although I am sure that you would not admit anything to me if you were involved. Not that I am suggesting you were." Ashleigh was gabbling and Simon thought that she probably added the last sentence realising that she had no reason to suspect him of anything at this stage.

Simon listened to Ashleigh's explanation for the call and was somewhat taken aback at her blunt suggestion that Graham's wife in some way suspected him of involvement in the matter. Or was it Ashleigh who felt like that and was using her sister-in-law as cover? Whichever it was, he needed to quash that possibility before it developed any further.
"First of all, Ashleigh, I can assure you that I had nothing to do with Graham's death. I was as shocked as you must have been when I heard, particularly as your brother and I had only spoken a couple of days earlier and, as you say, had planned to meet when I came to London last Friday."
"I probably should not even be calling you like this," said Ashleigh, "I am sure the police would take a dim view of it if they found out."

Which, thought Graham, makes me wonder even more why you are calling me. However, he did not want to let this opportunity pass, especially as he had not expected to have the chance to speak with one of Graham's family so soon after his death. He fully concurred with Ashleigh's view that the police would be very displeased to learn of this phone call taking place and once again the voice in his head told him that this was yet another opportunity to back off and stop meddling where he should not. The other voice told him that it was too late for that, he was involved, and no matter what common sense told him, he would continue to dig and try to find out what had happened to both Gerry and Graham Binns.

"I am pleased you did call, Ashleigh," said Simon. "I promise you that the reason I contacted Graham was a totally innocent one. I just had this mid-life thing about families that lose touch and decided if I did not act my kids would never know who the Binns family were. I know that probably sounds spooky, but it is the truth. Then Graham and I met for dinner and after that he seemed to decide that I was a good listener and someone he could share his suspicions with. That was why we were to meet on Friday. I swear that there was nothing more than that and I certainly played no role in what happened last week. In fact, my work colleagues can provide the confirmation that I was in Yorkshire the whole day of your brother's death."
"Were the suspicions you were to meet him to do discuss to do with my dad's murder?" asked Ashleigh.
Simon had been unsure whether Graham had said anything about the planned meeting to his sister but did confirm that this was the main reason for their second meeting.
"He did not share anything concrete with me (I mentioned our sibling rivalry), but it seems he did tell Sarah some details of what he had found, which is how I learned about this last week. I was shocked, both that he had not discussed such fundamental concerns with me given that it was my Dad, too, and that there exists the possibility the police got it so wrong when arresting that man Spedding. I am not sure on what basis my brother came to his conclusions, but it would be pretty incendiary if he is right. An innocent man spending 25 years in jail and all that."

Simon asked if Ashleigh would like him to briefly explain what Graham had told him over the phone. When she said she would, he told her about Graham finding their father's possessions in a suitcase which included a doctor's letter and their mother's birth certificate together with Gerry's comments and hypothesis as to what these documents meant. It seemed as if all of this had led Graham to a shocking conclusion. It was this that he wanted to tell Simon in person rather than on a call.

"I so wish that he had told me the full story when we last spoke on the phone," said Simon in conclusion. "That way at least I would have known what the anomaly was and would now be in a better position to understand things. I don't suppose what I have described means anything to you, does it, Ashleigh?"

Ashleigh said that it meant nothing to her, but that if whatever secret Graham wanted to share was in any way linked to his own demise, it must have been a dramatic revelation. Simon agreed with her.
"I need to go now," said Ashleigh, "my boss is hovering and I do not want him to hear me on the phone with you. Thank you, Simon, I feel better having spoken with you and will tell Sarah about our conversation. Bye."

The line went dead. Simon sat staring at his phone whilst a myriad of thoughts went through his head. On the one hand, he was sure that Ashleigh really had called him to 'check him out'. Her brother was murdered shortly after someone with whom he had not spoken for forty years reappears out of the blue and arranges to meet him the very week he is killed. On the other hand, Simon was sure that something else must have triggered the call. With the police handling the murder investigation, why would the victim's sister call a potential suspect with all the risk that this entailed unless she was trying to confirm or check out something which might help to explain what had happened? What could that be?

As Ashleigh ended the call, a similar stream of thoughts had disturbed her mind, too. When Simon's name was mentioned to her by Sarah, a montage of long-buried memories suddenly came flooding back to her, memories that she had forgotten with the passage of time, but which were now as clear as if they had happened earlier that day. Were they linked to Simon's reappearance after all these years? More importantly, was there a connection with the murder of her brother? Surely it was just a coincidence. Or was it?

Only time would tell.

28

CHAPTER 27

07 September 2016

"So, how was your trip to Leicester, Keith? How many extra barrels have you sold?"

It was the first time that Simon had seen his uncle since he had returned from his London trip, and he was in the sort of mood that almost made him want to pick an argument with the Chairman. The events of the past few days had weighed heavily on his mind, and he was seeking an outlet to release all the pent-up pressure he was feeling. The reference to selling additional barrels of beer was a direct mimic of the way Keith Steele used to challenge the brewery's sales reps in his days as CEO.

"Right, lad. So, you have driven 1,300 miles so far this month and you are presenting an expense claim for £137. I make that about two hundred and seventy quid of costs in total. How many extra barrels have you sold?" The poor, quaking salesman usually found his or her ability to speak frozen by Keith's aggression and managed nothing more than a blubbering noise that sounded as if they were submerged below water.

"What is that supposed to mean?" Keith's belligerence was as clear as day.

"Just making sure that we are all walking the talk, Keith."

"Well, that is bloody rich coming from you. The man who scoots off to London trying to flog our company as if it was a second-hand sweater on e-bay. You challenge me for building relationships that will have a positive impact on our business whilst gallivanting around trying to ruin all the good work I have done over a lifetime of devotion to this business."

This time, Simon was not prepared to take his uncle's comments without a robust response.

"Anyone would think you had something to hide, Keith. Maybe this was more than just a jolly?"

The chairman's face went several shades of crimson and spittle formed around his lips as he glared at his nephew.

"What the hell are you suggesting? If you think I am lying about something, then say it and let's tackle it like men."

Simon had expected a reaction, but Keith's response had been far more brutal than he had anticipated, and he wondered which nerve his comment had touched. Was the chairman seriously about to challenge him to a duel as if they were both medieval horsemen?

"Clearly a tetchy area, so I won't say any more. Especially given that we have important matters such as the Board next week at which we need to take a definitive position on the potential sale of the company which is something we all need to be focused on. My scooting off to London, as you so elegantly put it, was productive in helping us to understand the two expressions of interest as you will see when I circulate the Board pre-reading materials over the weekend."

The mention of selling Steele's brought the predictable response from the chairman which made Simon feel much better inside even though it was entirely predictable. It reminded him of a toy bear he had as a child which laughed every time you tickled its tummy.

"They will carry me out in a box before this company is sold to anyone. And I mean anyone."

"So where did you and your friends go in Leicester? I know the city quite well having worked in the East Midlands when I first joined Steele's." Simon pressed on with his questions.
"Don't be so bloody nosey, my activities are none of your business."

Mixed in with the pleasure Simon was deriving from this little spat with his uncle, which he told himself he must do more often, was an element of intrigue, even concern, as to why Keith was being so aggressive and evasive. In Simon's view, Keith was undoubtedly deficient in the sense of humour area, nevertheless he had been surprised at how an ostensibly innocent enquiry about his uncle's trip, even given his intent to provoke, could have engendered such a vehement response from the chairman. Did Keith have something to hide? What had gone on in Leicester that Keith did not want to share?

As these thoughts flowed through Simon's mind a far more sinister question occurred to him.

Had Keith actually been in Leicester at all?

29

CHAPTER 28

14 September 2016

The Steele's Board meeting the following Wednesday was every bit as confrontational as Simon had expected it to be. He reported back on the second meeting with Peter Westmann and informed the Board that, based on these discussions, his recommendation as Chief Executive was to progress discussions with both potential suitors with a view to understanding more about them and their proposals. This would then be reviewed at a suitable future Board meeting. Keith was predictably against this course of action, and as usual spoke in an animated tone about the family heritage, but in the end the Board voted in support of Simon's recommendation and instructed him to work closely with Westmann Buck to move the project forward. Keith threatened to resign over this decision, but as usual, once he had calmed down, said that he would agree reluctantly to stay on as the company needed his experience, and that his presence would be invaluable as a counter-balance to those who were disloyal and unpatriotic to the family crest.

Feeling pleased with himself at having gained the Board's agreement to his proposal, Simon headed back to his office to spend a couple of hours catching up on his outstanding admin tasks before heading home. The past couple of weeks had been full-on even by Steele's standards and he had a long list of mundane but important tasks to attend to. As he worked his way through the list, Simon's mind drifted to the recent call with Ashleigh and the so far unanswered question as to what really drove her to ring someone who to all intents and purposes was a potential suspect in the case of her brother's brutal murder. There had to be something that had triggered a recollection in her mind that led her to take such a risk and phone Simon. As he was mulling this over, his office door opened and Jude entered.

"There is a Detective Inspector Allan Broughton on the line asking to speak with you. Should I put him through?"

"Yes, Jude, please do."

"Mr Letwin, Allan Broughton here. I wanted to let you know that we have checked out your movements for the 31st of August and we are happy that you were indeed in Yorkshire all day meaning that you could not have committed the crime in London yourself. Clearly, you could have worked with an accomplice but for the moment we are assuming that this is not the case. We may, of course, need to speak with you again as the investigation proceeds given that you were in contact with Mr Binns and planning to meet with him during the week he was murdered. If there is anything else that occurs to you that you think might be relevant to this case, please do not hesitate to call me. Otherwise, I advise you to keep your counsel and leave us to do our job."

Simon felt a gush of embarrassment at the policeman's final remark as if the man was exceptionally perceptive and knew that Simon was unlikely to be able to simply walk away from this intrigue. He was also pleased that Broughton had followed up swiftly and spoken with Mark and Jude, whom he had provided as his two witnesses for confirmation that he had been at Steele's at the time of the murder. It was certainly a relief to get any whiff of suspicion lifted from him which meant that he would not need to explain to Dani why, despite her clear message to him that his further involvement with Graham Binns would not be tolerated, he had chosen to proactively call

Scotland Yard and then subsequently to meet with them, lying to her for good measure by inventing a fictitious Marketing agency meeting to cover his tracks.

Having ended the call with Allan Broughton, Simon returned to his To Do list or rather to thinking through why Ashleigh had called him and what his next course of action would be. Although the police would be investigating Graham's murder they would not be revisiting the events that led to his father's death in 1991. Simon was now convinced that the two incidents were somehow linked. In his mind, there was something from the past which had led Ashleigh to call him and he really wanted and needed to understand what that was. Quite how he was going to do this remained to be seen, and he had to make sure that whatever he did would not jeopardise his home life and ultimately his marriage.

Three hours later the To Do list had barely shifted. This was because Simon had spent ninety per cent of the time thinking about the Binns family and what on earth had happened to drive one individual to end the life of his second cousin. Two murders, twenty five years apart, somehow connected. What did Simon know about the murder of Gerry Binns? Certainly a lot less than he would have done had Graham lived long enough to meet him on the last day of August. He made a summary of the things he had gleaned from Graham;

- Graham believed that the situation of his grandmother Elisabeth's pregnancy and some shocking revelation surrounding that could probably explain his father's murder
- to Simon, it simply did not make sense that a small-time local criminal like Michael Spedding would murder Gerry Binns unless there was a connection between them that Graham and the Binns family did not know about. Gerry did not keep money in the shop so presumably robbery cannot have been the motive. Spedding had never previously shown any violent side to his character

- if Simon was right that there was a link between the two murders, then Michael Spedding could not have been the perpetrator. He was still incarcerated after the 1991 killing of Gerry having been refused parole in 2011 following a judicial review. Either the two murders were not linked, or Spedding was innocent of Gerry's death

When Simon looked at this he had to admit that it was pretty scant in terms of substance, nevertheless the key facts seemed to him to point in one direction. Michael Spedding did not murder Gerry Binns because whoever did commit this crime was also responsible for the recent death of his son. This view, however, was almost certainly not shared by the Metropolitan Police who had convicted Spedding twenty five years ago and would have no reason to believe that they had got this wrong. There had been cases of police forces who had fabricated evidence or ignored information that was at odds with their preferred conclusions resulting in innocent people spending time in prison. Was this the case with Michael Spedding? Did the police, in the quest to ensure they solved the case as quickly as possible, find a likely suspect and build a case against him that ultimately saw him convicted? In which case, would they be able to solve Graham's murder if they viewed it as a stand-alone event rather than being linked with his father's demise? Why would anyone want Graham Binns dead? So many unanswered questions.

Simon's view, based on his recent meeting and phone calls with his second cousin, was that Graham was an ordinary, professional and law-abiding man. Maybe there were reasons that would drive someone to want to end his life, a customer who felt wronged perhaps or a creditor that remained unpaid. These seemed fairly mundane matters and certainly not ones that normally lead to murder. Had Graham himself caused a death and was this retribution? That seemed a very far fetched explanation for what had happened. Or, as Simon was led to believe, had he simply discovered something about Gerry's murder and intended to share his theory when they met, thus threatening to expose someone for what had happened in 1991? That might lead this someone to see silencing Graham as the only way to protect their secret and their liberty.

Simon's head was buzzing as this multitude of thoughts and possibilities occurred to him. Scotland Yard would be investigating Graham's death and it would likely be almost impossible and certainly very dangerous if he stepped on their toes by trying to carry out his own inquiries. The situation regarding Gerry Binns' murder was entirely different. Allan Broughton and his team would not be considering what happened a quarter of a century ago because to them the case was closed at that time and the guilty party was currently in jail serving his penance. If Simon could prove that the man found guilty of that crime was in fact innocent by identifying the real perpetrator, that might be a very important development in helping to solve the riddle of who was responsible for Graham's death.

As he thought this through, Simon was suddenly accosted by a little voice in his ear that reminded him of his promise to Dani. His face reddened as he realised that he had not thought about his wife at any juncture during the afternoon whilst he examined the two Binns' cases. The problem was that he now felt totally invested in what had happened to Gerry and Graham and he knew that he would not be able to walk away from his involvement however damaging that might be for his work and personal life. Crazy as it might seem, he felt he owed it to Graham to do everything in his power to find out what really happened at Binns' Cycle World on that fateful day in 1991 and to try to see how this was connected to the awful events of two weeks ago. He would need to tread carefully, both in order not to alert Dani and also not to raise the suspicions of Detective Inspector Broughton, which could see him arrested for interfering in a police investigation and potentially perverting the course of justice. Like an addict he was now hooked and he knew that he could not stop himself.

Whatever the consequences of that decision might be.

30

CHAPTER 29

18 September 2016

Ashleigh Percival had spent a considerable amount of time since her call with Simon thinking about the long-buried memories that had resurfaced when her sister-in-law mentioned his name. She was transported back to the summer of 1985 and the town of Ingleby where she was on holiday with her parents. Her brother Graham was not there as he had chosen to go on a trip with some university friends believing that this would be a far more exciting way of spending the Summer break. She could not remember the name of Simon's grandparents at whose house they stayed but she did remember that Simon's grandmother, a lovely woman as she recalled, had died the year before. In fact, this was to be the final holiday that the Binns family took in Ingleby since William Steele was badly affected by his wife's death, so much so that he himself passed away a year later.

She also vividly remembered the 16-year old boy that she noticed for the first time that year despite the fact that she had met him a couple of times during previous visits. She was 18 and had dated two school friends but neither had developed into a proper relationship. When she met Duncan she felt differently even though he was two years younger than her. He seemed mature for his years and there was a hint of badness about him which she found exciting. Although she was only in Ingleby for three weeks, she managed to meet Duncan on a couple of occasions in between family trips to see places in the area. He was, she remembered, related to William and Margaret Steele but she could not remember exactly how. At the end of the holiday they committed to writing regularly to one another and to hopefully meeting again soon. Ashleigh wanted to invite him to visit her in Ilford but her parents were not keen on this idea. She toyed with the idea of going back to Ingleby herself without telling her parents but decided that it would be almost impossible to do this without them finding out given the family ties. So, they wrote to each other for a couple of years before Duncan's letters suddenly stopped. Ashleigh wrote two more letters in the hope that he would resume their correspondence but that did not happen. She wondered if he had met a local girl and did not have the heart to tell her and for a while she felt pangs of jealousy assuming that this was the case. Then she met David Percival and after an initially slow burn their relationship blossomed and they ended up marrying in 1994.

A few years after their final holiday in Yorkshire and totally out of the blue, Ashleigh had received another letter from Duncan. After a couple of brief questions asking how she was (with no explanation as to why he had suddenly stopped his correspondence), he proceeded to tell her that he had the opportunity of a lifetime to move to Europe and set up a new business. The venture was being funded for him by someone who was in his debt, and he wondered whether Ashleigh might be interested in coming with him to help manage it together. Typical of the Duncan she remembered from 1985, spontaneous and direct she thought, smiling to herself. She wrote back thanking him for his kind offer but politely refusing it, asking him to explain more about the intrigue that he had suggested lay behind this opportunity. She heard nothing back from him. No attempt to clarify what he had hinted at. Maybe he was upset or offended that she had turned him down. Based on the short time she had known him in his younger days he was certainly self-confident and so may have simply decided to stop the communication there and then. From that day until now she had heard nothing more about Duncan and his business venture.

The truth was she had no reason to think about him now that she was a happily married woman. And yet when Simon Letwin's name resurfaced two weeks ago, Ashleigh immediately thought of Duncan and of their short but enjoyable teenage liaison thirty years earlier. Why was this? True, he was an attractive boy but they were just kids and she had now met and married the person she intended to spend the rest of her life with. Could it rather be the mist swirling around the circumstances of Duncan's business that had never been revealed to her? Ashleigh was an avid fan of crime fiction and had even tried her hand at writing her own novel, although she had struggled to find enough time to make much progress with it. Maybe it was that her internal antenna was tuned to anything that had a whiff of intrigue about it.

As she sat contemplating these matters, Ashleigh could not help thinking that there might be a connection between the reappearance of Simon Letwin after all this time and the activities of the roguish boy who had captured her heart for a brief period all those years ago. Was she being ridiculous? No, she decided that she was entitled to consider anything that might in some way help to contribute to solving the brutal murder of her brother which was having such a dramatic impact on her family following a similarly vicious attack on her father years before. Although Duncan had refused to reveal any details of the circumstances that provided him with his opportunity, there was certainly more than a hint that his good fortune was the result of him discovering something untoward. Quite what that might be Ashleigh did not know. Should she try to locate Duncan and re-establish contact? Would she even know where to start? Should she call Simon and see if her suspicions resonated with him?

Or should she just forget the whole thing and leave the investigation to the police?

31

CHAPTER 30

18 September 2016

Following the Board meeting and trying to put the matter of the double Binns murder out of his mind at least temporarily given he had other issues to focus on, Simon spent the next few days following up with Peter Westmann on the matter of the potential sale of the Steele's business. He agreed with the adviser that they should immediately revert to both suitors with positive feedback from the Board and start the process which would allow them both to move forward with their due diligence on the company. Vinbrew had been unhappy not to be given a period of exclusivity to do their own assessment but had reluctantly accepted the situation given that the alternative was for them to walk away from any potential deal. Mark agreed to take charge of providing both companies with access to the Steele's data room, the repository of critical information which would allow the two interested parties to do their evaluations of the family business. The data room covered everything from financial reports to operational summaries to legal documentation in such areas as company ownership and leadership team biographies. Initial face to face meetings with both suitors were arranged for the first half of October which would allow both to observe the Steele's operation first-hand and ask any questions they may have once they pored over the company information provided to them. Mark had commented earlier that this process would take a lot of their time and Simon was beginning to appreciate just how accurate his brother's assessment had been.

Alongside his work commitments Simon had also promised himself that he would make a concerted effort to spend more time at home or at least to ensure that whilst he was at home his attention was firmly on Dani and the kids. They usually ate separately in front of one of several televisions in the house, but Simon insisted that they had dinner together so as to catch up on each other's day. Initially, Hannah and Greg seemed suspicious of their father's motivation for this but both did admit that they had enjoyed listening to his updates on what was happening at Steele's.

"And what about the murder, dad? Your friend. Have the police made any progress?"
Greg looked expectantly at Simon as he asked the question. Simon glanced in Dani's direction before answering and saw the look of wariness etched across her face.
"I don't know, Greg. I have been busy with work and since they are the experts, I should leave Scotland Yard to investigate." As he spoke the words sounded hollow and fabricated to him. He hoped that this was just his feelings of guilt and that Dani in particular did not see them in the same way. He thought that he had just about got away with his deception.
"This spaghetti is amazing," Simon continued, smiling at Dani, "what do you guys think?" There was a general murmur of agreement around the table as mouths were filled.

Once dinner was over, Simon's suggestion that they watch a movie together was roundly rejected by both children. Hannah wanted to watch a Korean drama on Netflix and Greg made a beeline for his room where his ongoing affair with Spotify would no doubt continue.
"Looks like you and me only then, babe," said Simon, reaching for Dani's

hand and leading her into the lounge. Seemingly reassured by his demonstration of being a good father and husband, Dani relaxed and they spent an enjoyable couple of hours watching two episodes of their favourite series. Simon was about eighty per cent focused on the drama, the other twenty being spent thinking some more about what his next steps should be in the Binns case. Having concluded that the best way forward was to focus on Gerry's death rather than Graham's, one very logical course of action would be to try to arrange a meeting with Michael Spedding. He needed to understand more about the man and his involvement in the events of 1991 which seemed to be where everything had started. He was unsure whether Spedding would agree to see him, but if Simon could make a viable case as to why he should, then maybe the prisoner would agree. Tomorrow, following his Monday colleague and customer phone calls and the weekly product tasting, Simon would start work on making this visit happen.

* * *

"Is that Whitmarsh prison?" Simon had managed to find out where Michael Spedding was serving out his sentence for the murder of Gerry Binns, discovering that it was at a Category A site in the East Midlands. Category A prisons housed the most dangerous inmates, those who posed a real threat to the public should they manage to escape. Often, a prisoner who started in a Category A institution and demonstrated good behaviour could be transferred to a less secure and more open environment but this had clearly not happened in Spedding's case. That coupled with his failed parole hearing in 2011 made Simon wonder if the man was indeed the kind of violent individual who could have disposed of his victim in cold blood rather than an unfortunate petty criminal who just happened to have been in the wrong place at the wrong time.

"This is Whitmarsh, how can I help you?"

Simon introduced himself to the man on the other end of the line, explaining that he would like to visit Michael Spedding as he had some very interesting new information to share with the prisoner about a long-lost relative of his. He did not mention Spedding's crime nor did he indicate that he was himself a relative of Gerry Binns which might well have caused the prison authorities to believe his visit was something of a revenge mission and to refuse to sanction it.

"I will need to speak with his key worker here in the prison, Mr Letwin. Mr Spedding, like all prisoners at Whitmarsh, is categorised as dangerous and I will need to appraise him of your request. Can I give Robin Daubney your number in case he wishes to call you back?" Key workers were members of the prison staff who were given the responsibility of supporting a prisoner during their custodial period. Simon assumed the aforementioned Daubney to be the key worker assigned to Michael Spedding.

Simon thanked the switchboard operative and hung up. He did not have long to wait before Robin Daubney phoned him.

"Mr Letwin, I understand that you wish to visit Michael and that you have information he may be interested in hearing? Have you met him before? Are you in any way part of his family or circle of friends?"

"I am not a friend, Mr Daubney, and he currently does not know me from Adam. I happen to have uncovered some information which I believe he may wish to hear although I would prefer to discuss this with Michael directly." Seeking empathy, Simon referred to Spedding by his first name as Daubney had earlier done. He had decided that in order to gain Spedding's acquiescence to a visit he would need to have a strong, attractive and persuasive reason to put forward. It was a stretch to say that he had new information about a relative of the prisoner to impart, but if it needed a white lie to achieve his objective of meeting with Michael Spedding, he was happy to create one.

"Mr Letwin, whilst it is not my job to discourage non-family members from visiting a prisoner, I am going to say here and now that I hope you are not a journalist trying to whip up a story or someone whose visit will disturb and upset one of our inmates."

Simon tried to reassure the key worker by telling him that he was a senior manager in a professional business and had no intention of upsetting anyone. He did not volunteer where he had come across the information he wanted to impart, but Daubney seemed to be as satisfied as he was ever likely to be.

"Right, I will speak with Michael and put your request for a visit to him. If he accepts to meet with you, I will call you back and we can confirm a suitable time and date."

Two hours later Robin Daubney was back on the line, informing Simon that Spedding had agreed to the visit. The proposal was that it should take place the following Tuesday at 11.00. Simon smiled as he heard the positive news and thanked the key worker for getting the appointment for him. As he ended the call, he realised that his next challenge was how he could absent himself from Ingleby in order to drive the two and a half hours needed to reach Whitmarsh, meet with Michael Spedding, then drive back to Yorkshire ideally all in the one day. It did not take him long to come up with a solution. It was several months since he had last been out in the field making customer visits with the sales team, so he was due a visit, particularly as he kept saying to the Board how important it was that the leadership team was out at the "sharp end" and not sitting in the ivory tower at Ingleby. Things had been very busy recently with the takeover speculation but that was no excuse. As his thoughts developed, part of Simon started to feel guilty about the lie he was going to have to tell. For the second time in as many weeks he would be creating a fictitious meeting to justify to Dani why he was travelling south. It also struck him that Jude would be making the arrangements so how was he going to maintain the pretence of working with the Steele's sales team when he was actually going to be at Whitmarsh prison? Once again, he hit on a solution. He would book a two-day field visit and work with the sales team on the first day before telling the Sales Manager that evening that something urgent had come up requiring him to return to Ingleby. That would allow him to travel to Whitmarsh, meet with Michael Spedding and return to Ingleby that evening as planned. Nobody should be any the wiser.

An hour later and the trip was confirmed. Simon would leave Ingleby early next Monday morning and meet the local Sales Manager, Jake Archer, in Nottingham. They would visit customers in and around the city area before staying overnight in a local hotel. Whitmarsh was only about an hour's drive from their Monday night location so Simon would leave early on Tuesday morning for the second leg of his trip. Provided that Jake Archer did not speak with anyone at Ingleby or vice versa, the plan seemed foolproof.

What could possibly go wrong?

32

CHAPTER 31

July 1949

She was so excited when her tenth birthday finally arrived and she could proclaim to her family and friends that she had at last reached double figures! Nine was such a little girlie age, but ten...that was a sign that she was really growing up! She woke up very early as her excitement robbed her of further sleep and she sat in the kitchen waiting for her parents to appear. She had been disappointed in the past few weeks that neither her mother nor her father seemed to be as excited about her upcoming milestone as she was, and she hoped that they had not forgotten to get her a card and a present. She had dropped enough hints about wanting a proper painting set after she had won a painting competition at school and she really hoped that her parents were perceptive and supportive enough to oblige.

As an only child she in theory enjoyed all of the parental affection on offer, but even at her relatively tender age she found herself wondering why her parents often seemed to forget she was around and hardly ever demonstrated the sort of love she believed other children got from their mother and father. Whenever she discussed this topic with her friends at school (being very careful not to suggest that her own parents were at all deficient in this area) she was always struck by the apparent gap between the way most of their parents apparently interacted with them and the way her mother and father behaved towards her.

With these thoughts occupying her mind as she sat alone with a glass of orange juice waiting for the sound of the floorboards creaking above her, a smile crept onto her lips at the thought of seeing her aunt and uncle later that day. They would certainly have a card and present for her because they had told her that she should come round and see them after school so that they could give her something special for reaching the momentous age of ten. Strange as it may seem, and she was not really sure why, the young girl had always felt very close to her aunt and uncle. There seemed to be some bond there that was stronger even than the one with her parents and she often found herself wondering why this was. Was it her fault? Was there something that she was doing which drove her parents to be reticent and to hold back on their affection for her? Were they simply not the affectionate type? It was a lot for a now ten-year old to cope with.

As she thought about this, another thought crept into her mind. Why was she an only child? Did her parents realise after she was born that they really were not the parenting type and decide not to have any more children? Had she been a contributing factor to this decision? She snapped her fingers and shook her head, telling herself to stop these thoughts which were threatening to turn what was supposed to be a joyous and momentous day into one of sadness and self-doubt. Of course her parents would get her a nice present and make sure that she had a happy day.

Yet this thought did not stop her willing the hours to pass quickly so that she could visit her aunt and uncle and really feel wanted and welcome.

33

CHAPTER 32

26 September 2016

The day in trade visiting a selection of the brewery's customers in and around Nottingham was an enjoyable one and Simon realised just how much he missed the cut and thrust of the field. Every time he got the chance to meet with customers, which regrettably had been far too infrequent of late, he was transported in his mind back to 1988 when he joined the family business after graduation and took on the role of Sales Account Manager. This was his first experience of managing customers and if he was honest it was probably one of the most rewarding and enjoyable times of his career. He managed a portfolio of pubs and free trade outlets in the Leicestershire area living in a rented flat in Loughborough. The location was ideal; far enough away from Ingleby to be independent, close enough if he wanted some home comforts on the occasional weekend. And what a happening city Leicester was in the late 80s! So although the main reason for Simon's visit to the East Midlands was his agenda for the following day, he genuinely enjoyed his time working with Jake Archer. The young sales manager reminded him a lot of himself at that age and he made a mental note to make sure that HR had Jake's career development firmly on the radar.

As the two men sat in the restaurant at the hotel that evening Simon put his pre-determined plan into action. He told Jake that he had received a message with an urgent request to return to Ingleby which he planned to do first thing in the morning.

"I'm gutted, to be honest," he told his young colleague, "I really enjoyed today, and I was looking forward to seeing more customers tomorrow. I will have to ask you to apologise to those we informed of our visit and I will call each of them myself in the course of this week." As he trotted out this blatant lie, Simon inwardly self-criticised his behaviour, which he would willingly admit was disgraceful. The only mitigation that he could muster, and he felt it was a reasonable mitigation, was that he was doing it with the best of intentions in mind, namely trying to understand what had led someone to murder Graham Binns. Nevertheless, it was beyond unprofessional to do this to one of the Steele's team, and he winced as he thought about what the Board might say about their CEO were they ever to find out. Hopefully that would never happen. Never mind the Board, his thoughts continued, what would Dani say? The prospect of that was truly unpalatable, and he quickly blotted out the associated images from his head.

"I understand, boss," replied Jake, "it has been great having this opportunity to work with you today. I have learned so much."

The genuineness of Archer's words contrasted sharply with Simon's lies, and he felt even worse as a result. They finished their dinner discussing football, a passion they apparently shared, before Simon made his excuses and headed back to his room for an early night. He called Dani to catch up on happenings at home and was informed that nothing remarkable had happened since he left that morning.

"Nothing remarkable ever happens these days," his wife said. The thinly disguised jibe was not lost on Simon.

* * *

CHAPTER 32

After a fitful night's sleep, Simon was up and about before 6.30 and by 7.15 he was on the road heading north east towards Whitmarsh. He had identified a Premier Inn hotel on his route and decided that a decent full English would be an enjoyable way to start the day. It would also allow him to sit and deal with some emails and phone calls before he headed for the prison for his meeting with Michael Spedding. As he worked his way through his inbox, Simon suddenly realised that his phone was ringing and since he had put it onto silent mode whilst in the restaurant he had not seen the call initially.

"Hey, bro, what are you looking for so early on a Tuesday morning?" Simon was not sure what led him to take this jovial tone with Mark but suspected as he thought about it that it could be the feeling of guilt that he was not doing what he said he would be today.

"Morning, Si. I was hoping to catch you before you got into customer visit mode." It was good that Mark could not see the shade of red pasted all over his brother's cheeks as he gave this entirely innocent reply.

"I know that you will be back in tomorrow, but I just wanted to flag something to you and ask for your advice. It concerns Keith."

With all of the issues that had been swirling around both within the business and in his life outside Steele's Simon had not given a second of thought to his uncle for some time now. In fact their last interaction was after the trip to Leicester where Simon had goaded the older man and even questioned whether he had actually been in the East Midlands city at all.

"What has happened now, bro? Don't tell me he has been ranting about the takeover again, he really is becoming worse than a broken record."

"No, he has been strangely silent on that score. Which probably means he is plotting his next move so we had better beware. The reason I called you concerns what might just be a minor point, but he sent in his expenses for for his recent trip to Leicester and did not provide any receipts. When I challenged him on it, given the sensitivity with the auditors, he claimed that his train, hotel and food and drink receipts had been in an envelope in his briefcase and that he now cannot find it and assumes he must have dropped it somewhere on the way home. I was tempted to suggest that it might have been whilst he was pissed, but I bit my tongue and refrained."

Simon frowned as it was made clear to all employees that no expenses would be reimbursed without the appropriate receipts. The taxman came down hard on companies that did not follow procedure and as CEO Simon was ultimately responsible for making sure that it was. Mark continued to explain.
"The total claim is for £935. The biggest item will be the hotel because they apparently did most of their eating and drinking there and only ventured into the city itself on the second evening. I reckon that bill will be well over $700 since the train fare was $78 and he thinks the bill for the pub in town was no more than £120."
"Can he not get copy receipts for these things? The hotel should certainly be able to provide a copy invoice, the train app, assuming he is not a total tech dodo, would still have his journey details and so maybe the only one that would be slightly harder to get would be this city pub. It is not as if his days are overloaded, so he should get off his chubby arse and follow the company rules that he himself put in place." Simon was not prepared to sit back and watch Keith flaunt the regulations that everyone else adhered to so rigidly.

"Well this is where it gets a bit worrying, Si and is why I needed to call you since he is pushing to get reimbursed. He claimed he did not have enough time to call around chasing receipts and said that, since he was the Chairman and a respectable upstanding character, we need not worry about the auditor. I decided that if I needed to get Jude on the case I would as I am not at liberty to decide whether anyone, including the chairman, can be allowed to ignore the company rules."
"Good idea, Mark," said Simon, "you should not have to do that but we as the leadership cannot afford to be seen as breaking the company rules and processes. So did she manage to get the receipts?"
There was a moment's silence before Mark replied to his brother's question.
"Well here's the thing. Jude called the Mercury Hotel in Leicester and requested the copy invoice only to be told that there was nobody of that

name staying at the hotel on the dates provided. Jude told the lady that maybe she had looked at the wrong dates and could she please check again. The receptionist did so and told Jude quite categorically that there must be some mistake.

Nobody called Keith Steele has stayed at the Mercury since it opened in 2012.

***

Simon sat motionless and with a deep frown etched across his face after ending the call with Mark. He had told his brother not to pay Keith's expenses claim today and that he would pick this up with their uncle once he was back in the office the following morning. His first reaction had been one of anger that the chairman felt that the rules which were clearly defined and which had actually been introduced by Keith himself when he was CEO did not apply to him. Simon hated the chairman's arrogance, and saw it as a terrible example to set to more junior members of the organisation. Yet as he thought through the ramifications of what Mark had just shared with him, it was not so much the failure to adhere to due process which worried him but rather the possibility that there was something at play here with far more sinister overtones. Simon recalled the exchange he had had with his uncle after he returned from this trip. Keith had been pretty evasive and refused to play along with his nephew's attempt to lighten the tone after his question about how much beer Keith had sold on the trip. Keith's aggressive responses had shocked him and led him to conclude that maybe he had not been in Leicester at all. At the time, that doubt was more of a rhetorical question than a serious conclusion but now, with this expenses issue raising its ugly head, maybe there really was substance to Simon's theory.

It was of course possible that Keith had indeed lost the receipts, but was that really likely? If his uncle had placed the envelope into his briefcase, it was difficult to see how it could have fallen out or been lost under normal circumstances. So, if the receipts were not lost, where were they? The only possible explanation was that for some reason or other his uncle did not want to present them so had invented an excuse, namely that he had mislaid or lost them. Why would he do that? If he had spent a lot on drinks nobody would pull him up for that. He was the Chairman of a brewing company and entertaining clients and other stakeholders was part of his role. The only other reason Simon could think of was the one that had occurred to him during the conversation with Keith. If the receipts were not made available because they revealed that he had not been to Leicester but to somewhere else, he would not be able to justify claiming the expenses for venues in Leicester. If he had made the trip to a different location, he could still make a claim for costs incurred during that visit. Unless……Simon was finally forced to seriously consider the only explanation that made sense.

Keith did not want to reveal where he had been for reasons best known to himself.

***

Simon checked his phone and realised that it was time he left for Whitmarsh. He would need to park his thoughts about Keith's expenses and pick this up again later. The journey to the prison was largely uneventful and he arrived for his appointment twenty minutes before schedule. This gave him time to recap in his mind what he wanted to get out of the meeting with Spedding and to make sure that he approached the interview in a way that met these objectives. Satisfied that he was ready, he went to the prison reception desk and announced his arrival. After completing the formalities, he was taken through to the prison meeting room and soon after found himself sitting opposite Michael Spedding. Given the security levels at Whitmarsh, a thick glass window separated the two men although in truth Simon did not feel threatened despite the being in one of the most secure of Her Majesty's institutions. Simon smiled at his interlocutor and began.

"Michael, I hope you do not mind me calling you Michael."

"Why would I? It's my name."

Simon winced internally and hoped that this response was not going to be a precursor of the conversation to follow.

"Thanks, Michael. First of all, I want to say thank you for agreeing to see me today. You do not know me and in your position I might be very suspicious, so I am really grateful."

Spedding looked across the table at Simon, his face nondescript and difficult to read. Eventually he spoke.

"I am suspicious and I also hope that you are not one of these do-gooders that come in lording it up and using the idea they are helping me only to further their own agenda."

To Simon this was a perfectly normal and understandable reaction from a man who had been locked up for 25 years and had a parole hearing conclude that he should not be released. If he was going to get anything from this meeting he would clearly need to demonstrate to Michael Spedding that the reason for his visit was a genuine one.

"Michael, I promise you that my reason for coming here today is because I have discovered something that I believe may help you, not because I am trying to do anything beneficial for myself."

Spedding's face betrayed a clear message to Simon that he remained extremely sceptical of his motives, but the words he uttered gave Simon hope that this could work as he had planned.

"Okay, I am listening. I suppose I could not be screwed any more than I already have been by the whole system, so what the hell? You told Robin that you had discovered something I might want to hear."

"Yes, Michael, and now that I am here I do not know where to start! Let me say up front that what I have learned casts a shadow of doubt, in my mind at least, over the crime that you were accused of committing." Simon had decided that he might as well say this early in the conversation as this might catch Spedding's attention and convince him that his visit was genuine and in his interest.

"So you think I am innocent? Well that would be novel because no other fucker thinks I am."

If Simon was looking for a hint of how his opening gambit had gone down with the prisoner there it was in blazing technicolour. He had to admit that he could not blame Spedding for being sceptical, and his sarcastic response was likely honed on a quarter century of being incarcerated including being denied his freedom by the parole board after serving twenty years behind bars. Simon had spent quite some time planning this visit and what he was going to tell Michael Spedding. What he was not going to tell him was that he was related to Gerry Binns, which was something he felt might make the other man clam up and refuse to speak, believing that some kind of revenge was the motive for this contact out of the blue. He needed to get Spedding talking and potentially telling him something that he had omitted, consciously or otherwise, from his original statements to the police. He also had to keep an open mind since Spedding might be as guilty as sin, even though Simon had severe misgivings that that was the case.

"Let me cut to the chase, Michael. You might be wondering how I ever got to know about you and about what happened in 1991. Somewhat by chance, I recently met a man called Graham Binns. If you do not know of him I am sure you can see by the surname that it is the same as the man you are in jail for killing. In fact, Graham was Gerry Binns' son."

Michael Spedding raised his eyebrows as he listened to Simon, who took this as a sign of interest in what he had just communicated.

"I say was, you may not be aware that Graham Binns was murdered earlier this month."

If there was any doubt that Spedding was paying attention to what Simon was relating, it dissipated with the sharing of this piece of news. He did not say anything, but the look on his face left no room for doubt. Simon pressed on whilst he had the man's full attention.

"I would really like you to tell me a bit more about what happened the day that Gerry Binns died. Then I can share some additional information with you."

Michael Spedding looked at Simon as if he was evaluating whether this request was a trick to get him to reveal something that he should not. After a few moments of silence he started speaking.

"I told the fuzz everything exactly as it happened but they chose not to believe me and here I am twenty five years later. I am not guilty, it wasn't me that topped Binns, I was just unlucky to be in the area at the wrong time."

"I know you told the police everything, Michael, but please tell me what happened from your perspective as sometimes you remember something that you had forgotten to say first time round."

"Okay, but I am not sure what it will change. Anyway, it is not as if my calendar is full of appointments today so what the hell?"

With that, Spedding gave Simon a blow by blow account of the day's happenings from his point of view. The visit to the pub next door to Binns Cycle World, the discovery as he left the pub that the cycle shop was closed, the cycles lying on the ground inside the shop, his decision to check out what looked like a disturbance, the discovery of all that blood pooled around Gerry Binns' body. And the individual sitting in the coffee shop window seemingly watching him before all of this started.

'I mention the geezer in the shop last because the way he was watching me before I went into the Nags got me a bit riled. He was staring at me as if I had two heads which I haven't. When I came out of the pub after me pint he was gone. I took particular notice because if he had stared at me again I would have gone in an 'ad it out with 'im."

"You didn't recognise this person? Are you sure it was a man? And maybe you just caught him as he looked across the road. Could have been totally innocent, right? "

"Never seen 'im before. And yes, I am pretty sure it was a bloke. You can tell, can't you? And there is no doubt in my mind that he was deliberately giving me the eye." Simon did not think it was always so straightforward to make these assumptions especially in these gender fluid times, but he did not say so. He was also not convinced that this person was necessarily watching

Spedding, but if he (or she) was it was clearly an important part of the story. He moved the conversation on to the cigarette butt found inside the cycle shop.

"So the main piece of evidence used to convict you seems to have been the cigarette butt they found inside the shop. Is that right?"

"Yeah, it fucking was. And I swear, as I told the police, I never set foot inside the bloody shop. I never got further than the back yard and all that blood. It was awful." The look that crept across the prisoner's face as he mentioned the blood looked genuine enough to Simon, although Spedding would not be the first convict who was also a distinguished actor. He continued with his story.

"I might have dropped the fag butt outside in the street because I would certainly have been having a ciggie before I went for me pint. But no way did I go into that shop and no way was I smoking anywhere near where they found the fag butt. I reckon I was stitched up."

Simon was pleased that the discussion was now touching on the important parts of the events of that day. He was also happy and pleasantly surprised at Spedding's level of engagement now that he seemed to have got past his initial hesitation. Whether Simon was any more convinced of the man's innocence was entirely a different matter.

"Two questions," said Simon. "Why would anyone stitch you up, and why were the police so convinced that it was you who had murdered Gerry Binns?"

Michael Spedding looked at Simon as if he had just asked him if seven was greater than six.

"Bloody obvious isn't it? If the guilty party could shift the blame to me they would escape scot free. That is what happened, I think. And the rozzers don't give a shit about people like me if it helps to solve a case quickly and get the hoi-polloi off their backs. They probably figured I am a loser anyway, so what fucking difference does it make if I lose in 'ere rather than on the streets?"

Simon was shocked but probably not surprised to hear the man's explanation. People like Spedding were part of life's unfortunates, but that did not make them into doormats to be stood on and for others to use to wipe their dirty boots. He decided it was probably time to introduce Graham's misgivings about the original verdict.

"Thanks for sharing all of that, Michael. Let me explain a bit more about why I came. I told you I met Graham Binns and that not long after our meeting he was seemingly murdered. I say seemingly because the police are still working to establish the facts surrounding the case. One of the things we discussed was his father's murder – don't ask me how the topic arose – and the fact that he was not convinced that what the police say happened is actually what happened. In other words, he was unsure whether you committed the crime or not. I would like you to keep what I just said between us for obvious reasons."

Michael Spedding stared at Simon as if he were trying to decide if what he was saying was genuinely what he believed or whether it was some kind of ultimate piss-take designed to rub even more dirt into his face.

"Why would he think that? And why, if it's true, did he wait twenty five years to open his gob about it?" Simon had to admit that this was a very fair question.

"I think if you look at it from his point of view, Michael, it must be awful to lose a family member in the way he did and the easiest thing once someone has been arrested for the crime is to accept it and try to move on, if that is ever possible. Taking it upon yourself to try to do the police's job is a big ask and so you accept what has happened. But that does not mean you cannot have reservations and doubts. He did not actually tell me what those doubts were because he was murdered shortly after we met"

"Fuck." Spedding only uttered a single word but the message was clear. Simon's words had definitely hit a nerve.

"So you think that this Graham guy was topped because he was about to spill the beans about me?"

"I am not quite sure what his concerns were, but he told me he did not think

you were the guilty party. Which is a pretty bold statement to make."
"And now he is dead so if he did have some evidence that someone else did it I guess that has disappeared with him. Which is fuck all use to me."

Simon felt sorry for the man. Having spent all this time in prison for someone to seemingly offer you hope and then have it torn away by the reality of the situation must be difficult to stomach.
The prison warden assigned to the meeting room approached the desk and informed Simon that there were five minutes left of the allocated time.
"Well, Michael, thanks very much for meeting me today. I do not know how I am going to take this forward, but I promise you that I will do everything I can to see what else I can find out about the events of 1991. I owe that to Graham Binns if not to anyone else. I do not know if it will ultimately make any difference but I am damned well going to try."

Michael Spedding did not say anything but nodded in what Simon took to be a kind of acknowledgement. Rising from his chair, Simon nodded back at the prisoner and left the meeting room. He collected his possessions including his phone from reception and exited the prison gates, switching the phone on and checking his messages as he did so. He had 23 emails and a handful of messages plus three missed calls from his brother Mark. One of the messages was also from Mark and as he read it Simon closed his eyes and realised he had some explaining to do.

"Simon, where the hell are you? Not with Jake Archer, that is for sure. Call me."

34

CHAPTER 33

24 September 2016

On a Saturday morning almost four weeks after the murder of her brother, Ashleigh Percival was sitting with her best friend in the kitchen of her house feeling frustrated at the apparent lack of progress that the police were making in their pursuit of her brother's killer. She had personally met with the investigations team three times and she knew that her sister-in-law Sarah had been interviewed on more occasions that that. It was natural for the police to focus initially on close family members given their proximity to the victim and the perception that they were likely to have a stronger reason for wanting a relative dead than a non-family member would. However, Ashleigh knew from a TV documentary she had watched recently that with male murder victims a significant percentage of the perpetrators were friends, acquaintances or strangers rather than relatives. With this in mind, she hoped that Scotland Yard was also mining the list of contacts obtained from Graham's phone and from names that she and Sarah had provided them with. The police would obviously not share details of who else they were speaking with, not least because both Ashleigh and Sarah remained on their list of possible suspects, but she wanted to feel reassured that progress was being made.

"It is hell, Georgie," she told her friend, "as far as I can see they are no closer to identifying who was responsible for this. They always say that the best time to solve a murder is in the first 24 hours. If the police do not have a suspect, a lead or an arrest in that time frame, the chances of solving the crime are halved. God only knows what the chances are after 24 bloody days!"

Georgia Robinson had been friends with Ashleigh since their days at Ilford Academy and her friend had been shocked and saddened by Graham Binns' death and the impact it had had on his sister, even if she knew that they were not as close as siblings usually are. Ashleigh herself would not have described their sororal relationship as particularly strong, a combination of the usual rivalry that tends to exist between siblings and the fact that their interests were about as diametrically opposed as it was possible to get, nevertheless it was unthinkable to Georgie that Ashleigh could have had anything to do with her brother's murder. Since that awful day at the end of August she had been trying to help her friend to keep a positive mindset whilst recognising that achieving that at a time like this was nigh on impossible.

"They may be more advanced than you think, Ash," said her friend in an attempt to introduce a more upbeat tone to proceedings. "Given that you remain a suspect, as you say, they will not tell you what they are up to but who knows, they may be about to make an arrest." If Georgie had been asked to bet her house on the Met having a suspect she would have declined, but her objective was to cheer her friend up. It was clearly not working.
"The last time I spoke with them, that would have been last week, I got the usual piece about following up several lines of inquiry which roughly translates to 'we haven't got a bloody clue'. I keep asking myself what will happen if they cannot solve this."

"Come on, Ash, it has only been a few weeks and sometimes these things can be very complex if there is no obvious suspect. As far as we know Graham did not have any enemies, at least not ones whose grudge would extend to murdering him, so the police will have had to more or less start with a blank page. That will take time." It was the best Georgie could do to try to make her friend feel slightly better, but she realised it was unlikely to work.

"I have also been thinking about that relative I mentioned to you, Simon Letwin. My second cousin to be precise. Despite what he told me when I called him, there must be some connection between him showing up after 40 years, meeting Graham for dinner and arranging a follow up meeting, and Graham being murdered two days before that second meeting. I know coincidences happen but this one is just too coincidental. Especially, as you say, there is no obvious suspect with a real motive. That kind of leads me to conclude that he must be involved in some way."

"What about that boy you mentioned last time we spoke. He was related to this Letwin guy wasn't he?" Ashleigh had briefly shared her reminiscences about Duncan with her friend but had not gone into much detail.

"He is or was. I do not even know if he is still alive. I cannot remember the relationship because to be honest we spent most of the holidays up there with mum's aunt and uncle and hardly ever met the rest of the family. To be honest, Georgie, I think I am going to try to find him and see if he can shed more light on Simon's potential involvement. He told me that his business venture had been funded by someone that owed him and I understood by this that there was a major scandal involved. What if that someone was Simon Letwin? If it was, we might be well on the way to explaining Graham's murder."

"Do you have his contact details? I thought you said he stopped writing and did not even tell you which country he was going to. It was somewhere in Europe, right?"

Ashleigh sighed. "Yeah, that is the problem, I have no phone number for him and emails did not exist in those days. He could be anywhere."

"I suppose asking Simon about him might be a risky strategy if he was the person that killed Graham. You could be putting Duncan's life at risk,

too. On the other hand, Simon's reaction to you asking might give you a good indication of whether or not he is involved." Georgie had always been insightful in Ashleigh's view, and she really valued her friend's opinions.
"I think that is risky. I did consider ringing the brewery to ask if they had his details but that might be equally risky given that Simon is apparently the boss there. Anyway, as I understand it Duncan was a bit of a black sheep, so it could well be a case of out of sight, out of mind. Looks like it just might just not be possible to find him."

Georgie felt sorry for her friend. She was clearly trying to do everything she could to come to terms with what had happened and to find a rational explanation for why it had. Losing a brother in this violent way having earlier lost a father in a similar fashion must be totally unbearable.
"Do you still have his letters from that time? Is there anything in there that might help you to contact him?"
"I don't think so. And anyway, I can't imagine what they might contain that would help me to locate him after 30 years. As I said, I would not really want to contact any of his family given what he told me. I don't want to put myself in danger if any of them were involved in what happened to Graham."

It seemed as if this was not going to be an avenue that Ashleigh would be able to explore. Then Georgia suddenly had an idea.
"Would your mum remember anything? I know that the dementia is getting worse, but you told me that her long-term memory is still quite sharp."
Ashleigh considered what her friend was suggesting. It was true that in common with many dementia sufferers her mother could often not remember what she had eaten for lunch but had a crystal clear recollection of things that happened half a century earlier. Whether she had any information on Duncan that Ashleigh herself did not have seemed unlikely but not impossible. It was certainly worth asking. Ashleigh knew that her mother had been very close to her cousin – what was her name? – so might have been told something by her that would help identify where Duncan had moved to. There was certainly nothing to lose by asking her. She was planning to visit

her mother at the weekend so made a mental note to broach the subject.

"Thanks, Georgie, you are a star. I can't go on like this, in some kind of limbo, so I will ask mum when I see her next Sunday. If Simon Letwin is responsible for what happened the sooner this is confirmed the better. I have exposed myself by contacting him, and for my own safety he either needs to be ruled out as a suspect or locked up.

It is as simple as that."

35

CHAPTER 34

27 September 2016

"What the hell are you doing in Whitmarsh when you are supposed to be visiting customers in Nottingham? Simon, what on earth is going on?"

Mark's usual calm, rational approach to things had been abandoned as a result of his sheer fury.

"We have been chasing you for the past hour to discuss an urgent matter regarding the takeover discussions. I called Jake Archer when you did not respond to be told that you had returned to Ingleby to handle a critical matter that had cropped up. I then find out that you are still in the Midlands doing Lord knows what. So go ahead, I am listening."

Simon had rarely heard his brother speaking to him like this. In fact, he could think of only one other occasion, a time when Simon had neglected to tell Dani he would be away for the night sparking calls to the police by his frantic wife fearing that something terrible had happened. Realising that whatever he said was unlikely to appease his brother, Simon took a deep breath and began.

"First of all, Mark, I owe you a huge apology, which I know is an easy thing to say when you have screwed up. Actually, I am not sure if I have screwed up as much as being deceitful, which is probably worse. Although if you ask me if I regret what I have done, I do not think I do." Simon paused to see what reaction his opening gambit got. The answer was total silence, which he took as an indication that further explanation was demanded and expected.

"Let me tell you the truth about what I have been doing. And please let me finish before you say anything else. To answer your unasked but obvious question, I have been pursuing the Graham Binns thing in spite of all the words of warning from you and Dani. I am convinced that things are not straightforward, starting with the murder of Graham's father, which may not have been committed by the guy currently serving a sentence for it in jail. If my inclination is correct, solving the mystery of who did actually do it might help to highlight who is responsible for Graham's death. As it stands there are two different killers which I just do not believe. So, this morning I visited the so-called murderer of Gerry Binns in prison to see if I could find anything else out to shed light on what really happened that day. Having spoken with him I think my scepticism surrounding his guilt may well be justified, although I do not have any concrete evidence yet on which to base that view."

The silence at the other end of the line continued. Just as Simon wondered if the line had dropped, Mark spoke.

"I am not sure I need to say anything, Si. You could probably say it for me." Mark's tone was more measured and controlled than earlier in the call but the message was clear and unequivocal. To say he was unhappy about what his brother had done was like describing a serial killer as a naughty boy. Simon told his brother that he was setting off for Ingleby right away and would be in the office first thing. In the meantime, he asked Mark to fill him in on the urgent happenings that had led to his earlier call.

"Oh, I see, so you do still remember the small matter of the future of our business which needs to be managed whilst you swan around playing the big detective? Good to know that the Steele's CEO has his priorities in the right order." The acerbic tone shocked Simon, although he had to admit that

Mark's position was entirely valid.

"Look, Mark, let's not have this conversation now. You are totally justified in your criticism of me, but can we get to the point of the call?"

"We will discuss this tomorrow, Si, and don't think for one minute that I am dropping it. Anyway, we have a pretty serious issue to deal with on the potential acquisition front. Peter Westmann was desperately trying to reach you earlier to fill you in. Apparently, both Vinbrew and Eldrich Global have received anonymous letters purporting to come from someone familiar with Steele's warning them that the underlying state of the business is not as strong as the numbers would indicate. It seems that he received worried calls from both of them early today asking for clarification and an explanation. Peter's reading of this is that someone is clearly trying to suggest to them that their offer should reflect this or, even more dramatically, that they might want to consider whether they should even proceed with their interest in acquiring us. I called Peter back when Jude informed me that he had apparently been unable to reach you."

Simon listened to his brother with a growing sense of alarm and disbelief. Who would have done this?

"Mark, that is ridiculous. Is there any clue as to who might have sent the letters and why?"

"That was what Peter wanted to discuss with you. I told him that I had no idea of who or why, and we agreed that he would speak with you as soon as you were available."

"Okay, Mark, let me call him now and arrange for a Zoom meeting tomorrow morning which we can both attend. We obviously need to try to get to the bottom of this as soon as we can before it takes on a life of its own. I need to let the Board know, too, unless you already did that." Mark confirmed that he had not discussed the matter with anyone including the Board. He also informed Simon that Peter Westmann had emailed them both a scanned copy of the letter sent to both companies which seemed to be identical.

Simon ended the call with Mark and immediately called Peter Westmann. The

M&A advisor gave essentially the same story that Mark had already shared and it was agreed that the meeting to discuss next steps would take place at 10.00 the following morning. With that, Simon drove out of the car park and set off on his long journey back to Ingleby.

* * *

Despite being tired after his two-day trip, Simon was at his desk before 8.00 and his first task was to read the letter that had been sent to their two suitors. He had intended doing this when he arrived home the previous evening but a combination of fatigue and the guilt-ridden feeling that he should spend time before bed with Dani meant that this did not happen. When he got to it, the letter was not a long one and was almost entirely devoid of detail to back up the headline claim that Steele's financial situation was nowhere near as robust as was being portrayed. There was a second claim, namely that there was a potential time bomb ticking, hidden inside the company organisation, which would undoubtedly cause a major problem for any acquirer who would obviously be responsible for handling any fallout if and when it ever came to light. The clear intent behind this letter was to create significant doubt in the minds of the recipient companies and ultimately to persuade them to drop their interest in acquiring the brewer. Reading and re-reading it, Simon's initial reaction was that this seemed to be the work of someone with an apparent grudge against the company but who lacked any proof to validate the claims he or she was making. As CEO, Simon knew that the Steele's financial statements they had shared with the companies through the data room were accurate and robust, so the claim that something was being hidden or covered up was simply untrue. As to the assertion that there was a smoking gun hidden somewhere in the business, Simon had no idea what that could be referring to so, if such a threat did indeed exist, it was something of which he as CEO was unaware. Given his role as the head of the business, he believed that this was highly unlikely. Nevertheless, truthful or not, the two claims being made in this letter were very serious and unless they were debunked there was a potential risk that both Vinbrew and Eldrich Global might withdraw their interest in acquiring the company.

The meeting with Westmann Buck focused not so much on the content of the letter but firstly on reassuring Peter Westmann that there was no substance to the claims being made and, secondly, on what needed to be done to provide comfort to the two suitors that this was indeed the case. On the first point, Mark, as CFO of the company, gave a categorical reassurance that all of the financial information shared was accurate and a true indication of the state of the business, having been professionally audited in line with the requirement. Peter was happy to hear this confirmation and said that he himself was totally reassured. On the matter of the supposed time bomb, Simon could only state his view that he was unaware what this might refer to and, again, the advisor seemed mollified.

The far greater challenge lay in how to reassure Vinbrew and Eldrich Global that the letter might be the work of either a crank or of someone, a disaffected current or former employee for example, who wanted to harm the company for their own reasons. The good thing was the the letter contained absolutely no information that substantiated either of the claims being made, in addition to being sent anonymously which was a further indication that this could be nothing more than baseless subterfuge. Peter Wetmann steepled his fingers and rested them on his chin as he seemed to be considering what he had just been told.

"I think having listened to your explanation that the best course of action is for me to respond to both companies telling them that I am satisfied with your reassurances and that this matter can be tackled as part of the face-to-face visits that are planned for the next couple of weeks."

"And on my side," said Simon, "I have asked for an emergency Board meeting so that we can discuss our response to this. We have to bear in mind that our employees do not know about the external interest in acquiring Steele's, so I will not be sharing anything with the wider workforce at this stage."

With that, and agreeing that Peter would update Simon and Mark once he had spoken with the two companies, the meeting ended.

***

The call had taken place in Simon's office and it was very clear from Mark's body posture and the look on his face that he had no intention of leaving until the matter of his brother's actions the previous day had been thoroughly discussed. Simon had spent time during the drive from Whitmarsh to Ingleby thinking about what to say to his brother when they met and he now took the bull by the horns.

"Mark, I know you are angry about yesterday and you are right to be so, but something about this whole thing is not right and the police will struggle to solve Graham's murder unless they look at the bigger picture. I want to help them to do that because I owe it to Graham."

Mark looked at his brother as if he were deciding whether to bludgeon a wasp that was buzzing around him or just keep an eye on it to make sure he did not get stung.

"You are obsessed with this, Si, and you seem blind to the impact this is having or could have on our business and on your marriage. You cannot carry on like this. Let the police do their job. I am sure that Graham Binns would not want you involved if it ruined everything else you supposedly hold dear."

Simon looked out of the window, avoiding Mark's gaze as he considered what to say next. It was true that this was becoming something of an obsession for him but one that he was powerless now to stop. He was convinced that the person who had killed Gerry Binns had also killed Graham, almost certainly because the latter was getting too close to uncovering the truth about Gerry's murder. This meant that Simon also had to be very careful not to provoke the killer and put himself next on the list.

"Mark, I am committed to both Steele's and to Dani and I will never allow the Binns saga to alter that. However, I cannot abandon Graham even if he would want me to do that because there is a man who has spent 25 years in prison for a murder he did not commit and a killer on the loose who so far has got away with every evil thing he has done."

Mark shook his head slowly and sighed. He realised that it was a waste of breath trying to talk Simon down at this stage. Simon had always been the bigger, more alpha of the two and, despite his occasional outburst, like the one he had unleashed at Simon a day earlier, Mark was destined to be the younger follower rather than the instigator. The best he could do was to continue to watch what Simon was doing and intervene when things looked like getting out of control. His final attempt to rein his brother in had failed.

Quite what that meant for the company, his brother's marriage and for Simon himself only time would tell.

36

CHAPTER 35

29 September 2016

Two days later the members of Steele's Board of Directors were assembled for the hastily convened extraordinary meeting in the company boardroom. Keith, as Chairman, had initially asked why a Board meeting was required for this matter given that the company was not going to be sold. Simon informed him that the sending of a malicious letter regarding company performance was important enough for a formal Board gathering with or without the matter of the potential takeover. Keith had then objected to the timing stating that such short notice made attendance difficult for him (Simon's unspoken response to this was to wonder what else Keith actually did that would make him unavailable), but he relented when he was reminded that four of the five directors attending would be a quorum meaning the meeting could proceed without Keith, even though he was the chairman of the board. Clearly it was preferable that he did attend, but constitutionally it was not an essential requirement.

"Good afternoon everyone," Keith began, "and thanks for making the time to be here today. The CEO wanted us to meet this week to discuss recent events even if I am not convinced this is at all necessary, so I do want to recognise your flexibility in being here." Keith proceeded to lay out the content of the letter that had been sent to Vinbrew and Eldrich Global, peppering the discourse with his own well-known views on the topic of the potential acquisition.

"I do want to say before we discuss this as a Board that I would request the CEO to formally confirm to us that the company financial statements are, to the best of his knowledge, accurate. I know that the accounts are audited, but the auditors do rely to an extent on what we give them. I think before any external communications are made that we as the directors of our beloved family business are confident in what we have reported."

Simon was stunned by his uncle's words. Was Keith questioning Simon's integrity? Was he seriously asking in his role as Chairman that the CEO reassure the Board that the financial reports of the company were accurate?

"Mr. Chairman, " he responded, "I am very happy to confirm to the Board that all of the reporting under my stewardship has been transparent and representative of the true state of the business. I would also like to make clear that I am extremely surprised and unhappy that the chairman has felt it necessary to ask this question in the manner he did in this forum. If there is indeed even the slightest concern amongst you, my fellow directors, that my integrity is anything less than 100%, I will offer you my resignation with immediate effect."

As he spoke these words, Simon glared at Keith almost daring him to continue with his challenge.

"Well, the writer of this letter certainly believes there is something up so I just wanted us to formally record that the CEO and his team are confident that this allegation can be rebuked. I am also a bit surprised, Simon, at your sensitivity in what is a very routine request. Anyway, if you feel twitchy we can move on since you have provided us with the confirmation I asked for."

Simon was seething. He was about to say something when Alastair Rundle, one of the external non-executive directors, moved to calm matters down.

"Mr. Chairman, I think that maybe your request, which in itself is not entirely unreasonable, was expressed in a way you probably did not intend. It sounded

accusatory and I believe that none of us, yourself included, believe that our excellent CEO has anything to reproach him."
Keith Steele's eyes narrowed and spittle started to form on his lips as the barely disguised rebuke hit him like a boxer's left hook. Rundle was a strong advocate of exploring the potential sale of Steele's, and Keith immediately saw his support for Simon as inextricably linked to their shared view.
"Alastair, thanks for your contribution. With all due respect, I think it was a reasonable question to ask and I would ask it again in exactly the same way. However, it is time to move on and conclude so that we can get back to more productive pursuits."

Simon looked at his fellow directors and it seemed as if the other three shared Simon's utter amazement at Keith's tone and attitude. How could he talk of "more productive pursuits" as if the matter of the letter was a triviality on par with deciding whether to have red or white wine with a meal. Someone was deliberately attempting to derail the due diligence process and in so doing to infer that Steele's was not the professional, well-run organisation it purported to be. If that was not a matter of the utmost gravity requiring full Board attention Simon did not know what was.

The Board proceeded to discuss the letter and how to handle the matter internally. Peter Westmann was following up with the two potential acquirers and the Board's view was that they needed as a matter of urgency to identify who had sent the letters and why. This was clearly easier said than done. Firstly, the letters had been posted in Richmond which hardly narrowed down the list of potential suspects given that it was the main town in the area where Steele's was located. Secondly, the general workforce was unaware that management was entering into talks with potential purchasers of the business and, whilst the news would eventually either leak out or be announced formally, the Board judged that for the time being it was best to remain silent and avoid causing unnecessary panic and speculation amongst the employees. It was decided, therefore, that the company would employ the services of an expert to examine the letter and see if there were any tell-tale signs which could point to a particular person or type of person. The letter and envelope had been produced on a computer so there was no handwriting to analyse which would naturally have made identification far easier. Keith had initially suggested that the company waited to see if further letters appeared rather than spend money on this analysis now but he was a lone voice. Simon was charged with taking this forward and keeping the Board fully informed of progress.

As the meeting closed, Keith asked Simon if he had a minute for a chat. Simon was taken aback by this as he could not remember the last time he had spoken directly with Keith, and it was longer still since his uncle had asked him for his time rather than simply barging into his nephew's office unannounced. Simon was quite pleased that this opportunity was presenting itself as he had been waiting for an opportune moment to tackle Keith on the matter of his Leicester trip expenses.

"Yes, Keith, let's do it now. We can stay here since the meeting is over. I also wanted to discuss something with you, this matter of your expenses. We can kill two birds."

"Has that still not been paid? I told Mark that I could not find the receipts so I gave him the estimates of what I spent. Is someone questioning the Chairman's honesty?"

"Keith, it is not a question of your honesty. We have to follow the audit rules which demand that a receipt must accompany every claim for a business expense. That is not my decision, it is the system. And I seem to recall that it was you who first started to implement this when you were CEO."

Simon had discussed this matter with his brother on his return from the East Midlands and agreed that he would pick the topic up with Keith. He had since been wondering at what stage he should drop into the conversation the fact that the hotel Keith claimed to have stayed in had no records of him ever having been there. He had decided to leave it for the moment and push Keith to provide documentary evidence to support his claim. If he could not do that, and if he was lying about visiting Leicester, there would come a time when this little nugget would need to be produced and for Keith to be forced to come clean.

"This is ridiculous, Simon. Are you telling me that if I cannot find the receipts that I will not be reimbursed? Are you actually saying this?"

"Yes, Keith, that is the company process and I cannot arbitrarily flaunt the rules for you or for anyone else. You could presumably call the hotel and the train company and ask for duplicates. I can ask Jude to help you if you need support." Simon dropped in the final suggestion as a way of testing the water given what Mark had told him earlier. If something really was awry, this might help to flush it to the surface.

Keith humphed, a look of utter disdain written across his face.

"It's OK, no help needed or expected. I will try to find the receipts and if I can't it seems that I will have to swallow the cost myself. A bit bloody rich when the chairman works so hard to build and grow the business only to find that the CEO thinks he is a liar."

Simon bit his lip and suppressed the desire to let rip at his uncle for what was a totally outrageous comment to make, preferring instead to draw a line under the matter since the ball was now very much in Keith's court.

"So, what was it you wanted to speak to me about," asked Simon, moving the conversation to his uncle's agenda. Keith hesitated briefly and then spoke.

"I remember you telling me that you had met the Binns lad a while back, the one that used to come and stay with your grandparents during the Summer."

Whatever he had been expecting Keith to want to discuss, this was certainly not it. A myriad of thoughts passed through Simon's mind at what was coming next.

"Yes, Keith, I did. We met in London for dinner when I was down there on business. Why do you ask?"

"I suppose you saw that he was dead, murdered apparently. Awful thing to happen. I wondered if anyone might have contacted you?"

"Like who?"

"Well, maybe his family. Or the police. I would have thought that they would want to speak to anyone who had met him around the time of the incident." Simon had no idea where this line of questioning had come from, nor where it was leading, but for someone who had previously expressed derision, telling Simon to be careful where Graham Binns was concerned, Keith seemed suddenly to have acquired an unexpected interest in the matter.

Simon decided not to reveal his discussions with Allan Broughton, which had happened after he had instigated the contact with the police, nor the call from Ashleigh Percival, since he had no idea what Keith intended to do with this information.

"Nobody has called, Keith. I only met him for dinner which hardly qualifies me as a prime suspect." He did not add that he had been due to meet Graham again two days before the murder which would have shed a whole different light on things.

"OK, well let's hope they catch the bastard who did this soon, lock them up and throw away the key."

With that, Keith turned around and marched out of the board room leaving Simon standing there alone, a look of complete puzzlement on his face. What was that all about? As he reflected on what had just happened, a series of dark thoughts invaded his psyche. Why was Keith suddenly interested in his cousin's son having earlier been so dismissive when Simon told him about their dinner? Why was Keith unable (or unwilling?) to produce receipts for his recent trip to Leicester? Why had the hotel he had apparently stayed in never heard of him? Why had he acted so dismissively regarding the recent letters to their potential acquirers alleging impropriety in the company of which he was chairman? And more generally, why was his uncle so utterly opposed to Steele's even considering the possibility of a sale if the right deal for shareholders was on the table?

Simon had no answer to any of these questions, but he did have the distinct feeling that he very much needed to get some sooner rather than later.

37

CHAPTER 36

02 October 2016

The approach of Winter was chillingly evident on this October Sunday morning as Ashleigh Percival drove from her home on the outskirts of Ilford to The Hedges residential care home in the leafy village of Boxleigh some fifteen miles away. Her mother Sonia had been a resident at the home for the past two years since her Alzheimer's had considerably worsened rendering her unable to cope with living alone in the opinion of both Graham and his sister. They had chosen The Hedges for its idyllic location in one of Essex's prettiest villages and for its reputation as a friendly place with dedicated staff. They had certainly been pleased with their choice, and Sonia seemed very much at home there which was, after all, the most important thing.

The outside temperature was displayed on the car's computer as being 8C but with the wind chill factor it felt much colder. Ashleigh had driven to Boxleigh with the heating on full blast and wearing a thick overcoat in an attempt to stay warm. She tried to visit her mother once a fortnight although in reality she had to admit that she had largely failed to reach that frequency. Since Graham's death she had promised herself that she would spend more time with Sonia, but a combination of her own struggle to cope with the aftermath of her brother's demise and the fact that her mother by and large failed to grasp the fact that her eldest child was actually dead, found her continuing to create excuses not to go. This particular Sunday was an exception given that she had a clear objective, namely to ask Sonia about Duncan.

The Hedges was a small but tastefully decorated home and Sonia had a large, well equipped bedroom on the first floor. Ground floor rooms were reserved for residents with mobility issues so Sonia, who was still a physically fit individual, was happy to climb the stairs which at least ensured she got some daily exercise. She rarely spent time in her room during the day, however, and as usual Ashleigh found her in one of the common sitting areas chatting with two of the other residents. So engrossed in their discussion were the three of them that it was only when Ashleigh spoke that her presence was noticed. Even then, Sonia looked quizzically at her daughter as if it was the first time she had seen her.

"Hello, mum, how are you today? It is certainly warmer in here than it is outside."

"Hello, love, I didn't expect you today, did I? Did you phone?"

Ashleigh smiled although she wondered if this was her mother genuinely implying that her visits were sporadic or just another sign that her memory was playing tricks with her. "I don't usually call you, mum, because you are always here! Anyway, you are looking good and I am obviously interrupting the three of you trying to put the world to rights!"

Sonia laughed and pointed at her mother's two co-residents.

"These two are always arguing about politics so it takes me to make sure they don't come to blows! I would make an excellent hostage negotiator."

For the next few minutes Ashleigh listened to the three of them continuing with their debate until she decided she needed to move things forward.

"Mum, I need to ask you something so maybe we can go to your room?"

"It is okay, you can ask me anything here. Gerard and Mary are very discreet even if they cannot agree what to be discreet about!"

"I would prefer us to be alone, mum. Anyway, I brought some flowers so we should take them upstairs and put them in water." She produced a bouquet

that she had bought at Tesco on the way over, and the sight of this sealed the decision to head up to Sonia's room.
"Ooh, aren't they beautiful," she said as she stood up, "it is amazing how they can grow when it is so cold outside." Ashleigh stifled a laugh and resisted the temptation to tell her mother that these flowers probably came from Kenya or Ethiopia which were two of the largest exporters of flowers in the world.

"I am really glad to see you socialising, mum," said Ashleigh as she sat down on the bed.
"Oh, I am the life and soul of this place," her mother replied, "some of them would never speak to anyone if I didn't start a conversation."
One thing Ashleigh could certainly vouch for about Sonia was her ability to talk. She remembered from childhood how her mother would dominate any family conversation to the point where one of the others would have to simply interrupt to ask her to give the rest of them a chance to speak.
"So why did we come up here, love? Is it time for my bath?"
"No, mum, you remember I said I wanted to ask you something in private and also put these flowers into a vase." Ashleigh opened the bouquet and stood it into a beautiful crystal decanter before standing it on the table next to Sonia's armchair.

"I wanted to ask you about our holidays to Yorkshire when we were children. We stayed with your aunt and uncle, I think."
"Every other year, dear. The alternate years they would come down and stay with us."
Sonia smiled as if this question had evoked fond memories which had been hidden in the mists of time.
"My aunt and uncle had a caravan in a park next to the sea and as part of our trip we would go there for the weekend which for me was the highlight of the trip. It was a bit of a squeeze but we all mucked in." Sonia proceeded to regale Ashleigh with a litany of random memories from her trips to Ingleby and the Yorkshire coast which Ashleigh was happy to let her do before she honed in on the main point of her visit.

"Mum, do you remember a boy called Duncan who was a part of the Ingleby family?"

Sonia considered the question for a moment before she answered.

"You mean the one that you had a soft spot for?"

Ashleigh was both surprised and not a little embarrassed by her mother's observation. She had thought that she and Duncan had kept their little friendship relatively under wraps but that was apparently not the case, at least where Sonia was concerned.

"Erm, yes, we...we were quite friendly, mum."

"He used to write to you, too". Another surprise. Ashleigh had monitored the post each day and thought she had intercepted Duncan's letters without anyone else seeing them but again it seemed she was wrong.

"I wanted to contact him, mum. Don't get the wrong impression, this has nothing to do with rekindling the friendship or anything like that, I need to ask him about something really important from the past."

Sonia's look suggested to Ashleigh that she was dubious about her daughter's motives to say the least. The younger woman continued.

"It is actually to do with Graham's death, mum. That is why I was hoping you would remember something that would allow me to find Duncan."

"What's the matter with Graham, love? I haven't seen him for a while."

Ashleigh decided not to go down that road knowing that her mother's short-term memory was impacted by her Alzheimer's. She wanted to focus on the purpose of her visit.

"Do you have any idea how I might contact Duncan? I cannot even remember how where he fits in the family."

"He went off abroad somewhere but I am not sure where. A bit of a rum lad to use a good old Northern saying. Mind you, his dad was a strange one as well. That was why Carmen never got on with her brother, so I didn't really ever get to know him either."

"Wooahhh, hold on, mum. These are names I am not familiar with. Who is

Carmen? And her brother?
"Carmen is my cousin and one of my best friends. We stay with her parents who are my aunt and uncle. Her brother is Keith. Actually he is also my cousin but I do not see him like that. Strange boy."
Ashleigh was concerned to hear her mother speaking of this period and these people as if it were now rather than from a time in the distant past. This was a key indication to her that her mother's Alzheimer's was really starting to take hold.
"So where does Simon fit into all this, mum?"
"Now Simon is a nice lad. He is Carmen's eldest son. I think he has a bright future if he decides to join the brewery."
Ashleigh was trying to assimilate all of this information that her mother was providing.
"So Duncan is Keith's son, right?"
"Yes, two peas in a pod, those two," said Sonia, "very different from Sally-Ann."
"Mum, who is Sally-Ann? You are losing me with all of this ancestry!"
"Sally-Ann is a lovely girl, I often wondered if June had had a fling with the milkman to produce her. June is Keith's wife before you ask."

Ashleigh had taken a notebook from her handbag and asked Sonia if she could run through all of this one more time so that she could make some notes. Once she had done that, she studied the list of names and their relationships. This was all very well, but it did not seem to be taking Ashleigh any closer to being able to find a way of contacting Duncan.
"So, mum, do you remember the background to Duncan leaving England and moving to somewhere in Europe?"
"Carmen told me about it, although I don't think she knew the real reason he managed to do that. Seems strange a lad of 21 being able to up sticks like that."
"That does not help me with trying to contact him, though. I suppose after all these years of no contact with their family it might be impossible."
"Sally-Ann probably knows where he is. He is her brother however much

like chalk and cheese those two are." Sonia chuckled as if more memories were flooding back to her.

"That is great, mum, but how do I speak with Sally-Ann? Every possible road I arrive at proves to be a dead end."

"Oh, I know where Sally-Ann is" said Sonia in a very matter-of-fact voice, "she still writes to me regularly after I helped her with her candle making."

***

Half an hour later after a full expose from Sonia on the art of making candles and how Sally Ann had now turned this into a lucrative cottage business, Ashleigh left The Hedges armed with a phone number and email address for Sally-Ann. She had forgotten that her mother had learned to make candles when she was at school and had pursued the hobby throughout their childhood. She certainly had no idea that Sonia had been in regular contact with one of Simon Letwin's family for all these years. Sally-Ann would be Simon's cousin. This meant that Duncan was also Simon's cousin - was this another sign that there might have been a link between Duncan's good fortune all those years ago and what had recently happened to her brother? It seemed that she might be one step closer to being able to contact Duncan which was certainly a positive step in the right direction.

Arriving home twenty minutes later, Ashleigh met her son Ollie and her husband David pulling into the driveway ahead of her after Ollie's regular Sunday morning football. The 15-year old was a exceptionally talented player and had recently started to play for a men's team in the one of the local leagues.

"We won 2-0, Mum, and I got an assist!"

Ashleigh had no idea what an assist was, but she was so keen to contact Sally-Ann as soon as possible that she wanted to avoid her son's long explanation and simply told Ollie that it was amazing and he should feel so proud of himself as she did of him. She had decided an email to Sally-Ann would be a better approach than a phone call, even if that might mean waiting longer for a reply. In fact, she did not have to wait long at all for the other woman to respond. Expressing surprise but delight at hearing from her second cousin, Sally-Ann suggested that a phone call would be more personal and far more efficient than typing things out longhand. She was unable to have the call today, so they agreed to speak the following afternoon. Since it was Monday tomorrow, Ashleigh would be at work, which was not ideal, but she could not pass up the chance to see if she could finally get the contact details for Duncan Steele.

The following day, as she waited impatiently for the call with Sally-Ann, Ashleigh found herself reflecting on the current state of the police investigation into Graham's death. She was sitting in the Operations office of a major supermarket chain where she was a senior supply chain scheduler for fresh produce, but the truth was her mind was currently elsewhere rather than on oranges, avocados and purple sprouting broccoli. The investigating team at Scotland Yard had continued to liaise regularly with the family, primarily Ashleigh and Sarah, partly because they naturally remained suspects until a successful arrest was made and partly to support them as they went through the natural grieving process. It was a strange mix of suspicion and compassion. Whilst the police remained relatively tight lipped about their progress in the investigation, Ashleigh continued to hypothesise that they were no closer to making an arrest than they had been the day the murder happened. She was sure they must have spoken with Simon Letwin given his sudden reappearance in their lives after forty years, and the fact that he had not been detained led her to assume that they must have discounted him as the potential killer. Quite who else might be in the frame she had no idea. What if the police simply could not solve the crime? Would they continue to keep the case open or would it become one of those cold cases that might reappear in a TV documentary in thirty years time? Ashleigh winced at this worst of all possible outcomes.

As these thoughts squirrelled themselves into her head, Ashleigh tried to focus on her work priorities but this was proving difficult to do. Her boss had already asked her twice today if she was okay, and she knew that she needed to make a conscious effort to appear as normal as she could. He would no doubt assume that it was the strain of recent events that was the cause, which meant she would receive sympathy rather than criticism, but she was a conscientious person and wanted to make sure that she did not let her colleagues down by making silly mistakes or delaying urgent matters through a lack of attention to detail.

As the agreed time for phoning Sally-Ann approached, Ashleigh took herself off to the small meeting room she had booked on the pretext of having a confidential business call. As she dialled the number she felt nervous, not knowing whether the discussion would advance her search for Duncan or be a complete waste of time.

"Hello, Ashleigh," chimed the unmistakably Yorkshire voice that answered the call, "I hope everything is okay with you. I must admit I was not expecting to hear from you or anyone from your family and even had to try to remember how you were related to us!"

There was no expression of sorrow about what had happened to Graham, which made Ashleigh wonder if Sally-Ann even knew what had happened.

"Thanks for agreeing to speak with me, Sally-Ann, it is a bit strange to be calling my second cousin whom I do not really know anything about! I did not realise that my mum was still in contact with anyone from your side of the family. It has been difficult as you might imagine since Graham's death."

"What happened to him?" The half shriek that accompanied Sally-Ann's question confirmed that she was indeed not aware of recent events in the Binns family. Ashleigh spent the next ten minutes giving her as brief a summary as she could of what had happened including the reappearance out of the blue of Simon Letwin.

"That sounds weird, Simon turning up like that. To be honest, I have never really got to know him and the others either even though they are my cousins. Dad and my aunt Carmen apparently hated each others guts so we hardly ever got together as kids before we all moved on with our separate lives."

Ashleigh was surprised to learn this, and realised that asking Sally-Ann about Simon was unlikely to yield anything new. She decided to move the conversation to the main point of the call.

"Sally-Ann, I contacted you because I want to get in touch with your brother to ask him about something that happened years ago when we used to visit your grandparents in Ingleby. I thought that maybe you have contact details for him." Ashleigh had been unsure how to pitch her request, worried that her interest in the Steele/Letwin family following immediately on the back of Simon's unexpected reappearance might set alarm bells ringing in Sally-Ann's head. Her response suggested that it possibly had.

"Why on earth would you want to do that? I didn't realise you even knew who Duncan was. What could have happened back then that might be in any way relevant today?"

Ashleigh needed to think on her feet. The last thing she wanted to do was to scare Sally-Ann off, but equally she needed to get in touch with Duncan. His sister was currently the only potential link she had who might be able to help her to do that.

"You may not be aware that Duncan and I became quite friendly and used to write to each other. Anyway, he told me about the business he was going to set up - I am not sure which European country it was in - and mentioned something about falling on his feet and that it was being financed by someone who owed him a debt. I want to check something with him to make sure that it is not linked with what happened to my brother Graham."

There was silence on the other end of the line. Ashleigh wondered if she had been cut off, but eventually the other woman spoke.

"I am not sure that I can help you, Ashleigh. I also do not understand exactly how my brother managed to move to Spain and set up a business like that at such a young age. Anyway, you seem to know as much if not more than me." All of a sudden Sally-Ann had become very defensive, and Ashleigh thought she sounded frightened. Did she really not know about the origins of Duncan's business or was she simply trying to shut the subject down?

"The one thing I do not have, which you might have, Sally-Ann, is a contact for Duncan. That is all I am asking of you."
Again there was silence. Ashleigh waited patiently on the line, starting to consider her options if Sally-Ann did have her brother's details and refused to share them.
"I really.....oh, this is..."
Ashleigh decided it was time to lay her final card, like a poker player who risks everything in an attempt to draw an opponent out.
"I understand this might be difficult for you, Sally-Ann. You hardly know me. In some ways I maybe should not have involved you but it is too late for that now. Graham was brutally murdered and I am trying to understand why because the police do not seem to be making much progress. My worry is that someone else might know something about the killer which could put them in grave danger. That is why I was hoping you would help me if you have what I need. I am not playing games with you, I promise."
The ploy worked. Sally-Ann did have Duncan's email address and a Spanish mobile phone number.

"Ashleigh, I hope that I am not making a terrible mistake sharing these with you. I am prepared to trust you as a distant relation and as someone who is trying to understand more about your own recent family tragedy. Please don't make me regret this."
Ashleigh thanked the other woman profusely and promised to keep her updated on any progress made. They ended the call wishing each other all the best. Ashleigh looked at the contact details she had just been given and a cold chill passed across her as she considered the words that she had used that had finally led Sally-Ann to share them. She had subtly hinted that Duncan or even Sally-Ann herself might be in danger if the killer felt threatened by something they knew. She now realised that in contacting Duncan, without knowing whether he himself was involved in Graham's death, she was potentially putting one other person in grave danger.

Herself.

38

CHAPTER 37

03 October 2016

Duncan had always loved the fact that the weather in Marbella was so pleasant throughout the year, the protection of the Sierra mountains providing the double benefit of keeping summer temperatures cooler whilst winters were warmer and more temperate. October back in Ingleby would be foggy, cold and generally miserable whereas temperatures in this corner of Spain hovered in the mid-twenties. He had just been for a swim in the clear blue sea and was now sitting on the terrace of his bar enjoying a double espresso before the lunch service began. It was obviously quieter at this time of year, but there was still enough custom to justify keeping the place open. He usually closed the bar for the majority of January, as much to get over the hectic Christmas and New Year period as to reflect a shortage of custom as people made their resolutions for the coming year.

On this particular Wednesday morning something other than the glorious weather and planning for the upcoming festive season was occupying Duncan's mind. The previous evening he had received an email out of the blue from Ashleigh Percival and it had taken him a few minutes to figure out exactly who she was. By the time he did, he was far enough into her letter to realise that this was not just a "Hi, how are you" communication from a forgotten friend, but rather something much more serious, ominous even, that required his full attention. As he had read through the email the previous evening it gradually dawned on Duncan that the events of that fateful day in 1991, buried from sight for twenty five years, were potentially about to be dug up and re-examined in the quest to understand what had recently happened in this year of 2016, events that he himself had not even been aware of. As he sipped the strong coffee, Duncan opened his laptop and re-read Ashleigh's email;

"*Dear Duncan,*

Firstly, I hope you are well and that you remember me! I also hope that you do not mind me contacting you out of the blue like this. I got your details from Sally-Ann.

I am not quite sure how to approach this or even if any of it is actually relevant! Sorry, that sounds weird, so let me explain.

I am not sure if you are aware, but my brother Graham was murdered a few weeks ago in London. As I write, nobody has been charged with his murder and I do not know how much progress the police are making to identify the guilty party. As I have been trying to make sense of what seems to have happened, I suddenly remembered you and the time when you told me that you were setting up a business overseas and that it was being funded by someone in your debt. This was around the same time as my father was murdered by a man called Michael Spedding. The reason you came to mind was because your cousin, Simon Letwin, who is also my second cousin, suddenly reappeared in Graham's life forty years after their last contact in the days when our families used to spend our summers together. Shortly after he did, Graham was brutally killed. This could all just be coincidence, but I can't help thinking there might be more to it than that, which is why I am taking the liberty of writing to you.

Reading what I have written, I am a bit worried it all sounds ridiculous, but I cannot just sit here doing nothing. I guess the nub of my question, and you may not be able or prepared to answer this, is whether there might be a connection between what I have described about Graham's death and the events leading to you having the opportunity to open your business in Spain (Sally-Ann told me that is where you are). You may decide to ignore this email altogether, but hopefully you will reply, if only for old time's sake :)

Regards,

Ashleigh

Duncan stared at his laptop screen as a number of different thoughts and emotions competed for his attention. He was shocked to learn of Graham Binns' murder which had obviously not made the news in Marbella. His initial thought was that there must surely be some connection with the death of his father Gerry in 1991 based on what Ashleigh had said. Duncan knew exactly what had happened on that particular day in Ilford, indeed the reason he was in Spain with a thriving business was entirely thanks to what had happened that day. He had also believed that with Michael Spedding locked up as the confirmed perpetrator of the crime, that the events of a quarter of a century ago were buried for good alongside Gerry Binns.

What was Simon Letwin's role in all of this? Why would he suddenly seek out the Binns family if he had really not seen or communicated with Graham since the 1970s? It seemed now, with this news, that the ghosts of the past might be about to be reappear and that a spotlight might once again be shone on that fateful day at Binns Cycle World. What if it was? Would this be a problem for Duncan? Or rather did this new piece of news and a second murder present him with a further opportunity to monetise his knowledge? He had been living comfortably for the past twenty five years so perhaps he should just be grateful for that and ignore the content of Ashleigh's email. After all, if he did want to turn this to his advantage he would need to do some investigating, make some phone calls and involve people he had not had much contact with since he moved to Spain.

He loved the occasional game of poker with its element of risk and with the challenge of understanding how good a hand you were holding. He considered the Binns saga and realised that he would need to decide on his next move. There were only two choices.

Stick? Or twist?

In the event he decided to stick. Despite his 'devil may care' approach to life in general, Duncan could see no reason to stake what he currently had for something that may not even be true. He was fairly sure that the person that had recently murdered Graham Binns must have been the same one that had killed his father all those years ago, but the more he thought about it, the less inclined he became to try to find out. Letting sleeping dogs lie was definitely the wisest course of action.

Choosing to stick, however, was not quite as simple as just deciding to do nothing. Like it or not, Ashleigh Percival, still very much a Binns, was now clearly on the trail of the truth regarding this latest tragedy in her family, and was unlikely to be satisfied until someone was convicted for the crime. The more he thought about it, the more Duncan realised that this was potentially very dangerous. If Ashleigh managed to work out who had murdered Graham, even if the police did not, this could lead to a re-examination of the circumstances surrounding Gerry Binns' death. Whilst he, Duncan, had played no role in the earlier murder itself, he had used his knowledge of the incident to persuade the guilty party to bankroll his business. Blackmail was a serious crime, and it was unlikely that his victim, with whom he had scarcely had any contact since 1991, would fail to implicate him should the police realise that the wrong person had been convicted for the crime.

"Shit." His earlier mood of optimism had vanished to be replaced by the dawning realisation of how potentially damaging this new development was. Far from seeking to exploit the new incident, Duncan now needed to ensure that the events of 1991 remained consigned to the vaults of history, and that Michael Spedding remained consigned to his life sentence. He would have to start by responding to Ashleigh in a way that ensured that his objective could be achieved. How to do this was not yet clear to him, but do it he must.

And quickly.

39

CHAPTER 38

04 October 2016

The handling of the letters crisis with Vinbrew and Eldrich Global had clearly been a success given that both companies had agreed to go ahead with their due diligence visits to Steele's and that both subsequently remained interested in firming up their acquisition offers according to Peter Westmann when he reported back to Simon. The advisor confirmed that he had set a deadline of 31 October for the submission of firm offers for the business and warned Simon that there was likely to be a lot of toing and froing before then as both companies requested further information to help them to finalise their documentation. Whilst their potential suitors were putting together their offers, Mark was leading the process within Steele's of aligning on what kind of offer from either company would tempt them to consider selling. A Board meeting had been set for the third week of October to discuss the options and to agree on a final set of conditions. It was going to be a hectic few weeks, especially since the financial year end was also approaching rapidly meaning there was a strong focus on making the budgeted sales numbers whilst keeping costs within the agreed parameters.

The matter of who had actually sent the letters, however, remained a mystery. Simon had contacted an expert and shown him the documents, but the only thing he could tell from what he saw was that they had been typed in Word, which narrowed the list of potential suspects to just about 95% of laptop users in the country. He suggested that if Simon believed it to be an inside job, he could deploy a specialist to analyse a number of documents from each person, and look for telltale words and sentence construction that might point the finger of suspicion at the guilty party. Simon's view was that this was an expensive needle in a haystack proposal, and so politely declined the offer. They would need to keep looking for the culprit but it would be a fairly low-key matter now that the two would be acquirers seemed to have been satisfied.

Despite all of this activity, Simon found his mind increasingly fixated on developments following Graham Binns' murder including the growing odd, even suspicious behaviour of his uncle. He had heard nothing from the police since the call from Allan Broughton telling him that his alibis checked out. He was very grateful for this as it meant that Dani would hopefully remain in the dark as to his extra-curricular activities, although as a consequence of this he had no idea if the Yard was making any progress towards solving the case. Nor had there been any follow-up to his phone conversation with Ashleigh Percival. He had half wondered whether he might receive a call from Graham's wife, Sarah, who apparently had her suspicions about his links to Graham, and whom he thought might have been using her sister-in-law as something of a stalking horse.

As he sat at his desk considering what he could do next to advance his investigation, Simon knew what he should really do was to forget it and focus on the far more pressing matters of closing the company's financial year on a high and preparing for the Board meeting where the future of Steele's Ales would be under the microscope. He also knew that forgetting it was no longer an option available to him.
He was in it up to his neck and would be until someone had been arrested and brought to justice for the crime.

***

Ashleigh Percival was in the middle of a work meeting reviewing with her team how they could manage the present shortage of certain fresh fruit and vegetables which were stuck on the Spanish/French border as a result of strike action by Spanish lorry drivers. With no end to the dispute in sight, the Operations team at the supermarket chain would need to plan on an allocation basis trying to eke out the reduced quantities so that all of their shops at least had some produce to sell. She was already receiving emails from irate store managers and knew that this was only likely to get worse over the coming days and, heaven forbid, weeks. Ashleigh's phone buzzed indicating the arrival of a message to her private account, and, glancing at the screen, she saw that it was from Duncan Steele. Tempted to invent an excuse such as needing the toilet in order to read the email, she nonetheless managed to stay focused on the task in hand and it was only forty five minutes later, when the semblance of a workable distribution plan had been completed, that she was able to find some solitude back in her office and to open the new communication. She was pleased to see that Duncan had replied to her recent email and proceeded to read it with anticipation.

"Hola Ashleigh,

Hey, it was great to hear from you after all this time. Of course I remember you, how could I ever forget? Wink, wink!

I am very sorry to hear about your brother, I was shocked. Of course, I am not really in touch with events in the UK any more so did not know about this tragedy until I received your email. Not sure what else I can say. I cannot think how there could possibly be a link between my business set-up and Graham's murder because, as I say, I have not been back home for at least eight years. It is too bloody cold and depressing! On the other hand, I was very curious to hear about my cousin Simon suddenly contacting your family after so many years. It must be at least 30 years since I last heard anything from him, so God knows why he would be contacting your brother out of the blue. To be honest, he was always a bit of a strange guy so maybe I shouldn't be surprised. Have you spoken with him and asked him the same questions? It seems a weird thing for him suddenly to be interested in you again just before this tragedy occurred. Anyway, far be it from me to cast suspicion, I am sure you can investigate this yourself.

If you ever fancy a trip out to sunny Spain my earlier offer still applies!

Take care,

Dunc

Ashleigh finished reading and began to process what Duncan had said. He had been at pains to distance himself and his past from any connection with Graham's death whilst at the same time suggesting to her that Simon Letwin's behaviour was, to say the least, suspicious. Ashleigh still had no idea of what the indebtedness that had forced some unknown individual to fund the setting up of Duncan's business might be, and she still could not help but think that there could well be some link between this and her father's murder given the proximity in time of the two events. On the other hand, exactly the same point could be made about Simon's actions and Graham's recent death. She let out a heavy sigh. She was convinced that somewhere in the middle of all of this lay a pointer to the truth, but she had no idea of what or who to believe.

On the face of it, notwithstanding the proximity of the timeline, there was no clear evidence of a link between Duncan's good fortune back in 1991 and the brutal killing of her father that same year. If anything, the possibility of a link between Simon Letwin's reappearance, seemingly without a convincing explanation beyond his claimed mid-life fear of the Binns and Steele families being cast asunder from each other forever, and Graham's murder seemed far stronger. That despite the fact that Ashleigh had no idea of what the shocking secret might be that her brother had intended to share with his second cousin at their planned meeting.

As she mentally assimilated all of the information she had recently learned, both from Simon Letwin and now from Duncan Steele, Ashleigh was convinced that she had within her grasp the explanation as to why Graham was murdered if only she could join all the pieces of the jigsaw together. It was also looking more and more likely that her brother's death and the murder of her father were inextricably linked. This, she believed, was also the view of Simon Letwin. Did she trust her second cousin? He seemed to be genuine enough and if, as he claimed, his work colleagues had confirmed his alibi for the day of Graham's murder, it might be time to pool resources and share what else they knew. She wondered if Simon had really had no contact with Duncan Steele these past decades. Was Duncan telling the truth or lying to protect his own skin or that of someone he was closely involved with? Duncan had seemed to hint at Simon's possible involvement in recent events but perhaps that was to divert attention from him and whatever shady dealings had led to his unexpected windfall shortly after her father's death. As these possibilities swirled around inside her head, Ashleigh reached a decision. She needed to call Simon Letwin again and see what he knew about Duncan Steele and his business in Spain. In doing this, she might be laying herself open to enormous risk, but she craved clarity on what had happened to her family in both 1991 and 2016 given that nothing was clear. Furthermore, the police seemed nowhere close to understanding why Graham had been murdered.

Simon seemed her best shot at managing to do this, so call him she would.

She hoped that this would not prove to be the biggest mistake of her life.

40

CHAPTER 39

06 October 2016

As the clock ticked towards midnight on a balmy southern Spanish night, Duncan Steele was sitting on the terrace of his bar as the last of the locals chatted and laughed and enjoyed their final drinks of the day in the relaxed atmosphere usually found across most of the Sierra Blanca. Business was very good at the moment, but it was not this that occupied his mind this evening. It had been two days since he had replied to Ashleigh Percival's email and he had been wondering ever since whether his response had satisfied her and put her off his scent. At the same time, he had done his best to point the finger in the direction of Simon Letwin, taking full advantage of the fact that his cousin's reappearance in the life of Graham Binns after forty years of silence was bizarre to say the least. Ashleigh had naturally seemed so desperate to understand why her brother had been murdered that this had seemed to Duncan like a perfect opportunity to take the spotlight off himself and, as importantly, off the person who had actually murdered Gerry Binns. The person who, Duncan now believed, was also very likely responsible for the death of his son, Graham.

Although he was keen to know if he was off the hook in the mind of Ashleigh,

Duncan had decided that he would not contact her again and would simply wait to see what, if anything, happened next. Keeping his head below the parapet seemed the most sensible approach in the circumstances. What he did not yet know but was soon to find out was that another sniper was currently hidden in the undergrowth, a sniper who if they got Duncan in their sights would prove to be far more dangerous to him than Ashleigh Percival. If Duncan did end up in this person's line of fire, he and anyone he was currently protecting was very likely to be in the gravest danger.

***

Ashleigh had also spent the previous two days thinking things through, in her case about how best to approach Simon Letwin to discuss what she had learned from her exchanges with Duncan. She was pretty sure that Simon was not involved in Graham's murder, which also meant that he had likely had nothing to do with her father's demise. If she could believe him, and she was beginning to think that she could, then he was as keen as she was to see justice done in both of these cases. Aware of how busy they both were at work, she texted him asking when would be a good time for her to call about a very important matter. She did not give any more details at this stage, eager to see how keen Simon was to follow up on their previous conversation. He replied within five minutes, which confirmed to her that he was indeed keen, and they agreed to speak the following afternoon.

"Good afternoon, Simon, how are you? I know you are a busy man."
The understatement of the year, thought Simon, but he did not intend going into too much detail on that with Ashleigh.
"Yeah, got it in one, Ashleigh. We are involved in a potential takeover at the moment which is sucking up most of the time I have." He winced at the lie, but at least Ashleigh was in no position to challenge him on this. For some reason, Dani's voice echoed in his mind, and if his second cousin had been able to see him she would have seen his cheeks flushed red.

CHAPTER 39

"Thanks for making time for me again, " said Ashleigh, "I have been doing some digging of late and wanted to share a few things with you. I know you have been doing your own investigations, and maybe some of what I have learned you have not yet found. It could be that we look at a potential collaboration to try and get to the bottom of this whole thing depending on how you see this call when we are done."

Simon was surprised at how forthright Ashleigh seemed to be considering that her brother had recently been brutally murdered. He had not expected to be able to speak to anyone from the Binns family so soon, and was pleased that she was clearly reaching out to him with a clear purpose. It also seemed to indicate that she trusted him which, in his opinion, was another positive sign.

"I am all ears, Ashleigh. What have you discovered?"

"Have you spoken with your cousin, Duncan, recently?" Ashleigh decided that getting on the front foot rather than talking in riddles was likely to be the best approach with Simon, and so it proved.

"Wow, there is a name from the past! How on earth did he get onto your radar? It must be thirty or more years since I even thought about him. He moved abroad as far as I remember, although I have no idea where he went or what he went to do. And to be honest, I have had little interest in finding out."

Ashleigh was encouraged to hear Simon confirm that what Duncan had said about decades having passed with no contact between them was seemingly borne out by Simon.

"You may not be aware, because when we came to Ingleby it was more your grandparents that we saw rather than you, but I got quite friendly with Duncan when we were teenagers and we wrote to each other for a while after that. He contacted me in 1991 shortly after my father's death to tell me that he had come into a cash windfall as a result of someone being seriously in his debt and was using this to set up a business abroad. I discovered recently that he was in Spain." Ashleigh omitted to add that Duncan had invited her to join him out there partly out of embarrassment but equally to distance

herself from Duncan so as to get Simon talking without suspecting her of possible duality.
Simon frowned as he listened to his second cousin talking about his own direct cousin whom he hardly knew. He was keen to learn more about this intriguing and potentially worrying development.

"Have you spoken with Duncan? From your question to me, I am assuming you have. Do you have any idea who was in his debt and what the reason for this was? It sounds interesting and, well pretty dodgy to be quite frank about it."
"We exchanged emails because I am trying to make sense of what happened to Graham and I am struggling to make much progress. It also seems that Scotland Yard is struggling too, which is adding to my stress levels. Like you, I have had no contact with Duncan since he moved to Spain, and I have to confess to you that it was your sudden reappearance in Graham's life that made me think of him again. I may be making a huge mistake in telling you this, Simon, but the family is desperate to understand who killed my brother and I am prepared to take some risks to try to find this out. The reason I thought of Duncan after all these years was as a result of you suddenly contacting Graham for what seemed like such a flimsy reason, excuse me for saying so. I thought that you might be the person in his debt, and that this might have had something to do with dad's murder. If you are, then I am clearly in real danger, but I decided to call you again because I do not think you are that person. You also seem to believe that the two murders are linked which is now my view too."

Simon was so shocked that for a few moments he was unable to speak. He had not for one minute imagined that Ashleigh, or, for that matter, anyone else, might regard him as a murder suspect. Yet when she put it like she had he could begin to see just how she could have arrived at that conclusion. Eventually he found his tongue again.
"Let me reassure you, Ashleigh, that I was not involved in either your father's or your brother's deaths. I have been trying as desperately as you to get to

the bottom of what happened to Graham largely because I am worried sick with guilt that what he wanted to share with me is the reason that someone was driven to kill him. I am continuing to do this despite the warnings from my wife, Dani, that she will divorce me if I do not desist."

"Oh, God, Simon, that sounds awful. I really do believe you now, if that helps at all."

Simon gave a half-laugh and sighed.

"Now you have added another angle by dredging up Duncan Steele. What exactly did he tell you in his email?"

"Well, not too much in reality. He claimed not to have heard about Graham's murder until I told him, and then said that he had not been back to the UK for at least eight years so did not see how he would be in a position to help me. Oh, and when I told him about you recontacting my brother out of the blue he did suggest that you might be a better person to ask since you always were a strange guy. I suppose that means he considers that you could be a potential suspect or at least wants me to believe that you might be."

Simon was horrified. How could someone who hardly knew him cast such aspersions and describe him to a third party as being strange, meaning suspicious? It seemed as if Ashleigh herself now believed him, Simon, when he said that his decision to contact Graham after decades of not speaking with her brother was entirely innocent. So what was his cousin Duncan trying to do by pointing a finger in his direction? Why would anyone, let alone a family member, do this unless they were trying to protect themselves, or protect someone else? Or had Ashleigh misunderstood Duncan and was his cousin's reference to Simon being strange merely said in jest and not as an accusation? As these thoughts hit him like a taser shot, he realised that he really needed some time to think this through and to decide what his next move should be.

"Ashleigh, I am really sorry, I need to run as I have a visitor waiting to see me. Let me reflect on what you just told me and let's speak again in a couple of days time."

There was no visitor, but Simon needed to get off the phone and organise his thoughts. As the call ended he stared out of the window where the afternoon had turned dark and the rain had started to pour down. He remembered from school that when the weather outside mirrored the state of your thoughts it was known as the "pathetic fallacy".

There were certainly storm clouds gathering around him and he was worried that the thunder and lightning would follow soon unless something quickly changed.

41

CHAPTER 40

06 October 2016

"So, what is the latest on the takeover, hun, you have been strangely quiet on the matter for a while." Simon and Dani were sitting having dinner at the kitchen table the evening after Simon's latest call with Ashleigh. He had been trying to decide on his next steps after learning of her email to Duncan and was still undecided whether making direct contact with his cousin at this stage was the right thing to do given that he had no idea where, if at all, Duncan fitted into what had happened to Gerry and Graham Binns. He really needed to focus on matters at Steele's as the Board meeting to agree on their financial aspirations if the sale was to proceed was drawing ominously closer.

"Mark is preparing a series of reports for the board, babe, outlining what we would expect in order to seriously consider selling. The board meeting is next Wednesday so Mark and I will do a first review of the papers tomorrow." In fact, that was a lie because he had not put any date for the review in his calendar, but he knew that he needed to and, furthermore, he did not want his wife to think his mind was on anything else.

"Do you really think Steele's will be sold or will Keith get his way?"

That, in a nutshell, was the sixty four million dollar question, thought Simon.

"It is a clear possibility, babe. We need to look at all the angles and decide whether we would be better off continuing to operate independently or whether to look to partially cash in on what we have built and be swallowed up into a much bigger business. I think at heart we would all be like Keith in wanting to remain a family concern, but you also have to consider the way the industry is moving and make a call about where the most shareholder value lies. Clinging on to a vague ideal of retaining your independence whilst missing out on the big bucks might be a very costly mistake."

As he laid out these thoughts to his wife, Simon realised again just how monumental was the decision that he was about to be part of as a member of the Steele's Board and just how ridiculous it was that all of his energies were currently being expended on distant relatives that he hardly knew. Yet he was unable to let go of the Binns family drama now that it had got its claws so deeply embedded under his skin. He simply had to know what had happened to Graham and how that was connected to the murder of his father twenty five years earlier.

"I am glad that you are focused on this, hun, because it really is our financial future. I was so worried that you were going to get so deeply involved in that crazy Binns stuff that you forgot what was most important in life."

Dani stood up and kissed her husband and put the dinner plates into the dishwasher. It was a good job that she had her back to Simon as she did this because the colour of his face as she spoke these words would have told her a totally different story.

***

Spurred on by the events of the previous evening, with Dani's embarrassingly wide of the mark comments about him focusing on current matters at Steele's, and his additional good fortune that she had missed the tell-tale signs of guilt written all over his face, Simon decided that he simply had to contact Duncan. He needed to understand more about events leading to his cousin's move to Spain in 1991 and whether this was in any way connected to the dual tragedy that had engulfed the Binns family. The meeting with Michael Spedding had been informative but hardly conclusive, and Simon felt that his investigations may well be reaching a stalling point unless he found a real breakthrough soon. His cousin's reappearance literally from nowhere through the medium of Graham's sister seemed so far-fetched that it filled Simon with the hope that buried within the intrigue, there might lie a major clue to the recent murderous events in London.

The other matter which had been increasingly troubling Simon concerned Keith. Dani had mentioned him during their discussions over dinner and this had led Simon to recall the series of rhetorical questions regarding his uncle that had peppered his thoughts only a few days earlier. The trip to Leicester (or not), the missing expenses receipts (or not), his sudden interest in Graham Binns having earlier been so dismissive, and now his son Duncan reappearing like Marley's ghost through the mists of time. If one added to all of that Keith's vehement opposition to even considering a sale of the family business, Simon could not believe that this was simply a perfectly random set of coincidences. Rather it pointed towards something that fully deserved further examination in the context of his investigations into what had really happened within the Binns family.

***

"Dear Duncan,

I hope that this email finds you well and that you are not too shocked to hear from someone you last saw over 30 years ago! Maybe you won't be, because I got your details from Ashleigh, who I know recently contacted you out of the blue after many years of silence. You must be getting used to it!

I also understand from Ashleigh that you had not heard about her brother's recent murder. I am not sure why you should have known given that you have lived abroad for such a long time and, like me, you have had no contact with the Binns family for decades. I believe that she also told you about my communication with Graham, and the fact that we were supposed to meet, but that his death happened two days before that meeting was due to take place. We had re-established contact over Link Up, so it was obviously a total shock to me when he was killed so violently. As a result, I am now fully committed to trying to get to the truth as to why someone would want to commit such a vicious crime. I owe that much to Graham.

How is your business in Spain doing? I vaguely remember the time you moved away, but I really have no idea what your business is or how and why you set it up. I must admit, I was surprised (and impressed) that someone so young had both the skills and, probably more so, the financial resources to do this. Yet, it seems based on what you told Ashleigh, that someone may have been forced into helping you by bankrolling the new company due to a debt that they owed you. Obviously, this is none of my business, and I do not know what kind of debt this could have been, but if there is any chance that it might have something to do with either Graham's death or even that of his father, Gerry, I am sure the police would be very interested. They have already spoken with me and confirmed that I am not a suspect. They might want to eliminate you, too, if they get a whiff of potential wrongdoing.

It seems pretty strange being back in contact with you after all these years. On the one hand, I do not know you at all, but on the other hand I have worked closely with your father, my uncle, throughout my career! Maybe I should pop over and let you show me the little corner of paradise which you have made home! Hope to hear from you.

All the best,

Simon

CHAPTER 40

Having drafted his email to Duncan, Simon sat back to review the content to make sure it was striking the notes that he had intended. He had wanted to achieve two main objectives; to firstly establish his own innocence (confirmed by Scotland Yard)given Duncan's totally unfounded suggestion to Ashleigh that he might be involved. Secondly, to probe into how Duncan's business came to be set up with a view to (subtly) suggesting that if this was a dodgy deal the police may well become interested. He felt he needed to push things into what might be deemed a risky, even dangerous area in order to obtain the information he so desperately needed. He decided he was happy with what he had written and was ready to send it into cyberspace. Even so, his cousin might seek to ignore him and not reply. On the other hand, at least Duncan would see that Simon was serious, which was the best he could hope for at this stage.

***

If Simon was worried that his message might land on deaf ears, he would only have needed to witness the change in Duncan's expression when he opened the email and took in its contents to see how much impact his words had had. His cousin had started the day in a really good mood following a very enjoyable dinner and late night drinks with a new date. However, by the time he had worked his way through Simon's communication his demeanour had changed dramatically, and all thoughts of Maria Vicario had rapidly floated off into the ether. What was clear to him was that his cousin had decided to become Hercule Poirot which was his first potential problem. If Simon was going to push hard to understand not what had happened to Graham Binns, he would be all over not only Graham's murder but also what had happened to his father Gerry back in 1991. How easy it would be for Simon to unravel the Michael Spedding conviction and get at the real truth was currently unclear to Duncan, but avoiding any such meddling at all costs would be critical if he and the guilty individual were to continue to remain out of the glare of the spotlight.

The second problem was the police who, according to Ashleigh, were making little or no progress in solving the puzzle of Graham's murder. Any new lead, therefore, particularly one with unanswered questions, such as the origin of the funding for his business, was likely to be seized on by the strong arm of the law if it showed up on their radar. Whichever way he looked at it, Simon Letwin's unwelcome intervention was bad news for anyone, including Duncan himself, who desperately needed to keep the ghosts of the past firmly under lock and chain.

Much as he would have preferred to simply remain silent, hoping that the status quo would remain, he knew that he needed to respond to Simon's intervention to try to extinguish the emerging flames before they became a raging inferno.

42

CHAPTER 41

08 October 2016

Having by her own admission neglected to visit her mother as often as she should, albeit for reasons that she felt were at least partially justified, Ashleigh turned into the driveway of The Hedges for the second weekend in succession feeling slightly guilty that it was her agenda rather than her mother's that was the reason for the increased visit frequency.

Following her recent correspondence with Duncan Steele and her calls to Simon Letwin, she was convinced that the explanation for Graham's murder in some way or other involved one or both of them. If she believed what they said, and certainly in the case of Simon she did, she could not be so sure about Duncan as yet, neither of the cousins had actually committed the crime but that did not mean there was not a connection of some sort. The key to solving the mystery clearly lay in whatever her brother had wanted to share with Simon but had been brutally prevented from so doing. With that in mind, Ashleigh had decided to pay another visit to Sonia to see if her mother had any relevant recollections tucked away in the back of her mind.

"Hello, mum, I thought I would drop in and see you again. How has your week been?"

Sonia frowned as she looked in the direction of the voice, and it was clear that she did not recognise her daughter.

"Are you the girl that Carmen said she wanted me to meet? She told me all about you, you know."

"Mum, it's me, Ashleigh. Carmen is not here, only me." She only hesitated to add that her mother's cousin was unlikely to appear again any time soon because she was not sure what impact a statement like that might have on someone suffering with Alzheimer's.

"Oh, hello, love, did you just arrive? I was just chatting with Carmen, but I am not sure where she went."

Ashleigh could see this little exchange spiralling into a major discussion, so decided to close it down and move onto what she had come to speak with her mother about.

"I am sure she won't be long, mum. In the meantime, I wanted to ask you a few things about your memories of your childhood and your mum and dad. I have started to get really curious about my ancestors after I joined that family tree site recently." Ashleigh had decided that this little white lie was justified in order to get Sonia talking about the past without the need for her straying into areas she did not wish to go.

"I am not sure how much there is to tell, love, if I am honest. I come from a very uninteresting background, and as an only child I do not even have any siblings I can moan and groan about! Why are you suddenly interested?"

"Come on, mum, I am sure it is more exciting than you make out! I am interested because I feel there is so much that I don't know about you and what you were like when you were my age. For example, those family holidays that you went on with your parents to Yorkshire. I think that was Carmen's family, right?"

Sonia's eyes lit up at the mention of her cousin, no doubt accompanied by a string of images and fond memories from that time.

"I used to look forward to those trips more than anything, you know. Carmen and me, we were inseparable during those holidays, always wanting to go places together. And I really loved my Uncle William and Auntie Margaret, almost like a girl would love her own parents. Sometimes I used to wish they really were my parents, especially on the days when my own mum and dad seemed not to be that interested in me." As she spoke these last words, Ashleigh noticed a small tear in her mother's eye.

"Carmen had a brother, right?" Ashleigh wanted desperately to ask about Simon and Duncan, but decided to work her way gently towards that part. She wanted to make sure that her mother's memory remained lucid and believed that the best way to get what she needed was to go logically step by step. The look adorning Sonia's face at the mention of Carmen's sibling was a picture that painted a thousand words.

"Keith. He was a little devil, that boy. It is hard to credit that he and Carmen came from the same parents. I remember Carmen once speculating that perhaps her mother had been over-friendly with the postman when her brother was created!"

"I thought it was always the milkman who was blamed when the genes were not as expected!" Sonia laughed at her daughter's witticism then continued.

"It always surprised me that he ended up in charge at the brewery, although it is the family business so he had no competition. There is no way he would have got that job if it wasn't his by birthright."

Ashleigh saw her opportunity to move the discussion in the direction she wanted.

"He is retired, I think. Simon is now in charge. Did you know Simon well? He is Carmen's eldest son I believe."

Sonia frowned as if she was trying to match the name with the mental images she had of people she knew. Then she smiled.

"He was a sweet boy, so polite and so intelligent for his age. I remember he used to write stories at school and had won a regional competition for creative writing. Of course, we stopped going up to Ingleby when you were still quite young because William and Margaret died and Carmen did not have the room at her house to put us up. So sad."

"And what about Keith? He had two children I think?"

"Duncan and Sally-Ann. She was a lovely girl but that lad was strange. Then again, given that half of his genes were from Keith, it is hardly surprising."

"In what way strange, mum?" Ashleigh hoped that she might be getting somewhere.

"Well, we hardly ever visited them so I cannot say I saw too much of him. But when we were at their house, he was antisocial, usually in his room doing goodness knows what, and when he was downstairs he didn't have two words to string together."

"I was told that he moved to Spain when he was about 21 to set up his own business. I also heard that somebody owed him a large debt for some reason and it was this person that paid for him to establish it." Time to cut to the chase, thought Ashleigh.

Sonia frowned again and looked at her daughter. She shook her head.

"I am afraid I never heard about that. Mind you, we had probably stopped our visits by then so maybe he did and we just didn't hear the news."

"I think it was around the same time that dad died, mum." Ashleigh was hoping against hope that her mother recalled something, but it seemed that she did not. Mention of her husband's demise only resulted in the conversation coming to an abrupt end. Ashleigh felt a flush of frustration course through her veins. It seemed as if all attempts to understand if and how Simon and Duncan were connected with the deaths in her family were destined to end in failure. She was about to give up and leave when she remembered the reason behind the meeting her brother had planned with Simon Letwin, the meeting that never happened. Simon had told her what he knew of Graham's discoveries hidden away in Gerry Binns' old suitcase.

"Mum, maybe we can talk a little bit about where you were born and your very early years. I do not remember seeing many photographs of you and your parents. Did grandma Elisabeth have a good pregnancy? As you said, you are an only child." Ashleigh knew from the call with Simon that there was a doctor's letter which apparently contained a shocking revelation, and also that something about Sonia's birth certificate that seemed to be out of the ordinary, but that was all she knew. She wondered whether or not her mother would be able to enlighten her further.

Sonia Binns looked at her daughter and said nothing for a few moments. It was as if she was trying to decide whether to reveal her hand at cards or keep it to herself, believing a better time to do so would arise. Eventually, she spoke.

"I am not sure I should tell you this, but there was a bit of a scandal when I was born. I suppose it is OK now that you know, you are not a child any more!" Ashleigh resisted the temptation to laugh out loud at her mother's twee rationale. She really needed to encourage Sonia to spill some beans that might help her to better understand what had happened.

"Well, my mother actually got pregnant with me before she married my father, and so she had to go away from home in order to avoid the local gossip mongers and preserve the family reputation. My auntie Margaret went with her, I expect to keep her company so she did not get bored."

Ashleigh frowned as she listened to her mother recounting this story. Pregnancy out of wedlock was a very big issue in the 1930s, and she could imagine the potential shame that knowledge of this would have brought on her grandparents and great-grandparents.

"That is pretty shocking for the time, mum. How did you find this out? It is certainly not something that would have been freely talked about in the family, I am sure."

"Nobody ever talked about it, love. No, it was in my mother's diary which she kept religiously. Dad found the diary when we cleared her house out after she died."

A sudden burst of optimism hit Ashleigh.

"Mum, what happened to the diary? Was there anything else interesting in it?"

"Oh, I have it somewhere, love. It might be in a bag in that cupboard there."

Ashleigh jumped up and opened the wardrobe door. The place was crammed full of various bags and cases and it was difficult to know where to start. Ashleigh remembered the painful exercise of sorting her mother's possessions when they finally decided to sell the house. To be fair, Graham had done most of the work, but Ashleigh had helped and she had been amazed at how much junk a person could accumulate over the course of a lifetime. What she was looking at now represented but a small proportion of what was in the house, but it was still a fairly arduous task rummaging through in search of Elisabeth Croft's diary. It took a good half hour before Ashleigh finally dug out a somewhat dog-eared book that contained insights into the thoughts and activities of her maternal grandmother. It was a fairly weighty tome covering a period of several years, and it took Ashleigh a while to locate the period she wanted to read about. Her mother had been born in September 1939 so she started to read the diary entries from January of that year. The subjects covered were typically bland given that Elisabeth was a girl in service and had little or no life beyond working at Ingleby Hall. Most of the commentary was about fellow workers or the titled family who employed her, with a smattering of barbed comments about the daughter of the lord of the manor whom Elisabeth described unflatteringly as looking like a horse.

"What?" Suddenly, as Ashleigh read the entry for 26 March, she was stopped in her tracks. Elisabeth was in a happy mood that day and for a very good reason. "Our second wedding anniversary! I'm so happy I met Eric!"

"Mum, have you read this diary?"

"Not really, love. Your father found it and asked me whether I knew that my mother was pregnant before she was married. It was certainly news to me but not something I wanted to shout about, of course."

Ashleigh frowned and continued reading. After more mundanities, including reflecting on the arrival of Spring and opining on personnel changes at Ingleby Hall, reading the entry for 9 May brought another dramatic change to Ashleigh's demeanour. The subject of pregnancy was indeed the topic, but not at all in the way that Sonia had led Ashleigh to believe. She had to read the journal entry three times before she was sure that she had not misunderstood Elisabeth's written words. As she realised that she had not, her mind went into overdrive as she considered the possible implications of what she had just learned.

"Mum, can I borrow this diary? I am so excited at what it tells me about the way my grandma lived and thought in those difficult wartime years."

"Of course, love," said Sonia, almost dismissively. "I had forgotten that I had it, so I will not miss it, I am sure." Her mother laughed as if she had just told the world's funniest joke.

As she took her leave, kissing her mother and promising to be back soon, Ashleigh wondered if she should call Simon Letwin and share what she had discovered. Could she trust him? Did she need him? Most critically, could she make sense of this new information before someone who might have been involved in or even responsible for her brother's murder knew that she was firmly on their trail.

There was no time to lose.

Delay might literally be the difference between life and death.

43

CHAPTER 42

09 October 2016

"Hola Simon,

It was great to receive your email and to hear from you after all these years. I am not sure what to make of being contacted by TWO relatives who had basically disappeared off the face of the earth, but good to know you are all still alive. Actually, not a great choice of phrase given what happened to Graham Binns, so sorry for that and my condolences. I didn't know the guy but it's obviously a tragedy for the family.

It is nice that you are interested in my business, (which by the way is a drinking bar if you didn't know), but as I said to Ashleigh in my email I had nothing whatsoever to do with the killing of anyone, never mind a relative, and I will not let my name be blackened by such rumours. I moved here it is true helped by someone that owed me, but it is amazing that anybody would stretch it to make that a link with the Binns case. If the police have the money to waste coming out here to see me, they should put it to better use stopping real criminals like that murderer Spedding who killed old Gerry Binns. And since I have not even been to England since 2008, I cannot possibly have been involved in Graham Binns' death so I am as innocent as you claim to be.

Anyway please pass on my regards to everyone at Steele's and take care of yourself.

Duncan"

When Simon finished reading Duncan's email his first thought was "well, he would say that, wouldn't he?" His comment about Simon's and Ashleigh's reappearance on the scene was crass and hardly appropriate in the circumstances. Regarding the origins of his business, he was being supremely dismissive as if sticking two fingers up at people who might be assumed to be grieving. He might as well have told Simon to piss off because it was nothing to do with him. Finally, he was clearly at pains to distance himself from the murder of Graham Binns, claiming not to have been in the UK at the time, which Simon had no reason to disbelieve.

This was, as Duncan had pointed out albeit somewhat sarcastically, much the same situation as Simon, who had demonstrated to the police that he had been in Ingleby and not London on that fateful day. That did not mean, of course, that someone known to Duncan was not involved. At the same time, Duncan was taking the opportunity to remind Simon, if a reminder was required, that there was already someone in jail for the murder of Gerry Binns. The phrase that came into Simon's mind as his cousin made his point was "plunging the knife one more time into Michael Spedding". Simon's own recent meeting with Spedding had led him to question whether the police had got the wrong man all those years ago. If Duncan or one of his associates was responsible for Gerry Binns' murder, it obviously suited him to make sure the finger of blame remained firmly with the man convicted. As this thought landed, something that had been nagging away at Simon during his re-acquaintance with Duncan suddenly came into focus. The story Duncan spun of how someone who was so much indebted to his 21-year old self that they set him up in business in a foreign location was quite remarkable and, if true (and how else would Duncan, something of a wastrel according to what Simon could recall of their youth, get the money to establish his business?), hinted at something so serious, even perhaps something that was a matter of life and death. Something perhaps linked to the the two deaths that had so engulfed Simon's very existence in recent weeks?

As he thought more about this, Simon became increasingly certain that whoever had bankrolled his cousin's business all those years ago was very closely linked to the death of Gerry Binns. And by extension, since he believed the killer to be the same person, with the recent murder of his son, Graham.

***

Ashleigh Percival had spent most of the time since leaving The Hedges the previous day contemplating what her next steps should be. One thing that was unmistakeably clear to her as she thought things through was that she was still a suspect, however unlikely, for her brother's murder, and would probably remain so until the police made an arrest. This would severely limit her ability to carry out any investigations herself into what happened.

Unfortunately for her, she had taken a day's sick leave from work on 31 August and had spent the day at home alone. Ironically, she was not even sick, but wanted to finish a couple of jobs around the house, so had decided that since she had not had a single sick day in the past three years she was owed one. All of this meant that if she wanted to continue trying to identify Graham's killer she would need to find someone who could be more openly active in their investigations because they were not considered a suspect. One very obvious candidate came to mind. She had been debating whether to update Simon Letwin on her recent discoveries and to ask him whether he had made any further progress on his side.

Debate over, she told herself. Simon had already done a lot of work on this matter and, from their albeit limited interactions, he seemed as passionate and determined as she was about bringing this whole episode to a conclusion and making sure that the guilty party or parties were brought to justice. She had no choice but to trust him. She would call him as soon as possible to see if he was as keen to collaborate with her as she now was with him.

***

"So the first thing I stumbled on was the fact that my grandma Elisabeth apparently married my grandad in 1936, despite the fact that mum, who was born in 1939, insisted that her mother fell pregnant with her while she was still single. When I read that I thought that maybe it was her dementia kicking in although it is normally not the long-term memory that suffers with people who have Alzheimer's. Anyway, it was when I read the diary entry in early May that I realised something was not right at all."

Ashleigh had texted Simon the previous day after deciding that he was her best hope of being able to operate below the radar in parallel to the police investigation into Graham's death. She had expected a positive response from him to her proposal but nevertheless was still very pleased at the enthusiasm with which he had replied to her message. When he called her he thanked her profusely for wanting them to work together. For her part, Ashleigh spent the first few minutes outlining her visit to see her mother before getting into the detail of what she had recently found out.

"What did the May entry say?" Simon was keen to get right to the heart of the matter.

"Let me read it to you. *I am not supposed to mention this, it is a big secret, but today I am feeling very down. M is now very obviously pregnant and looks so healthy with her rosy cheeks! This is so unfair knowing that I will never experience this."*

There was silence at the other end of the line.

"Simon, are you still there?"

After a further period of silence, Simon eventually found his voice.

"I am trying to process what you have just told me, Ashleigh, and I am finding it hard to know where to start and what to think. This has to be linked to the revelation that Graham hinted at to me over the phone just before he was killed, the big secret as Elisabeth refers to it here. Based on what your mother told you, I can only assume that the M referred to here is Margaret. Your great aunt, my grandmother. Would you agree? And if it is the same Margaret, what the hell does that suggest? And why would Elisabeth never experience what M was experiencing?"

"My mind has been all over the place since yesterday," said Ashleigh, and Simon could hear the anxiety in her voice. "What indeed does all of this mean?"

"We need to find the doctor's letter and the birth certificate that Graham spoke of if we can," replied Simon. "I think they might just hold the key to this supposed secret. I am already forming a hypothesis on what seems to have happened, but those documents would hopefully confirm things. I don't suppose you saw either of these when you were looking for the diary, did you?"

Ashleigh said that she had not seen them, but that she could go back to The Hedges and take another look. Simon recalled from his last conversation with Graham that his second cousin had mentioned finding the two documents in a suitcase.

"Does your mum have your dad's suitcase with her at the home? The one I mentioned that Graham had found when you moved her out of her house."

"I didn't see it, no. I am sure she would not have got rid of it, though."

Simon thought for a moment, then had an idea.

"Perhaps Graham would have wanted to keep the suitcase himself having found the documents and your father's note. Especially given your mum's dementia. Could they be with his wife at their house?"

"That is a good point, Simon. I can certainly call Sarah and ask her. Let me do it now. I will ring you back when I have done that."

Simon took advantage of the time while he waited to hear back from Ashleigh to follow up on a message earlier that morning from Peter Westmann. The advisor had now collated the submissions from the two would be owners of

Steele's and wanted to arrange a meeting with Simon and Mark to dissect them and answer any questions the brothers might have. This would then allow the board to meet to discuss both offers and come to a definitive decision as to whether to sell or hold. As he realised how quickly the time to decide the company's future was creeping closer, thoughts of his uncle Keith came to mind, firstly because of his opposition to a takeover but also because he was still trying to rationalise the chairman's recent comments and behaviour on a number of worrying fronts. It was agreed that Peter would send the two proposals over before the end of the day, and that they would then meet virtually the following week once Simon and Mark had had the opportunity to thoroughly review the documents.

Simon left his office to make himself a strong coffee in the kitchen and, as he was taking the first caffeine-rich sip, his phone rang.
"Hi Ashleigh, just give me a minute to get back to my office." Simon hurried along the corridor and shut the door behind him. "Right, I am with you. Do you have some news?"
"In the words of the well-known TV show, Simon, have I got news for you!" Ashleigh proceeded to tell Simon that Sarah did indeed have the suitcase at her house and that she had never looked inside it since it contained only Gerry Binns' possessions which were frankly of little interest to her. Upon Ashleigh's request she had opened the case and riffled through it in search of a birth certificate and letter from a doctor both of which she had located buried amongst other papers, photographs and assorted knick-knacks. Sarah had then scanned both documents and emailed them to her sister-in-law.
"If you give me your email address I will forward them to you."

Five minutes later Simon sat looking at both documents on his laptop. As he read the contents his mind was filled with a mix of shock and bewilderment as he attempted to rationalise what was being said. The letter from a Dr Thomas Hawthorne dated 12 September 1937 to Mrs Elisabeth Croft was short but unequivocal in the message that it relayed. Following the recent tests that he had carried out on Elisabeth he was writing to confirm that she would indeed be unable to have children as she herself had suspected and feared. He offered her his best wishes and clearly did his best to soften this difficult news with a positive comment about alternative options such as adoption. The second document, the birth certificate of Sonia Croft, the future Sonia Binns, was no less dramatic in terms of what it revealed and in its effect on Simon. For some reason, which the document itself did not make clear, the name of Sonia's mother and father had been changed after her birth according to the note made in the margin. The amended details showed that the father was Eric Croft and the mother Elisabeth Croft. Sonia's actual parents. So why had the certificate needed to be changed? Whose names had been recorded on the earlier version? As Simon tried to make sense of what he was reading a shocking possibility infiltrated his thoughts. Eric and Elisabeth Croft were not Sonia Croft's birth parents. Which led inevitably to the next question.

Who were Sonia's mother and father?

44

CHAPTER 43

10 October 2016

"Yes, I know that we agreed that I would not contact you as a condition of setting me up in business, but things are taking a dramatic turn in the wrong direction and that could spell disaster for you and, by association, for me." Duncan Steele had really been spooked by the fact that not one but two of his relatives had emerged from the woodwork within days of each other both posing a real threat to the peace and tranquillity, not to mention the money, he had enjoyed over the past twenty five years. Given his promise never again to contact the person he was now speaking with, he had thought long and hard before making this call. It was true that the potential consequences for his interlocutor were far more serious than for him, but he felt duty bound to flag this threat and try to protect them both before events spiralled completely out of control.

The person on the other end of the line seemingly had one thought on their mind.

"What the fuck did you tell them? I know you, Duncan, you always were one to engage your tongue before that minute brain of yours had got its act together."

"I didn't tell them anything, I am not that stupid. But they seem to have

pieced some of it together and I am calling you to warn you and to give you time to develop a plan of action over there to counter any looming threat. I could of course have just said nothing and left you to find out yourself, by which time it might well have been too late." Despite the fact that this individual was his benefactor, Duncan did not see why he should take any crap from someone who had far more to lose than he himself did. It seemed that the other person was realising the same thing from the more conciliatory tone they employed when they next spoke.
"Okay, I get it. So what exactly do you think that they know?"

Duncan thought carefully before answering the question. He had, maybe inadvisedly, told Simon about the way in which he had been able to establish his business in Spain. This was something he certainly did not intend to share with the person he was now speaking with. In the end he chose his words carefully.
"It seems as if Simon Letwin has been in contact with Michael Spedding which is obviously not ideal. They also seem to at least be aware of police progress on the Graham Binns case - or the lack of it - which led Simon to suggest that if they knew about me they may well want to come and question me."
"Not ideal? Not bloody ideal? If they are digging into Spedding's real involvement, or lack thereof, "not ideal" is a flaming understatement!" And we need to make sure that the police do not identify you as a person of interest. The whole idea of me spending all that money was to shut you up, if you recall. Maybe I should come over there and finish you off as well if there is any danger that you will open your big gob."

"Don't you threaten me or I might just do that. I am telling you about the situation for your benefit not for mine. The best hand is still mine, just as it was all those years ago."
Duncan could imagine the look on the face of the other person as they listened to his words but he did not care. He had done what he wanted to do and would now resume the silence he had agreed to maintain. Knowing the other person

as well as he did, he was sure that they would now look to quell the threat that he had alerted them to, which had always been Duncan's primary aim in resuming contact. He hoped that he had done enough to deflect attention from himself and onto the two nosey parkers who deserved it.

If the person he had just spoken with was true to past form, Simon and Ashleigh were now in grave, even mortal danger.

***

As Simon drove into the office on Monday morning his mind was still engaged trying to figure out what the significance of the doctor's letter and birth certificate were. It was clear that Elisabeth Croft could not have been Sonia's birth mother due to her infertility, but it was less clear as to whether her husband Eric was or was not her real father. If Eric was Sonia's father he must have either been having an affair with the birth mother or perhaps there was some kind of agreed surrogacy arrangement in place. If Eric was not the father, that introduced a whole other set of possibilities and questions. Was Margaret Jones, who would become Margaret Steele when Sonia was already a toddler, somehow involved in this complicated scenario? Simon was unsure where the truth lay but he was sure of one thing. If he could piece this part of the puzzle together he was sure that the whole picture would come into view.

As usual on Mondays Simon planned to speak with a handful of customers before the product tasting session. Many of Steele's stockists were based in their traditional homeland of Yorkshire, but the popularity of their ales coupled with strong Marketing investment meant that in recent years their footprint had grown and they now had a presence in all corners of the country. The customer service team provided Simon with a random sample of six customers and he set about calling them with the problem of Sonia's parentage still buzzing around in his head. Having spoken with two Yorkshire free houses Simon noted with interest that the next customer's phone

number began 020. This was a London number and Simon was delighted to see just how far afield their products were distributed.
"Good morning, this is The Mitre and Sceptre, Camden. Darren speaking."

Simon was stopped in his tracks. Camden? The mention of the location hit Simon like a boxer's punch, memories of the awful events of a few weeks earlier forcing their way back into his conscience.
"Oh, erm, sorry, yes Darren, this is Simon Letwin, Chief Executive at Steele's Ales in Ingleby. I hope you are well and that business is booming. We are certainly delighted to have you as a customer."
"Wow, what have I done to deserve this? Two of the big wigs at Steele's getting in touch within a few weeks of each other. I know that I am the Chairman of the London Licenced Victuallers but I am honoured that you deem me important enough!" Darren let out a loud guffaw as if he had just told a pearl of a joke.
Simon wondered if he had misheard the publican and quickly asked the obvious question.
"Who was the other Steele's person, Darren?"
"Oh come on, how many senior guys do you have in the business? Keith, of course. I hadn't seen that old bugger in ages, so it was a real surprise when he dropped into the boozer!"
"Keith was in in Camden? When was that precisely, Darren?"
"Now you are asking me. No, actually I can tell you precisely. It was the 31st of August. I know because Arsenal were at home to West Ham and I was taking my boy to the match. Keith called in at lunchtime and we were talking about the prospects for the game. He is not much of a soccer fan but it made for polite conversation."
Simon was speechless as he realised the potential implications of what Darren was revealing to him. 31 August was a date indelibly etched into Simon's mind and for all the wrong reasons.

Keith was in Camden on the same day that Graham Binns was murdered.

At the very same time when he was purported to be in Leicester on a jolly with a group of his mates. A jolly for which he had failed to produce any receipts to support his expenses claim.

Was this just a massive coincidence or was there something more to his uncle's presence in Camden on the very day that the Binns family suffered its second tragedy?

"Did Keith tell you why he was in London, Darren?" Simon had to be careful not to arouse suspicion in the mind of their customer but he really wanted to try to get some insight into his uncle's visit that might suggest that he was there perfectly innocently and not for any dark, sinister reason.
"He said he was in London for a couple of days with a group of friends on brewery business. Apparently they had had a bit of a knees up the night before at the Holiday Inn and most of them could not face another pint that morning. Keith on the other hand seems to be a man with the constitution of an ox!"

Simon could not believe what he was hearing. It was possible that Keith had indeed been away with a group of his drunken associates but certainly not in Leicester as he had claimed. This was obviously why he had been unable to provide any receipts from the East Midlands city. A quick call to the Holiday Inn at Camden Lock had confirmed to Simon that his uncle had indeed stayed two nights at the hotel. Moreover, it seemed as if he had been there alone as he had not paid for any other guests as he claimed to have done when trying to get reimbursed for his supposed trip to Leicester. The rest of the call with Darren had been a discussion about the service the man received from Steele's, customer feedback on the beers and what else the company could do to cement its relationship with pubs like the Mitre and Sceptre. Although in truth, Simon's mind throughout this exchange was elsewhere and when he finished the call with Darren he decided to skip the remaining three calls as he needed to decide what to do with the information he had just received.

Two hours later, Simon was still sitting at his desk having thought through in detail everything he knew about the Binns case whilst trying to make sense of the parts that he still did not understand. Amongst the latter, hanging over him like a winter fog, was the question of what on earth was Keith Steele's role in all of this. His uncle remained violently opposed to any talk of a takeover of the family business, he claimed to have been in Leicester when in fact he had actually been in Camden, coincidentally on the same day that Graham Binns had been brutally murdered, and his general attitude, be it to the poison pen letters sent to Steele's prospective suitors or to Simon having had dinner with Graham Binns, was not what would have been expected of a company chairman. The more Simon thought about this and tried to find a rational explanation for it, the more he found it difficult to do so, meaning that ultimately Keith must in some way be involved at the very centre of this mystery. In Simon's mind the other critical piece of this complex jigsaw puzzle concerned the issue of the doctor's letter and Sonia's birth certificate and how, if at all, this was connected to the double murder in the Binns family. Was it possible that these two key elements of the mystery were connected? Could Keith really be linked to the demise of Gerry and Graham Binns, his distant relatives whom he hardly knew? If he was involved, what could have been the catalyst that led to this spree of violence and bloodshed?

Simon's thoughts were interrupted when Mark knocked and walked into his office. The younger man had intended asking his brother why he had missed the product tasting session (an event he never missed) but when he saw the look on Simon's face he simply stared. Eventually, Mark found his tongue.
"Whatever has hit you this morning must have packed a fair punch. You look as if you have just received notice that your world is falling apart."
Simon looked wistfully towards his brother.
"Mark, I know you have been telling me to forget all about the Binns saga and to a large extent you were absolutely right to do so. But what I discovered this morning suggests that far from being a case of distant relatives that we hardly know, the truth behind this whole saga lies far closer to home and, although I do not understand everything yet, the implication for you, me

and the business could be potentially explosive."

"Si, I gave up long ago trying to persuade you to focus on your marriage and our company because you are incapable of not scratching this other itch until it has been rendered red raw. What is this latest discovery that keeps you on your very own yellow brick road trying to find the end of the rainbow?"

Once again Mark's reprimand struck Simon full on but he was determined to prove to his brother that there really was something that merited his admittedly obsessive involvement in this matter. Over the next few minutes he outlined to Mark the growing list of unanswered questions concerning their uncle culminating in the information gleaned earlier that morning that placed Keith Steele in the very place on the very day that Graham Binns was murdered. Yes, coincidences happened, but this felt different. The chairman had lied about being in Leicester, that was now clear, what had not been clear had been why. With the knowledge that he had instead been in Camden, a potential explanation for his fabrication had revealed itself, however horrific confirmation of this might turn out to be. By the look on his brother's face, Simon knew that this revelation had struck a chord.

"I am trying to think of a reason why Keith being in Camden when he claimed to have been in Leicester could be something routine and innocent and not look highly questionable. I must admit I am struggling to think of a single explanation that does not suggest something potentially sinister." Mark shook his head as he spoke. Simon nodded and responded.

"It is difficult coming up with an innocent explanation, Mark. There is also something here linked to the fact that Sonia's supposed mother cannot actually be her mother since she was infertile and, according to Elisabeth Croft's diary, her future sister-in-law Margaret was pregnant out of wedlock. What I cannot yet work out is whether these two things are linked and, if they are, exactly how. I think I need to discuss this with Ashleigh and see if she can shine a light on this being closer to the family than I am."

"Well, before you go gallivanting in that direction, please remember we have a Board meeting in two days time that is without doubt the most important in the history of Steele's Ales." Simon knew full well that he needed the pragmatism and focus of his younger brother to keep him from chasing after what was doubtless important but nowhere near as urgent as the very future of the family business. He would do as Mark advised and make sure he was fully prepared for Wednesday.

But he knew beyond any doubt that once the Board meeting was over that he would pursue the Binns case on full throttle like a crack addict who could not function without his fix. .

45

CHAPTER 44

12 October 2016

Wednesday's Board meeting was every bit as tense and engaging as Simon thought it would be as the various views and opinions were aired about the two rival offers they had received. Details of each bid had been circulated in advance and Simon had been impressed at the monetary size of both offers which each valued Steele's at a significant premium to their own internal valuation.

Once again Keith mounted a robust if somewhat erratic plea for both offers to be rejected in favour of the status quo but the rest of the Board did not share his view, swayed by the fact that the impact of a sale on shareholder value creation was impressive. Of the two suitors there was universal agreement that the bid from Eldrich Global was the preferable one as it not only valued the company slightly above the valuation of Vinbrew but also guaranteed roles for the key Steele's executives. Simon would remain as CEO and Mark as CFO but not surprisingly the new owners wanted to appoint their own chairman meaning that Keith would be required to step down. True to form he went on the offensive immediately after the vote and the confirmation that he would be replaced.

"I would not stay on as chairman if they begged me. This is a very sad day for my family and I seem to be the only one that believes in family values. Our CEO and CFO clearly don't care about the heritage that put them where they are today." None of the other Board members commented on the chairman's comments and he himself said nothing more, possibly finally realising that this particular horse had already bolted.

After some post-decision chat around what the next steps would be, the meeting adjourned and Simon and Mark walked back to the CEO's office.

"Well, we have done it so there is no going back now." Simon raised his eyebrows as he stated the obvious but nevertheless using words that still sounded strange to him.

"It is kinda weird thinking that we will no longer own the company, " said Mark, "although it is a very nice thought that our bank balances are going to be somewhat healthier in a few weeks' time! How did you see Keith's behaviour and reaction?"

Simon had temporarily put the issues surrounding his uncle to the back of his mind but his brother's words brought the whole thing back into focus.

"Typical Keith. Admittedly, he was a bit less vocal and obnoxious than in some of his earlier objections to the sale but I think that might be because he saw the writing on the wall and even he, stubborn old git that he is, realised the game was up. I for one will not be shedding a tear for the fact that he will no longer be the company chairman."

"I guess the obvious question to ask is what he will do with his time now that he will have no role to play at Steele's." Mark's question was one for which there was currently no clear answer, but Simon's mind was now considering once again the possibility that his uncle had played a role, however unlikely that might seem, in the demise of Gerry and Graham Binns. To try to get closer to being able to answer this question he needed to speak with Ashleigh and pool his latest thoughts with hers. She would be at work now so he decided that he would try her before he left the office this evening.

***

By 7pm, having tried to reach Ashleigh several times over the previous hour, Simon decided he needed to go home to Dani who would doubtless be waiting to hear the full story behind the momentous decision that the Board had taken. He was slightly concerned that his second cousin had not answered her phone but he told himself that this was probably explained by the fact that she was working late or, alternatively, had a personal commitment and was not taking calls. He was sure that Ashleigh would see the multiple missed calls and contact him when she was free.

As Simon neared his house he was thinking how much, if anything, of what he had learned of Keith's presence in Camden and its potential implications he should share with his wife. There were certainly pros and cons to whichever route he chose. If he did share this latest news he would be admitting that, far from letting the Binns case drop as he had promised Dani that he would, he had continued to pursue it with vigour. The consequences for doing this, if his wife was true to her word, were dire in terms of their relationship. On the other hand, if his growing suspicions proved to be correct, there was the potential that he himself might be in danger which was surely reason enough to share this news with Dani. Having weighed his options Simon decided not to mention the latest developments regarding his uncle. He realised that this was probably a cop-out which he had chosen more to avoid a potential confrontation with Dani than because it was actually the better option but he convinced himself that this was the best choice since he could always tell his wife about Keith as and when he had more concrete information on the matter.

Over a dinner of lamb curry which was one of Dani's signature dishes, Simon talked his wife through the events of the day and the momentous decision of Steele's Board to approve the sale of the company. Financially it would be hugely positive for the members of the Steele and the Letwin families that were shareholders in the business, and Dani was clear in her opinion that this was only fair given the amount of blood, sweat and tears Simon and the others had expended over many years in building the company to where it was today. Payback, as she referred to it.

"And what about Keith? Presumably he did not have an epiphany just before the vote and embrace the sale with open arms." Dani laughed out loud as she asked her question.

"Definitely not, babe, and he still felt the need to turn down the offer to stay on as chairman which, of course, was never even made to him."

They both laughed which to Simon felt good after the stress and strains of recent weeks. Their laughter was interrupted by the shrill sound of Simon's phone. He glanced at the screen and saw that it was Ashleigh calling him. Should he take the call here at the dining table (which would immediately reveal to Dani his continued involvement with the Binns family) or move to his office where he could at least speak in private? He opted for the latter.

"Hello, Ashleigh, How are you? I tried to call you a few times earlier."

"Oh God, Simon, sorry I did not see your missed calls but I have had a terrible afternoon and evening. I am so scared."

"What on earth has happened, Ashleigh? Are you alright?"

"No I am not. I had two anonymous calls threatening me to mind my own business and let sleeping dogs lie. That is exactly what he said. And he also told me to keep away from you if I wanted to see another Christmas. It is him, isn't it?"

"What the hell? You say anonymous, but do you have any idea who it might have been?"

Ashleigh said that she had no clue as to the caller's identity because they had seemed to be using one of those voice distorters. It was definitely a man, though. Simon asked what specifically the person had said about him. Apparently, the caller had not referred to him by name but rather told Ashleigh not to get involved any further with the person she had been discussing her brother's death with. His exact words were that she should not jump in at the deep end when she was not a good swimmer.

"So, the reason I missed your calls was because I buried my phone in a cupboard for fear he would keep ringing me. Why did you call me?"
The study door opened and Dani stood there with her arms upturned in a gesture that said "what the hell are you doing, we were having dinner?"
"Ashleigh, dinner is ready here so let me call you in the morning, what I wanted to discuss can wait until then. Are you going to be okay tonight?"
"Yeah, Peter is home so I am fine, Simon. I have a meeting at 9 so ring me at 8.30 if you can."

"Who the hell is Ashleigh?" asked Dani when Simon had ended the call, "you leave the dinner table in a rush, presumably because you do not want me to hear the conversation, and I find you on a surreptitious call with some woman I have never heard of. Don't try to tell me it was a business call."
Simon's brain fizzed as he sought to urgently work out what the best (or probably least worst) response would be and realised that whatever he said his decision not to mention the Binns matter to Dani this evening was no longer an option. Ultimately, the truth was probably the best approach.
"Ashleigh is Graham Binns' sister, my second cousin. Now, babe, before you explode and shout at me, yes, I have been continuing my investigations into the two murders and I discovered something earlier this week that I think proves that I was right to do that despite my promise to you to leave well alone. And the call I just had with her only convinces me more that I am really onto something. She had anonymous threatening phone calls earlier today."

Dani stared at her husband, seemingly deciding what her response should be, before finally turning round and marching out of the room saying nothing.
"Babe, ..."
"Don't. You promised me , Simon, and you lied. I am sleeping in the spare room tonight whilst I decide tomorrow what I am going to do."
With that, she stormed upstairs leaving Simon standing there licking his wounds.

"What on earth is going on, Dad?" Simon had not seen Hannah enter his office and she was clearly alarmed at the raised voices and the sight of her mother stomping forcefully up the stairs.

"It is a long story, Han, and I am still not sure what the end scenario is going to look like. I have been investigating something and I promised Mum that I would drop it and I didn't. Actually I couldn't. On top of that we sold the Steele's business today. Don't worry, it will all come out in the wash!"

Hannah looked less than convinced.

"You and mum never have rows. I do not think I have ever heard you really raise your voices but this was clearly different. What the hell have you got yourself involved in, Dad?"

Hannah's question was not only logical, it was also spot on. Just what had he got himself involved in? Over the last few months he had had multiple opportunities to simply stop his digging but each time the lure of the Binns saga had proved too strong and he had de-prioritised everything else - family, business even his own sanity and safety.

And yet, despite his wife's reaction and the very real possibility that she might simply pack her bags (or more likely his) and the accurate observations of his daughter, he knew that he would continue to dig, maybe because he genuinely believed that he was nearing an understanding of what had really happened or maybe simply because, like a crack addict, he just could not stop himself.

***

And so, in search of his latest fix, Simon was at his desk in the office well before the appointed time to call Ashleigh. In truth, he had decided to leave home earlier than usual because he simply could not face Dani after the events of the previous evening. Cowardly maybe, but he wanted at least to speak with his second cousin before facing the music with his wife. He kidded himself that after the call with Ashleigh he might really cease any involvement with the Binns family but deep down he knew that this would not happen.

"Simon, good morning and I really hope that my call last night did not cause you any problems." Simon hummed which told Ashleigh everything she needed to know.

"Not your fault, Ashleigh, you were returning my calls. I am afraid Dani has not taken kindly to my broken promises so I am not sure as of now where I stand. Anyway, I trust you passed a peaceful night after your unsettling phone calls yesterday."

Ashleigh said that she had managed to get some sleep although it was fitful rather than deep.

"I have no idea who the caller might have been, Simon, but I am convinced it must have been the person that killed Graham. And if your theory is correct, that whoever murdered my brother killed my father as well, they must be late middle aged given that Dad died 25 years ago. And it surely cannot have been Michael Spedding unless he managed to access not only a mobile phone but also a voice distorter from his prison cell."

"I have a nasty suspicion that someone closer to home than we might think is implicated in this somehow. But I am not yet sure how or why. That is where I am hoping you might be able to do some more digging in your family to see if you can crack this puzzling code. "

Ashleigh gave an ironic laugh.

"My family now basically consists of mum, who has dementia, Sarah, who was not that close to my parents and Graham's daughter, Annabelle, who is too young to remember her grandad."

"It feels a bit like doing a complex jigsaw puzzle, said Simon. I am starting to see the outline but there are one or two key detail pieces missing. If Margaret was pregnant out of wedlock and your grandfather William wanted to hush this up due to the shame that this could bring on him and his parents I can see that he would grab at any solution that mitigated the problem. Your grandma Elisabeth could not have children but clearly has one, your mother.

And her name and that of your grandad Eric are clearly on your mum's birth certificate although we now know that they were not the parents named on your mum's original birth certificate. So let's assume that Elisabeth and Eric agreed to adopt their relatives' child to help them to avoid the shame, were they keen to do this or were they in some way obliged to play ball? If they truly wanted to adopt, would it not be more likely that they would choose a stranger's child rather than that of a blood relative with all the awkwardness that could lead to in future years? I know I would. Blood might be thicker than water, but taking on your brother's offspring just because he had been a naughty boy is a huge step."

Simon paused to allow Ashleigh to consider and respond if she had any comments on what he had said. There was silence at the other end of the line. Simon waited for Ashleigh to say something but the silence continued. Simon wondered if the call had dropped but eventually she spoke.
"Sorry, Simon, I was just thinking about what you said because when I spoke with Sarah about the diary and the birth certificate there was one other item she had found which shocked us both. I was trying to process how that might be a key piece of the jigsaw puzzle and based on your suppositions it certainly might explain why Elisabeth and Eric agreed to take my Mum. on"
Simon waited eagerly for an explanation, but none was forthcoming. He remained silent for a few more seconds before cutting to the chase.
"What was it, Ashleigh? Don't dangle a carrot and then snatch it away!"
"It was a greetings card." Ashleigh spoke slowly and deliberately suggesting she was still trying to understand the potential significance of this new information. "It was sent to someone called Eric so I assume it was my Grandad. I am not aware of any other Erics in the family."

Simon tried not to seem totally underwhelmed but he was thinking that this supposed nugget was not such unless he was missing something.
"Who was it from?" he asked. "I think greetings cards were fairly common in those days, too."
"You might view it differently when I tell you what it said."

"So come on, spill the beans."

Ashleigh took a deep breath before she spoke.

"To my darling Eric.

You cannot imagine how much I love and want you however impossible that might be. I hope we can continue to snatch moments like last week when you can get away.

Robert x"

"Holy crap!" It was as much as Simon found himself able to say.

"If we are looking for a good reason why Eric might have felt obliged to help someone, perhaps William and Margaret," said Ashleigh", "I think we might just have found it."

46

CHAPTER 45

12 October 2016

"You still look like you have seen a ghost, Si. What the hell is going on? I thought you would be more energised after the outcome at the Board meeting."

Simon had ended his call with Ashleigh and had sat for some time with his head in his hands, unable at first to take in the news his second cousin had given him. He had thought through the potential scenarios that this situation might have triggered and the consequent ramifications that each would have brought. The facts were clear; Eric was bisexual, perhaps even gay, and Margaret was pregnant out of wedlock, both of which were socially utterly unacceptable in the 1930s. Elisabeth was infertile, which was viewed as shameful and demeaning particularly for a woman, and William was an aspiring businessman who was no doubt desperate to avoid the stigma of making his girlfriend pregnant with a bastard child. As Simon mentally considered all of these pieces of the puzzle a full picture of what might have played out began to emerge in his mind. What if William had threatened to expose Eric's sexuality unless he and Elisabeth adopted Sonia? That would solve all three problems in one fell swoop and get him off the hook for fathering a child out of wedlock. Simon was pretty sure that this or something close was where the truth lay but, even if he was bisexual, what was the link between this act of deceit and the brutal murder of two men twenty five years apart? And if he was right about his uncle's involvement in the events that took place in Ilford and Camden, why would Keith Steele want Gerry Binns dead? Graham knew too much, which explained why the killer would want him silenced, but why murder Gerry, a relative that you barely knew?

As the various strands vied for attention in his mind, Simon asked himself which questions pertaining to recent events did not currently have a clear answer or rationale? Something else provided the glue that bonded everything together and he needed to find out what that was. As he considered this, three unanswered questions came to mind;

1. What was the truth behind Gerry Binns' murder? Michael Spedding had been fitted up for it, so who was the perpetrator and why kill a family man who appeared to have no enemies?
2. What was the real story behind Duncan Steele's business venture in Spain? Who had bankrolled this for him and why?
3. Why had Keith been so against the sale of Steele's Ales? Financially, the outcome made him a rich man so was it really family heritage that was driving his antagonism?

Suddenly it hit him, square between the eyes. It all made perfect sense now if one outstanding piece of information proved to be what he thought it was. He needed to find the answer to that as soon as he possibly could. He scrolled through his WhatsApp messages to view once more a document that Ashleigh had sent him recently and found what he was looking for.

"There have been many ghosts haunting my life these past few weeks, Mark. But I think I might be close to understanding what they are trying to tell me. I might need to make one more trip to check something out."

Mark looked at him warily.

"And where might that be to, bro? Outer Mongolia?"

Simon shook his head and took a deep breath.

"Minehead."

***

Having heard nothing from Dani since she stormed up to the spare bedroom the previous evening, Simon decided that before he did anything else he needed to tell her everything that he had discovered or surmised and get her approval for his final fact finding outing to Somerset. She might not let him do that, she might already have packed her bags but he needed to try. This was now so close to home that it would be remiss of him not to say something rather than continue to operate surreptitiously.

So at lunch time he decided to drive home and try to mend what had broken the previous evening. As he opened the front door the sound of 80s music could be heard from the kitchen. Ironically, the track playing was the Communards "Don't Leave Me This Way" and Simon hoped that this was not a portent of what was to come. He walked into the kitchen where Dani was in the process of stirring something on the hob. Unsure of what to say, Simon opted for what he thought of as humour, his default approach whenever the ice needed breaking.

"At least you are still here," he said, grinning, "I was worried you might have done a Houdini on me!"

Dani looked up from what she was doing, still a look of thunder on her face.

"If anyone frees themselves or leaves this house it will be you. I am damned if I am moving out given that you are the one that has lied and thrown our whole relationship into jeopardy."

Stung though he might have felt, his wife's reaction was totally as he had expected. He made that point to her, acknowledging that the fault was entirely his.

"Babe, I know I have behaved very badly, and you have every right to be angry, disappointed, pissed off, or all of these things. But what I need to tell you now will hopefully at least demonstrate to you that I had a reason for suspecting that all was not right with the Binns thing. With that, he outlined to Dani everything that he had found out and concluded with the potentially shocking news that the person responsible for the double murder

was someone very close to them.
"If I am right, I think you will agree that this is something that it going to impact you, me and everyone in the family."

Simon stopped speaking and looked at his wife. As he had been describing what he had found out he noticed that she was gradually paying more attention such that by the end she had stopped cooking and was fully focused on Simon's account of recent events. He waited, hoping and praying that her icy reaction of the previous evening might have started to thaw into something more understanding.
"This just sounds too far-fetched to be true. Are you sure that you are not adding two and two and getting five?" Dani was at least engaging which Simon saw as a distinct positive.
"Babe, I know this is a shock, and I do not yet have incontrovertible proof, but I really believe that this is what happened. There is one more thing I need to do to prove or disprove my theory. And for that I may need to go to Minehead."
"Where is Minehead?"
"It is in Somerset. I need to visit the births, marriages and deaths office to check something with Sonia's birth certificate."
Simon waited to see whether Dani would agree or fly into a rage again and tell him to pack his bags and get lost. After a few seconds where he thought it might go either way, his wife finally chose her side of the fence.

"I am not happy about this whole affair, Simon, but even I have to admit that what you have just told me, if it is true, is pretty nuclear. If this trip to Minehead brings the whole matter to an end one way or the other then you have my blessing. A thought - can you not phone them and ask whatever your question is without having to actually drive there?"
"I wish I could, but I fear this is not just a simple black and white enquiry. I need them to confirm something that happened in the 1930s and that I think can only be done in person. I probably need Ashleigh with me as well, given that it is her mother we are asking about. We may also need to tell a few

white lies to get the information we want."

"I thought I would ask before you set off on another wild goose chase."

The relief that swept over Simon at Dani's tacit approval was palpable and he threw his arms around his wife. She pushed back and wagged her finger at him, shaking her head as she did.

"I said you had my blessing to go to Somerset, but you are certainly not out of the woods in terms of the bigger picture. We need to talk about this once you stop playing Agatha Christie."

***

Back in the office and feeling much better about life, Simon set about contacting Ashleigh to see if and when she might be able to travel with him to Minehead. Surprisingly, she was free to talk immediately so he started by sharing with her the "aha" moment he had experienced after he had slotted the latest piece of the jigsaw in place.

"Wow, Simon, that is one hell of a theory. So how do we proceed from here?"

"That is the other reason for my call. The bit we need to check concerns the birth certificate - not the one we have but the original one that we believe exists." He outlined his proposal and why he needed Ashleigh to accompany him and was delighted when she said she would. They agreed to check their schedules and find a mutually convenient day. The trip was set for Thursday, and they agreed to meet at Bridgwater services on the M5 as close to midday as possible. To do that they would both need to set off early but neither minded given the importance of the task at hand. Simon sensed that they were so close to solving the mystery.

He hoped and prayed that they would both still be alive when the nightmare finally ended.

47

CHAPTER 46

13 October 2016

As Simon joined the M5 at the M42 intersection on his way to meet up with Ashleigh he was completely unaware that he was the third person to make this same journey to the Registrar's office in Minehead on matters concerning Sonia Binns (nee Croft). He had agreed with Ashleigh that they needed a credible story for the Registrar to approve their request and he felt that what they were about to ask was eminently reasonable. However, he was also aware that often a combination of process and bureaucracy ruled in institutions such as this so it was far from certain that they would be successful, however compelling their case. They had managed to sync their timing well and Simon had only been waiting for ten minutes at Bridgwater services before Ashleigh's Ford Focus swung into a parking space close to him. After a brief exchange and a hug given that this was the first time they had physically met in almost 40 years, the two cars rejoined the M5 to finish the final 28 miles of their journey into Minehead. Just over an hour later, they had managed to find parking and were heading for the Registry office of Births, Marriages and Deaths.

"Good afternoon, Madam, Sir, how can I help you?"
Simon was pleasantly surprised at such an ebullient and energetic welcome

from the lady whose name and role the brass plate on her desk announced as Marjory Jillings, Front Desk Administrator. He glanced at Ashleigh and nodded as a sign that their agreed spiel should begin.
"Thank you, Marjory, if you do not mind me calling you that." The smile in response to the informality told Ashleigh that she had the approval to do so.

"My name is Ashleigh Percival and my maiden name was Binns. I am here on behalf of my mother, Sonia Binns, who was born near here and whose birth was registered in this office in 1939. She is in her late seventies now and sadly suffering from a worsening case of dementia. We are researching the family ancestry and want to speed things up as we do not know how long mum's memory will hold out. The thing is, from her birth certificate we have deduced that changes were made after she was born which may suggest that her birth parents are not actually the couple named on the document. There is a side note saying that changes were made to the certificate so we wonder if this was indeed the case. We have come here in person to see if we can confirm what the changes made were."

Marjory Jillings looked at Simon and asked Ashleigh who "we" were.
"Oh, sorry, how rude of me. This is my second cousin Simon Letwin. His mum and my mum were cousins and the best of friends."
Marjory nodded and immediately a deep frown appeared across her brow.
"It's very strange, that reminds me of a similar case years ago when a man came in asking about changes to a birth certificate. That certificate had been changed, I remember, which suggested that there was definitely some skulduggery at play. Must be at least 20 years ago, but I have a razor sharp memory. It helps in this line of work, you know."

The Front Desk Administrator looked at both of her visitors and it was impossible from the poker face she wore following their request whether Simon and Ashleigh would get what they wanted or whether it would turn out to have been a wasted journey. The story of the man who decades earlier had made a similar pitch for information was all very interesting, and potentially

encouraging thought Ashleigh, but of little import to their own needs.
"We require the written consent of the person whose information is being requested in cases such as these. You already have the birth certificate for your mother, which is what you would be sent if you ordered it online." Marjory had clearly switched into official mode.
Simon, who had so far said nothing, decided he needed to respond.
"Marjory, Mrs Binns is suffering from acute dementia and would be unable to give you any meaningful approval. Without going into detail, there is a very serious reason why we are making this request and it would not be exaggerating to say that it could literally be a question of life or death."

Marjory Jillings looked from Simon to Ashleigh and then at the floor before seemingly reaching a decision.
"Please give me a few minutes, I am promising nothing but let me go down to the archives." She turned and disappeared through a door behind her desk.
Simon shrugged his shoulders.
"At least it wasn't an outright no."
They stood in silence and waited for Marjory to return. She eventually reappeared and it was clear from the look on her face that she had indeed discovered something out of the ordinary. Whether it was relevant to them remained to be seen.

"Well, well, " she began, "isn't it a small world?"
"Did you find something of interest? It sounds as if you might have done." Ashleigh tried to hide her impatience, seeking to empathise with the Administrator in the hope that she could and would help them."
"Indeed I did, at least in terms of confirming that I have a good memory!" Marjory wore a smile that said "aren't you impressed?" Simon and Ashleigh looked at each other then back at Marjory, willing her to get to the point. Eventually she did.
"Well it seems as if your mother is a very popular and in-demand lady! I just checked the archives and I recall very well that the gentleman I referred to earlier came asking questions about Mrs Binns too."

Simon's mind was racing and doing somersaults. Who on earth could have come here twenty odd years ago asking about Sonia? And why? As he sifted through the pieces of the jigsaw already in place there was only one person it could have been. Gerry Binns. If Gerry had also found the doctor's letter and birth certificate, he would of course be interested in knowing the truth behind these two apparently incompatible documents and how they impacted his wife. Had he discovered that the confirmation Simon was seeking as he sought to finish the jigsaw was the truth? Simon was dragged out of his reverie by Marjory Jillings.
"Are you alright, sir? You seem to be in a world of your own."
"I am fine, just a little shocked that the person I think you are referring to was brutally murdered in 1991. I am wondering if there is a link with his visit here and his subsequent. discovery, whatever it was."

Marjory looked visibly shaken. "Murdered, you say? That is shocking!"
Simon looked at Ashleigh , sensing that this might be the opportunity to persuade Mrs Jillings to share what she had found.
"What is more," Simon continued" "this gentleman's son was also murdered, just a few weeks ago, and we are sure that both deaths are the result of what that changed birth certificate might reveal to us."
Any resistance Marjory Jillings might have had in revealing what she knew was visibly melting as she listened to what Simon was relating. She might have worked in Births, Marriages and Deaths for thirty years but she was clearly still alarmed at the thought of someone she had met in her office apparently being brutally slayed.
"W-what exactly was the piece of information you were both seeking?"
Simon nodded to Ashleigh.
"The name of my mother's birth parents. We have a strong suspicion, but we need to be sure so as to be able to complete the jigsaw puzzle."

Marjory turned abruptly and headed back through the same door as she had done earlier. Two minutes later, she reappeared with a sheet of paper in her hand. The sense of expectation in the room was almost visible as she started to speak.

"Let me not prolong this any longer if this information was genuinely the reason that two people senselessly lost their lives. I have no reason to doubt you, even if I do not really understand the issues, so it is a procedural risk that I am prepared to take.

According to this birth certificate dated 8th September 1939, the one issued immediately after the birth of your mother as opposed to the document you already have which was issued when the changes were made, her parents were called William Steele and Margaret Jones."

48

CHAPTER 47

June 1947

From a very early age William Steele had wanted to have his own business. He had watched how, in the post-World War One years, his father, Horace, had studiously built up a flour mill on the outskirts of Ingleby into a successful operation which allowed the family to live in a large house in a very prestigious part of town.

William had joined a local brewery straight after school and quickly progressed to be a Production Manager in the company. As a young, single man he saved as much money as he could, driven by the desire to scratch the entrepreneurial itch he had seemingly inherited from Horace.

As the Second World War mercifully ended, William began to give serious consideration to his dream of becoming a business owner. He loved working in the beer industry, where he had learned his craft, and although rationing had been an omnipresent feature of recent years (and would continue to be well into the 1950s), beer had escaped relatively unscathed, being seen as a 'morale booster' for the population at large in times of such hardship. By 1947, with the war over and life gradually getting back to somewhere approaching normality, William had decided that he wanted to launch his own brewery, initially on a small scale, but with the dream of competing with the very best. His father agreed to lend him money to start the business and

William added the money he had saved himself, and so it was that in a small premises on the outskirts of Ingleby that Steele's Ales was born. As the first production run was put into the wooden casks, William stood smiling, the enthusiastic look of a man embarking on what would turn out to be a highly successful future.

It could, of course, have been so different had he not managed to successfully orchestrate events in 1939 when his fiance Margaret fell pregnant out of wedlock. As he thought back to that time, William was filled with a mix of embarrassment that he had caused a situation that almost ruined his plans and sheer relief that he had managed to prevent such a disaster. He knew that had he failed in this his father, a strict Christian who was dogmatic about the sanctity of marriage and would have viewed an illegitimate grandchild as a massive stain on his own character, would not have agreed to make the loan he recently had to help launch the brewery.

As it was, William had managed to both resolve the issue and to do it without anyone else being the wiser. Anyone, that is, except his son Keith, who had discovered the family secret quite by chance when his father handed over the running of the business in 1980. William had told Keith he needed to keep this to himself to avoid any potential problems down the line. This advice was given by William entirely to protect his own reputation and in no way out of concern for his son, nevertheless being as Keith would stand to inherit 50% of the brewery when his parents died rather than the 33% which he would get if the truth about his sister Sonia was ever revealed, it was very much in Keith's interests to follow his father's advice.

William's mind drifted back to Easter 1939 when the revelation that Eric Croft was having a homosexual affair provided him with his 'get out of jail' card. He smiled at his own little joke since he recalled that Margaret and Elisabeth had got hooked on Monopoly during their stay in Somerset. He had chosen to send Margaret to the West Country when another stroke of luck presented itself. The brewery where he was employed was looking to expand its product range to include cider and was looking for a supplier to work with. Since almost all the cider available was produced in Somerset the potential candidates all came from that area. William, as Production Manager, was the person chosen to work with the various suppliers to identify the one whom he felt was best placed to meet their needs. After several tastings and discussions on pricing and service William recommended to his manager that Thomas Perry Cider was his choice and the company agreed to move forward with them. Richard Perry, grandson of the founder, thanked William profusely and gave him an open invitation to visit and stay any time with his family in picturesque Middle Winton. So, when less than a year later William needed somewhere to hide his fiance until she gave birth and allow her future sister-in-law to accompany her, Richard was good to his word and seemed genuinely happy to help out. He even told William that the two girls would provide company for his daughter Mary who was an only child. Obviously William did not reveal the plan to Richard in its entirety but did tell him that he would appreciate him keeping the reason for the trip to himself to avoid any potential misunderstandings. Since the cider business under the new arrangement was going extremely well, Richard Perry, grateful and appreciative, was unlikely to rock the boat.

What William did not know on that day of celebration was that his attempts to cover up his duplicity would not prevent the truth finally emerging many years later. Long after he had handed over the reins at Steele's, this revelation would result in two brutal murders and the incarceration of his own son.

It is greed, as Democritus said, to do all the talking but not to want to listen at all.

49

CHAPTER 48

13 October 2016

Simon and Ashleigh looked at each other and neither spoke, words at this moment seeming unnecessary. For Simon it was not so much the surprise at learning the names of Sonia's birth parents (he had already guessed who they were from the news contained in Elisabeth Croft's diary), it was the confirmation of who they were and with that the shocking realisation that his growing suspicion regarding the identity of the double-killer was almost certainly correct. He was now also sure that he understood why Gerry Binns had been murdered. He turned towards Marjory Jillings who, having delivered the news that they had travelled to Minehead to seek, had stood in silence probably just observing the impact of the revelation.
"Thank you so much, Marjory, for your help and support. The police have been struggling to make headway with the recent murder and you might just have given us the information that will allow this awful case to be brought to a close."

Deciding that they should find a quiet place to debrief on the events of the morning, Simon and Ashleigh drove out of Minehead and pulled into the car park of a quaint village pub just off the A39. The kitchen was still open so they both ordered food and a Diet Coke and took a seat in the corner of the

main bar which was not too busy on this Thursday afternoon.
"So tell me, Simon," said Ashleigh, clearly wanting to cut to the chase. "We have confirmed that mum's parents were not Eric and Elisabeth but actually William and Margaret as you had told me you strongly suspected. What you have not shared yet is what that means with regard to Dad and Graham."

Simon had deliberately decided not to expound his whodunnit theory to Ashleigh partly because of the fact that it was her father and brother at the centre of this mystery and he wanted to be sure beyond any doubt that his suspicions were correct, but also because of who the likely suspect was and the need to have all the facts in hand before making any accusation. Even now he was reluctant to name names but realised that it was unfair to have dragged Ashleigh down to Somerset to help him confirm his suspicions regarding her mother's birth and to not then share the final piece of the jigsaw that this information suggested.

And so he laid out his conclusions to his second cousin and explained that there was one conversation that needed to take place to allow him to go to the police with certainty. As she listened, Ashleigh sat, mouth agape at what Simon was revealing. She could hardly believe who he was accusing of the double murder.
"So I will send him an email this evening when I get home and hopefully the little piggy will squeal!" Simon smiled and Ashleigh nodded as she saw how close to nailing the killer they had come.
"I really hope that he does," she replied, "he has certainly had his nose in the trough for all these years!"

***

Dear Duncan,

Since it was clear from your last email replying to my earlier note that you have no interest in the Binns murders beyond stressing your innocence, I will keep this communication brief.

The only point I want us to discuss is how a 21-year old with no qualifications manages to set up a bar like yours in a Spanish holiday resort. Of course, you boasted that it was paid for by someone in your debt but did not make it clear if that debt was financial or the result of something that your debtor wished to hush up and bury for good. You and I both know that it was, of course, the latter.

The problem for you, Duncan, is that I now know the truth about who the murderer of both Gerry and Graham Binns is, and it sure as hell wasn't Michael Spedding. What I am not clear about is precisely how and where you fit into all of this and how you managed to get the guilty party to buy your silence and get you out of the way. So now you are going to tell me because you have two stark choices given that being an accessory to murder, which includes covering up a crime, is viewed by the law as a very serious offence.

What are the two choices? Simple. Either you tell me the whole story, chapter and verse, or I will inform the Scotland Yard detective leading the hunt for Graham Binns' killer all about you and your ill-gotten Spanish gains. The first choice means that you might just stay below the radar, the second choice will definitely see you banged up in the slammer for a lengthy period of time. It is now Thursday evening, you have until Saturday at midday UK time to make your choice. If I do not get a response by then, I will by default move ahead with the second option. And do not be tempted to contact the murderer and suggest any funny business. There are two other people who know what I know and you would not get away with anything.

I am sure I will hear from you very soon.

Simon

50

CHAPTER 49

11 November 1990

On a balmy November morning in a year where the weather in general was warmer than normal, Gerry Binns was driving north on the A1, his destination a small town in North Yorkshire. Despite being a generally mild-mannered person, he was seething as a result of what he had recently discovered and was hell bent on having it out with his cousin. In fact, at the heart of the issue was the fact that his "cousin" was actually not his cousin but rather his brother-in-law.

The death of Elisabeth Croft earlier that year had been the trigger that had led Gerry to discover that his wife's birth parents were not Elisabeth and her husband Eric but rather Elisabeth's brother William and his then fiancee Margaret Jones. Despite being in possession of this potentially dramatic nugget of information, Gerry had initially been unable to understand the full implication of what this meant, assuming perhaps that Elisabeth and Eric had willingly agreed to adopt Sonia due to William and Margaret not wanting a baby. Since Elisabeth was unable to have children, a fact gleaned from the doctor's letter Gerry had found amongst his mother-in-law's possessions, that could have been a win-win situation for both couples. Only when Gerry had shared the basic facts of the situation with his good customer and friend

Ken Dawson, a self-confessed puzzle solver, did an alternative, potentially more shocking possibility surface. What if William and Margaret did want to become parents but also needed to avoid the shame of giving birth to an illegitimate child, a major social scandal in the 1930s?

If that was the case, how did they persuade Eric and Elisabeth to take Sonia on? It was possible that Eric and Elisabeth may have wanted a baby at that time and since Elisabeth could not conceive maybe they did agree to adopt Sonia. However, Ken thought that this would be unusual since adopting your brother's child might lead to relationship problems later on and it would be far more likely that a couple would seek a stranger's baby to bring into their family. So why did the adoption still happen? Were Eric and Elisabeth forced to agree to take Sonia for some reason? Did William and Margaret know something that they used to their advantage to get themselves out of their sticky situation?

Following his conversation with Ken Dawson which had come soon after his discovery of his wife's birth details at the Minehead registry office, Gerry had decided to see if he could find anything amongst Elisabeth's possessions which were still stored in a suitcase at their house. It did not take him very long before he came across a greetings card whose message read "Thinking of you, my love". Assuming this to have been a simple show of affection between husband and wife Gerry opened the card and read the message inside which stopped him in his tracks.

"To my darling Eric,

You cannot imagine how much I love and want you however impossible that might be. I hope we can continue to snatch moments like last week when you can get away.

Robert x"

Was this a joke? Was it some kind of prank? Gerry's mind fizzed into overdrive as he tried to assimilate what he was looking at. Nobody in the 1930s would dream up something like this, which meant that it must be real. And if it was real, what on earth were the implications and what impact did that have on the people involved?

Gerry sat motionless for a full five minutes as he considered the array of possible answers to the question he had just posed to himself. Gradually the pieces began to fall together and he started to develop a hypothesis. If William and Margaret needed to find a home for Sonia and knew of Eric's secret affair with someone called Robert, had they been able to force Eric and Elisabeth to take the newborn as their own in return for their silence? That seemed plausible given Ken Dawson's view that adopting a relative's child was fraught with future risks so maybe they were forced to take the child. The obvious follow-on question was that if they did take Sonia on did they legally adopt her? The birth certificate which had been changed referred to Eric and Elisabeth as the parents, but was it possible that this was just an arrangement of convenience? The less paperwork and legal interventions there were, the better, Gerry surmised. How could he confirm if Sonia had indeed been legally adopted?

Marjory Jillings! She had been helpful and prepared to bend a few rules to give him the information about the birth certificate. Would she be prepared to do him one additional favour? He called directory enquiries and ten minutes later was listening to the ring tone waiting for someone at the General Register Office to pick up. His luck was in, the phone was answered by Marjory herself. After a brief and heavily redacted resume of what had happened since he was last in Minehead, Gerry implored the Front Office Administrator to help with with one last task. His pitch to her was that she had already given him 90% of the information that he sought, but that he needed this last piece to complete the picture.

"Mr Binns, this really is out of order and you are seriously pushing your luck."

Gerry was about to get out the begging bowl when Marjory Jillings continued. "However, I am in a very good mood today due to the fact that my son has just been selected to play cricket for Somerset under 12s so I might be feeling more charitable than normal."

Gerry smiled to himself as he realised that this had been far easier than he had imagined. Marjory said that she would go and check the records and then call Gerry back. Fifteen minutes later the phone rang.

"Mr Binns, this is indeed a very strange case, I must say. At your wife's birth her parents were recorded as being William Steele and Margaret Jones. Shortly after this, a revised birth certificate was issued with Eric and Elisabeth Croft named as the mother and father. There is no explanation as to why this was necessary so I cannot tell you what exactly happened. My assumption would be that either that there had been some mix-up at the hospital at the time of the birth - it rarely happens, thank the Lord, but every once in a while it does - or that Mr and Mrs Croft had adopted the baby for whatever reason. There is no evidence of a baby mix-up situation so I have just checked the adoption records for late-1939. Mr Binns, your wife was never legally adopted by the Crofts.

Her maiden name was Sonia Steele."

Gerry Binns arrived in Ingleby and took some time to find the house he was looking for. He vaguely remembered visiting the place once before during one of the family holidays when Sonia, he and the children stayed with William and Margaret Steele. Eventually he arrived and parked in the driveway behind a very expensive looking BMW 7-series. He would normally never dream of turning up at someone's house unannounced but this situation was not normal.

As he climbed out of the car and started towards the front door his temperament had not improved one bit and his determination to have the planned conversation was as resolute as ever. He rang the doorbell and waited for a response. He had hoped that the person he wanted to speak with would be at home and was encouraged by the sight of the BMW parked in the driveway. A few seconds later the door was opened and Gerry found himself looking

into the eyes of the person he had come to see.
"Keith, good afternoon."
Keith Steele squinted as he looked at the man standing on his doorstep, not recognising who it was.
"Do I know you? I am busy at the moment and was not expecting anyone."
Gerry Binns gave an ironic laugh suggesting this was the welcome that he might have expected.
"Gerry Binns. My wife Sonia is your cousin you may recall although I think she was always much closer to your sister Carmen than she was to you."

Keith stood silently appraising the other man as if trying to work out if this was for real or some kind of hoax caller who had turned up to pull some trick. Gerry continued.
"Well, aren't you going to invite me in, *cousin* Keith? It was a pretty long drive up from Ilford." Without waiting for a response, Gerry Binns stepped forward and Keith had no choice but to step aside to avoid being knocked over. Not that he seemed pleased to see Gerry.
"It's nice of you to stop by," said Keith, although his tone suggested otherwise. "To what do I owe this pleasure?"
The two men were now in the large kitchen and Gerry closed the door. Keith looked put out but said nothing.
"I am not planning on staying here long," began Gerry, "but there is something very important we need to discuss."
Keith Steele looked at the other man. Was there a slight flicker of concern, even fear on his face?
"Basically Keith, I know that Sonia is William and Margaret Steele's daughter, not the daughter of Eric and Elisabeth Croft."

He looked Keith in the eye as he said this trying to gauge if the other man knew what was coming. It was difficult to tell.
"So rather than being your cousin, she is actually your elder sister isn't she, *brother-in-law*? Which basically means she owns one third of the shares in Steele's given that William's will stated that he left his estate to be split

equally amongst his children." Gerry looked at Keith as he spoke, wanting to see what impact his words were having. Keith's face was growing red and he gritted his teeth as he listened to the other man.
"You have known this all along, but you kept it quiet to suit your own selfish bloody purposes."
Silence.

"Well, we want our share of it now and we are going to get it. In fact, I will not rest until this wrong has been made right and I will do whatever is necessary to make it happen. You might want to keep this grubby little secret hidden from view, but I am sorry, the genie has been released from the lamp and there is no way to put it back. Sonia is a Steele and we will start the process to have this thing corrected immediately. Whatever the consequences."

Having said his piece, Gerry simply waited for a response. It was not long in coming and Keith Steele left Gerry in no doubt of his feelings on the matter.
"Your wife's parents are clearly Eric and Elisabeth who brought her up from birth. So I do not see any way in which you are going to succeed in robbing me of what I have dedicated my life to building. Actually, you've got some bloody nerve coming here and behaving like this when you are owed nothing."
It was now Gerry's turn to go red in the face. Pulling no punches, he told Keith that he was wrong in what he said about Sonia's parentage and that legally Sonia never became a Croft. He told Keith about the doctor's letter and Elisabeth's infertility, watching his brother-in-law's changing expression as the facts of the matter were laid bare. Keith was clearly in no mood to hear these truths and moved to shut down the conversation.

"If you dare utter one word about this it will be the last word you ever speak. I will not let you or anyone else ruin things. We can talk and see what we might be able to do, but what you are suggesting is never going to happen. I will personally make sure of that. Does Sonia know about this?"
"There is no way I am going away quietly now I know what happened and you had better realise that. I will not rest till we have back what is rightly

ours. Actually, I have said nothing to Sonia yet because firstly I wanted to be sure and secondly, since it will be a huge shock to her, I want to wait for the right moment to do that."

Like two heavyweight boxers slugging it out in the ring, the volume got louder and the tone more hateful.

"Right, I have said my piece so I won't hang around. This will need to be discussed by your Board and the appropriate action taken to right this wrong. My solicitor will be in touch so I will need the contact details for Steele's legal person." Gerry turned and started to head out of the kitchen.

"Sod you, you can whinge all you like but not one penny of the shares in my company are heading your way. Possession is nine tenths of the law, don't they say? Consider yourself warned, Mr Binns."

With the threat hanging ominously in the air, Gerry began the long drive back to Essex. He had made his point clearly, had received the feared but not unexpected rebuttal from Keith and would now take the matter legal. He would also need to decide the best time to break this news to his wife. He would wait a few days whilst he consulted a solicitor then tell her. He had been tempted on several occasions since Elisabeth's demise and this revelation to bring up the subject of her parentage but had backed off at the last moment each time.

What he did not know as he joined the A1 southbound was that he would never get to tell Sonia.

Within a few days he would be dead.

***

"It was you, wasn't it? I heard all that commotion in the kitchen a couple of Saturdays ago and then overheard Mum on the phone discussing the death of Gerry Binns with someone . It was Gerry Binns that was here with you, wasn't it? You killed him, Dad. You murdered him!"

Duncan Steele stood facing his father in the very same kitchen where the conversation in question had taken place. His face was a picture of horror and disbelief as he challenged his father. Duncan was what people in Yorkshire might refer to as a "rum lad" and he would freely admit to not being the best behaved pea in the pod. However, murder was altogether a different matter and the younger Steele was appalled that his father seemed to have committed such a crime. Keith Steele looked his son in the eye and calmly set about refuting Duncan's accusations.

"You are making a big mistake, lad. I am not sure what you thought you heard but it certainly wasn't what you think." Duncan could not believe what his father was trying to claim. He had clearly heard the argument and the accusations and he knew beyond doubt that Gerry Binns had been in their kitchen that Saturday afternoon. His father had a history of bullying Duncan into submission but that was not going to wash on this occasion. He had already thought through what he was going to make his father do to buy his silence and he would not allow himself to be fobbed off by a bunch of blatant lies.

"You must think I am totally stupid. I can quote you word for word what I heard. I know you have always had a fairly low opinion of me and you have hardly been a supportive and loving father, but this time you are going to dance to *my* tune rather than the other way round."

The first traces of doubt were etched on Keith Steele's face as his son prepared to reveal what exactly he wanted from his father.
"So basically, you have two choices. One is that I go to the police now and tell them everything I heard. Basically I shop you and you spend years in the slammer. The alternative is that you dip your mucky paws into your well stocked bank account and set me up in business. Option two guarantees my silence."

Keith's default reaction to being dictated to like this, especially by someone much younger, would have been to fly into a rage, spittle forming on his lips as he hurled profanities around like confetti. On this occasion, however, even he must have realised that such an approach would probably only make matters worse when what he needed to do was to think quickly in order to save his skin. In reality, there was only one choice. And so it was that Keith wrote a large cheque in Duncan's name on the proviso that his son left the country and did not return. Then, through a contact of his who had already moved to Marbella, Keith found the property that became Duncan's Den and, after some cosmetic renovation work, the bar opened for business in the Spring of 1991.

Simon finished reading Duncan's response to his email which had arrived on Saturday at 9am UK time, three hours before the deadline that he had set. The communication provided the clarity needed on how Duncan's Den had been financed and why Keith Steele had had little choice other than to fund the venture. Duncan's recall of the heated conversation between his father and Gerry Binns had filled in the small gaps that remained in Simon's hypothesis of what had caused the terrible chain of events that had led to not one but two murders in the Binns family. Duncan's subsequent confrontation with Keith was basically the nail in the coffin for Simon's uncle and there was no lingering doubt as to his guilt in the murder of Gerry Binns. The strong circumstantial evidence that linked Keith Steele to the recent slaying of Graham, his presence in Camden on the day of the murder being a key indicator, gave Simon enough to approach Andy Broughton with what he had discovered and then leave it to Scotland Yard to bring the case to a close. His next act was to call Ashleigh and fill her in on what Duncan had provided in terms of a testimony. Her reaction was a mix of relief and gratitude, the latter feeling because in the eyes of the police she still remained a potential suspect in her brother's murder.

As he ended the call with his second cousin, Simon breathed a huge sigh of relief himself. The past few weeks had been the most stressful of his life and he was still unsure of the status of his marriage after his lies and the obfuscation surrounding his behaviour. He was determined to spend this weekend chilling out and devoting time to his family.

The rest could wait for another day.

51

EPILOGUE

Three months later

It was the last week of January and Simon Letwin and his management team were sitting in the Steele's boardroom with the Chief Executive Officer and leadership team of Eldrich Global working on a strategic plan for the coming three years. The takeover of Steele's was progressing well and was expected to formally complete within a few weeks.

All but one member of the Steele's management committee had agreed to stay on and Simon and his team would continue to run the business with Eldrich Global management providing full support to their new colleagues. In the fullness of time there would likely be changes as synergies with other Eldrich businesses were identified and exploited, but for the moment the takeover process was proving to be extremely friendly and enjoyable. In Simon's view, it was the start of an exciting new era for the business rather than the end of a dynasty.

Whilst the takeover of the brewery business had self-evidently been a significant event in the lives of the Steele family, it was undoubtedly the potential indictment for murder of the company's chairman that took centre stage. Although Simon was absolutely convinced of his uncle's guilt, the case was far from being a slam dunk. After Duncan had opened up to Simon about Keith and the subsequent funding of his Spanish business, albeit only as an act of self-preservation, Simon had met with DI Broughton and shared everything that he had learned about the Graham Binns case. It had taken time for the police to decide that Keith Steele was a serious suspect because, although he was undoubtedly in Camden that morning, there was no actual evidence linking him to Graham's death. Simon thought it would be easier to convince the police of Keith's involvement in Gerry's demise and related what Duncan had revealed about the visit to Keith's house by Gerry Binns in 1991 and the subsequent threats made to the elder Binns by his father. Again, Scotland Yard were initially fairly unenthusiastic, pointing out to Simon that there was already a man in prison for the crime.

As often happens in criminal investigations, it was a stroke of pure luck that finally led to Keith Steele being viewed by Scotland Yard as a prime suspect in the Camden murder. The CCTV equipment in the lobby of the office block where Graham Binns had his business premises was faulty on 31 August so it had proven impossible to identify who had entered the building during the period when they believed Graham had been killed. There were two receptionists who worked on the front desk, one of whom had gone home at lunchtime on the day in question on the pretext of feeling unwell when she was actually going to buy a birthday present for her boyfriend before bunking off for the rest of the day. When the police questioned her colleague that afternoon, she panicked and, wanting to protect the other girl, told them that she had not seen her at all that day. Some time later, when both girls were subsequently questioned again, the one who had been absent finally admitted to the police that she was in fact in the building on the morning of the incident and had, fortuitously, taken pictures on her phone of all visitors as they entered. Apparently she had recently read a crime novel in which a CCTV camera had similarly stopped working and where the person on the front desk had done exactly the same thing. She burst into tears as she admitted this and had to be reassured by DI Broughton that she would not face prosecution for her actions.

Based on the photos on the girl's iPhone there had been a total of eleven visitors to the building during the crucial hour and a half period, one of whom was identified as Keith Steele despite the fact that he was wearing a cap in an effort to disguise himself. It took some time to trace the other ten visitors but eventually Scotland Yard spoke to each one and concluded that Keith Steele was the most likely perpetrator since he was not only related to the dead man but could not provide a verifiable reason for being in Camden on that day. The fact that he had submitted expenses claims for a trip to Leicester at the same time added fuel to the smouldering fire. What finally fanned the flames and caused an inferno was the forensic search of Keith Steele's laptop which led the police to find evidence of internet searches for Graham Binns and for his company location only days before he was murdered. This despite him not having had any kind of interaction with the Binns family for decades. In the face of such compelling evidence, Keith finally broke and admitted to the crime. He was arrested and remanded in custody in York pending a date for the trial.

Simon remained determined to see justice done for Michael Spedding, but had to admit to himself that this might take some time. He was conflicted regarding Duncan Steele who was clearly the only person still alive who could give a first-hand account of the events of that Saturday afternoon in his parents' house in Ingleby since his mother had been out shopping at the time of Gerry Binns' visit. Simon had given his cousin two options and the one he chose had resulted in his confession about the whole matter. Would Simon be prepared to renege on this and potentially put Duncan in the firing line as an accessory to murder? Or would he leave Michael Spedding languishing in prison, an innocent man? Time would tell.

One of the most perplexing elements of the whole case to Simon had been Keith's unwavering objection to a sale of the family business even when the financial benefits to Keith himself were obvious. Clearly unable to discuss this with his uncle, he had turned to Mark to see if he had any inkling as to why the chairman was so opposed to even considering the possibility of selling. Neither brother could come up with anything better than to believe that

Keith was afraid that in any due diligence performed on Steele's by potential purchasers, the truth about Sonia might surface. For obvious reasons, he wanted at all costs to keep that particular door firmly closed. In truth, the chances of this happening as part of a potential takeover were close to zero, so Simon and Mark came to the conclusion that it was simply the work of Keith's guilty conscience at play rather than anything more rational. The brothers also concluded that the poison pen letters sent to the two potentials acquirers of Steele's were also the work of their uncle, another attempt to derail the process and keep the past firmly hidden away.

"It is probably a good thing that the company has been sold given the fact that the former chairman faces a very long time in jail."
Five weeks earlier, the day after Keith Steele admitted his guilt in the Graham Binns murder, Simon was sitting in the kitchen with Dani, his wife being as pragmatic as ever. Although he would not have said such a thing to Dani after his visit to Minehead, given how precariously balanced his marriage was, Simon did feel a real sense of vindication and a justification for the way he had behaved. He could certainly have handled things better, particularly where his home life was concerned, but in his view that did not change the fact that he had managed to solve a case that the police had been unable to.

"You are right, babe," he replied, "he had no role in the new organisation so we have avoided what could have been a highly damaging situation had he still been chairman. I am still shocked that it was him even though I have suspected his involvement for some time."
Once the truth emerged about Sonia's birth parents and the fact that legally she had remained a Steele until she married Gerry Binns, a family conference had taken place to discuss and agree the division of the company sale proceeds between three not two qualifying parties. Ashleigh represented Sonia, who was judged to be better staying in the care home, whilst June Steele, Keith's wife, made a rare appearance in the wider family circle. The same could be said for Annabel, whose choice not to work in the family business and to live in a different part of the country meant she was generally

far less involved in family-related activities than her siblings Simon or Mark.

Amidst the tragedy and horror of the two murders suffered by the Binns family, one positive to emerge was the reconnection of Sonia's family with the Ingleby Steeles. Until recently nobody even knew that they were in fact all Steeles, and it was somewhat poignant that it had taken two brutal killings for this fact to finally emerge.

***

The first vestiges of Spring were starting to appear as Simon gazed out of his office window on another Monday morning. Since the takeover of the business he still dedicated the start of the week to his preferred activities, calling customers and Area Managers and doing the weekly tasting panel. He had shared this approach with some his new colleagues at Eldrich Global and surprisingly a few of them said they had adopted a similar approach to their Monday mornings.

He also remained a devoted fan of Link Up, despite the fact that the horrors of recent months had been triggered by his totally innocent use of the social media platform. Simon figured that sometimes a search for the missing link leads to happiness and success, whilst at other times, as on this occasion, it awakens some unexpected force that wreaks havoc and destruction. Then again, he thought, life itself is basically a series of gambles where you can win big but also lose spectacularly. He had succeeded in satisfying his curiosity concerning Graham Binns but at the ultimate cost to his second cousin. Did he regret what he had done? Of course he did. Would he do it again? Almost certainly.

And with that, Simon picked up his phone and dialled the first number on the list of customers.

Printed in Dunstable, United Kingdom

72282471R00161